Out of This World

Annette Mori

Out of This World

Annette Mori

Affinity
eBook Press
NZ
2015

Out of This World

Affinity E-Book Press NZ LTD
Canterbury, New Zealand

1st Edition

ISBN: 978-0-908351-49-7

Editor: Angela Koenig
Proof Editor: Alexis Smith
Cover Design: Irish Dragon Designs

Acknowledgments

As always an important person to acknowledge is Erin O'Reilly, because she always gives me the right amount of advice and encouragement. As my mentor, she is like a drug that I don't think I can ever wean myself from. Whenever I was stuck, she let me bounce ideas off of her and helped me think of ways to make corrections. Erin gives of her time freely, without the expectation of anything in return. I am honored to call her a friend and loved having a chance to meet her in person at GCLS.

I would also like to express my gratitude to Affinity Press and the wonderful trio (JM Dragon, Erin O'Reilly and Nancy Kaufman) who continue to support this new and somewhat unconventional writer. I am eternally grateful for the opportunities they give me to let my stories see the light of day.

On my journey, I elicited feedback from my older sister, Val who gave me valuable feedback that helped shape the final version of the story. She continues to be an incredible encouragement to me. My other beta reader and favorite fan, Gail Dodge continues to be one of my strongest supporters. She is the sweetest person and one of the first people to let me know how much she liked my writing. My other family members, who were also supportive, include my nephew, Aaron and his wife, Chelsea, and my little sister, Kim.

In addition to her talents as a cover artist, Nancy Kaufman was my beta editor and she is always a joy to work with. Thanks to Angela Koenig as the final editor and tightened the story even further. Inevitably, there are those pesky final errors that slip through and I am thankful that the final proof editor, Alexis Smith who caught those before the book went to print. Nancy Kaufman is a rock star with her covers. A triple help, Nancy is also a promoter extraordinaire.

Over the past several months, Rosie Moore and KA Moll have been wonderful supporters often sharing my posts. A huge thanks to all the other readers and fellow writers who have sent personal e-mails, written reviews and posted nice things on Facebook (you know who you are).

The Affinity authors are an especially supportive group and often share posts or send words of encouragement, especially Ali Spooner, Jen Silver, Lacey Schmidt, Renee Mackenzie, and Charlene Neil. Finally, my wife

Dedication

To all the readers like Gail who continue to support my books. To all the people who 'color outside the lines' and like to read unconventional books. To my wife who I love dearly for her patience when I get in a groove and ignore her during 'our' weekend time.

Also by Annette Mori

Locked Inside

Asset Management

The Incredibly True Adventure of Two Elves in Love
(Affinity 2014 Christmas Collection)

The True Story of Valentine's Day

Love Forever, Live Forever

Table of Contents

Prologue

My name is Mabel Butt and although the story I am about to tell may seem completely unbelievable to you, I swear every word is the God's honest truth.

I suppose with a name like mine, you think you'd know what it was like growing up, but I'm fairly certain you do not.

It's bad enough that my last name is Butt—a good strong German name my dad would tell you, but Mabel was the cherry that put it over the top for all those budding bullies. I don't think my parents intended to be cruel when they named me Mabel. I even heard stories that my dad fought hard against the name—at least he had some inkling what it might be like.

Mom can be a force to reckon with and I guess dad just gave in when I was born. Mabel was mom's favorite grandmother, and she was determined to have one of her children named after such an influential person in her life.

My older sister, Veronica, escaped my fate—lucky her. She also changed her last name as soon as she was old enough. I couldn't do that to dad after I saw his crestfallen face. He was so proud of his German roots and conveniently forgot all the names they had called him as a young boy.

The only person who never made fun of me was Sydney O'Donnell. She was my unlikely protector all through school, but she couldn't be there all the time. If it weren't for my name, I'm sure I could have blended into the background.

How could I not fall in love with Sydney? She was the only one who was ever kind to me. Everyone fell in love with Sydney so I definitely had no chance to win her heart. She had her pick of the school and I was the fruit left rotting on the tree—flawed and unappealing.

Chapter One

"Hey, Mabs. Whatcha reading?" Sydney leaned her long lanky body on the counter and gifted me with one of her slow sexy grins.

"Oh, hello Sydney." I quickly stuffed the book under the counter and away from her piercing blue eyes.

"Syd, all my friends call me Syd, how many times do I have to tell you that? You must be reading that book, *Fifty Shades of Grey*. I didn't think you had it in you." Sydney winked.

I'd been in love with Sydney since the fifth grade, but I was so far into the closet that even the Jaws of Life weren't able to pry me out.

I blushed at her teasing. "Um, no, it's not that book." I sat up and tried for my professional librarian look. "Can I help you find something, Sydney?"

She sighed. "I'm never going to convince you to call me Syd, am I?"

I shook my head. "You'll always be Sydney to me." I wanted to add, *Sydney, my hero and divine object of hidden desires*, but I didn't.

"Hollie wanted me to pick up that new lesbian romance by Janet River. Do you have it yet?" she asked.

I did have it. That was the book I'd just hidden under the counter but I couldn't tell her that. "We do, but someone just checked it out."

"Damn, I didn't think there were that many lesbians in our sleepy little town. Who checked it out? Maybe I can ask how long she'll have it and I can get it when she brings it back."

Busted. I thought of something quick and only felt slightly guilty for the lie. "Oh I'll just call you when it comes back in. You know, confidentiality and all that."

"Oh, sorry. Someone in the closet, huh? I just don't get it. Be out and proud. It's not like it's the fifties or anything. No one's ever bothered me."

Sydney was one of the beautiful people, popular, confident, and unfortunately, definitely spoken for, not that I would ever have a chance with her. Coming out was a non-issue for her. She just acted as if it was the most normal thing in the world to be a lesbian and it worked. No one ever challenged her. The fact that she began dating the head cheerleader, who happened to be the most sought after girl in high school, certainly didn't hurt. They were the golden couple. I thought she could do better because Hollie wasn't a very nice person, but maybe that was just wishful thinking on my part. I fantasized that one day she would realize she was really in love with me.

"That's because you're beautiful and everyone loves you. It isn't like that for everyone," I blurted out. If ever there was a time I wanted to be born a deaf mute, it was that moment.

Sydney quirked her eyebrow at me. "Are you flirting with me, Mabel Butt?"

Fortunately, at just that moment, the door to the library opened and the tinkling of the bell interrupted our conversation. I looked up and saw the most astonishing woman I'd ever seen in my entire life. I was speechless and I could tell Sydney was too. The woman had the kind of ethereal beauty that you almost never come across. Little did I know how accurate a description that really was. I wasn't aware at the time, but this moment would be the spark that changed my life forever.

Chapter Two

The strange woman nearly floated into the library and my mouth hung open just waiting for all the flies to gather inside and claim squatter's rights. Sydney was nearly my twin as she gaped at the woman.

She wasn't very tall, maybe five-seven, give or take an inch. Her hair was an unusual white blond and shimmered like silver, but it wasn't exactly the color of silver. Her eyes were what really captured my attention. They were a bright lavender color. People talk about Elizabeth Taylor's unusual eye color, but it wasn't like that at all. They were so bright, yet almost translucent. It's hard to describe the color. If Easter collided with Christmas, maybe you'd get that color, a sparkling light-purple in a shimmering Christmas ornament.

I was startled from my trance when her melodic voice reached my ears.

"I am looking for information on this planet, Earth. I am told the library contains the data I require."

Sydney blinked her eyes. I remember thinking she must have been in the same trance as me. I wondered at the time why she didn't take charge and introduce herself. It's what she usually did whenever someone new came into town. Sydney was always outgoing and, even though she never passed up an opportunity to meet a beautiful woman, she was fiercely loyal to her relationship with Hollie.

"I think I can help you if you can be a little more specific with what you are looking for. Do you want information on geology of the planet, geography, cultures, history?"

She cocked her head to the side. "Yes, all of it. I wish to study you as well. There is something special about you."

Even though her voice was appealing, her words were unusual and kind of alarming to me.

"What do you mean, 'study her'? She's not some lab rat. Who the hell are you anyway?" Sydney got in her face and glared at the strange woman.

I saw her lavender eyes capture Sydney's and then she did the strangest thing. She touched her on the wrist and a soft purple light spread from her hand all the way up Sydney's arm. I watched as Sydney's head turned into a kind of neon backlight and shimmered for a few seconds before I heard a pop.

Sydney smiled at her. "I'm sorry. I'm being rude. Of course you need Mabel's help. Mabs is the best. She can find information on just about anything you want to know, except for maybe herself, on that she's like a vault."

The strange purple light was a major clue and looking back, I wonder why I didn't figure things out from the very start, but I didn't. Even when she revealed all and I had a brief acceptance of the surreal, I quickly reverted to my safe and stubborn view of the world and its limited possibilities.

She tilted her head again and looked directly at me. I could swear that I heard her ask me if I was frightened of her, but her lips never moved and the words felt like they were just floating inside my mind. I shook my head as an answer to her mind question. That's what I called it because I didn't really have any other kind of way to describe it. I felt a lyrical laugh inside my head and then the words *mind question* reverberated inside my skull. I experienced an immediate sense of peace and then I laughed.

"I do apologize. I am not used to the primary Earth language. I am in need of a sponsor—an earthling to show me around." Her lavender eyes focused on me. "You are my choice."

I didn't realize I was answering her when the words just tumbled from my mouth. "I would love to help you find what you need." I looked into her beautiful eyes and I wanted to be her host. I felt flattered that she picked me. "I can show you around town since you're not from around here."

I convinced myself that she was just an eccentric out of towner who needed my assistance.

For the first time since I fell in love with Sydney, someone new drew me into her sphere. In that moment, I would have done anything this strange woman asked of me without question. Well almost anything. I don't think I would have murdered anyone for her, but for some strange reason I knew she would never ask me to do anything harmful to another human being. My initial assessment was that her beauty did not stop at her physical appearance. I suspected that she was truly beautiful—inside and out.

"Thank you. Is Mabel the name you wish to be called?" she asked.

No one had ever asked me that. I'd never been called anything else, except by Sydney. She called me Mabs and I liked how she would shorten my old fashioned name, but I didn't want this exquisite, exotic person to call me Mabs. I wanted a special name that only she would use and in my mind, I saw the name Bella. I was a huge fan of the *Twilight* series and I wanted a name that meant beautiful, something I definitely was not.

You are beautiful. I heard her say inside my head. Again, I ignored my inner voice telling me something was not matching up.

"I will call you Bella. It is an appropriate name. You may call me Celeste," she added in her lyrical voice.

Sydney seemed to be in a trance during the whole interchange between Celeste and me, but appeared to snap out of it when she heard Celeste call me Bella. She raised an eyebrow, but didn't say anything. I just stood there frozen with my mouth hanging open.

Celeste turned to Sydney. "Your Hollie is *throwing a hissy fit.* What is this hissy fit?"

Sydney blinked twice. "Um. What makes you think that? Do you know Hollie?"

Celeste brushed Sydney's arm and I saw a slightly muted version of the light I'd witnessed earlier.

"Oh, you want to know the meaning of the slang phrase *hissy fit.* It means she's not happy with me right now and probably expected me ten minutes ago. Gotta fly, Mabs. Can you recommend another book that I can appease her with or else I'm in deep shit?" Sydney asked.

I absently pulled the book I'd hidden from Sydney earlier from under the counter and handed it to her.

She looked at the book, scrunching up her face. "I thought you said someone had already checked it out."

I shook my head. "Sorry, they must have returned it and I just noticed it was queued up to be reshelved."

"Okay, thanks. Can you take care of the paperwork? Gotta run." Sydney waved as she ran out the door.

I turned to look at Celeste and she was smiling at me. I noticed her perfect white teeth lined up like miniature soldiers all in a very neat, straight, row. I felt my face flush and offered her a tentative smile back.

"Um, shall we start with geology?" I asked. For some reason, this thought popped into my mind. Geology was always a fascinating topic to me. I wasn't just a nerd, I was *the* definition of a nerd. I'm sure next to the word nerd in a dictionary, you can find a picture of me.

Her head inclined slightly. I took that as my cue to lead her to the section in the library where the books all about Earth's geology were located.

I took pride in my library, making sure that I aligned every book perfectly according to the old-fashioned Dewey Decimal system. First published in 1876 by Melvil Dewey, the system withstood the test of time after twenty-three major editions with the most recent in 2011. Nerd alert. I knew the most inane facts. No one gave a bleep about the history of the Dewey Decimal system.

I knew that paper books were becoming passé quickly with the explosion of e-books, but I still loved smelling the old leather and touching the pages. I would always want to handle the books. I just hoped that others would remain loyal to the printed page as the years and the technology grew.

I pulled *Earth: An Introduction to Physical Geology* from the shelf. It wasn't the most riveting book in the library, but it certainly had all the information about Earth's geology that Celeste might want. Just for grins I also pulled *Fingerprints Of the Gods*, a fascinating book I'd read suggesting that the history of mankind was far older than anyone previously thought. The author used tools like archaeoastronomy, geology, and computer analysis of ancient myths to support his theories. It was fascinating material to a nerd like myself.

"Interesting choices, Bella," she remarked.

"What other kinds of books would you like to check out?"

"How many am I allowed at one time?" she asked.

"You can check out up to five. I'll need to help you get a library card. Do you have a driver's license or some other kind of identification?"

Celeste did her cute little head tilt and I sensed that she didn't have any such thing. This was going to be a problem, but I was a master problem solver and decided it would be my personal challenge to help Celeste out.

"I don't suppose a computer chip containing my biological, physical location, and other necessary information will work?" Celeste touched my arm and I felt a warm, peaceful feeling travel up my arm and seep into my whole body.

Maybe she was teasing me, but deep down I knew her response was odd. Everything about Celeste was out of this world, but I didn't care. At first, I convinced myself that Celeste just had an unusual sense of humor. Later, I kept flip-flopping over what I believed.

"A computer chip isn't exactly a common form of identification recognized in this little hole-in-the-wall town." I was compelled to help, so I quickly added, "No problem, I can check them out under my card and I'll help you get a new license or some form of identification. I assume you just moved here from somewhere?"

"I am temporarily in this location," she offered.

"Okay, no worries. We can still use your temporary address to obtain ID. Do you have a piece of mail with you? Maybe a bill or something?"

"Address? Bill?" She quirked her head.

Okay, now I was getting a little concerned. *What am I getting myself into?* I frowned. "Celeste, where do you live? Temporarily, that is?"

"I live in my ship, of course, but you are not allowed to visit. We have strict guidelines." She touched my arm again and the peace flooded me.

She grinned.

Now I was sure she was teasing me. I liked it. No one, except maybe Sydney, had ever been playful with me before, because they always assumed I was too serious to enjoy joking around. I laughed at her, but then I got serious again because I thought that maybe she was homeless, although her appearance wasn't ragged like most of the homeless people I met on the street. Maybe she was just a traveler who had recently come into town and hadn't arranged for a hotel yet. She seemed kind of lost to me. It's amazing the things you tell yourself when you just can't embrace the truth. It's easy to fit nice little explanations into our narrow worldview and believe something even when it doesn't quite match. I absolutely did not want to think of any less desirable explanations. Either I was crazy or she was, and neither explanation was very appealing.

My Aunt Marie was a hoot, but she had several screws loose and I'd heard that mental illness was genetic. I sure didn't want to go there. It was a lot safer to believe that Celeste was an odd duck needing my help than that I was following in my Aunt's looney footsteps.

I didn't care if Celeste was some kind of escaped mental health patient. She didn't seem dangerous to me so I just convinced myself she was harmless. Besides, Aunt Marie was my favorite Aunt. She was the only person who could consistently get me to climb out of my cave and do crazy shit with her—like make sandcastles in the pouring rain.

"How long do you plan on staying in Roslyn?" I asked.

"As long as it takes," she answered cryptically.

Okay, I really wanted to help this woman, but she wasn't making it easy for me. It was a surprise to me when I blurted out, "Come on, if I can't go to your ship, then you'll just have to establish temporary residence with me. My place is not big or anything, but I have a guest bedroom and there's plenty of room for one more. Besides, having someone to talk to at night could be an adventure."

"I do have a place to rest, but I would enjoy spending more time with you. Are you sure this is not an inconvenience or against some rule?"

I really wanted this woman to stay with me. I didn't care if I might be enabling her delusions. It never hurt Aunt Marie. I blushed. "No, Celeste, I would really like you to come stay with me for as long as you want."

"Will you be able to let me read the two books you've chosen?" she asked.

"Sure. You can select two more. I already have one checked out, so with the additional two books, that will add up to the five I can check out. What else would you like to explore about Earth?"

"I would very much like to know more about ancient civilizations."

I grinned. This was another favorite subject of mine. "Oh, I love learning about ancient civilizations."

I walked over to another aisle and plucked two of my favorite books from the shelf. I showed her the books and she smiled and nodded. I headed to my desk to check out the four books I'd selected for Celeste. I typed my selections into the computer. I didn't need to record Sydney's book because it was the fifth book I'd checked out. No one needed to know I was secretly reading the book. I glanced at my watch and was pleased that I could legitimately leave without feeling like I was shirking my duties.

My little cottage was walking distance from work. I grabbed my jacket from the back of the chair and walked to the front door of the library. Celeste followed without saying another word. After I locked the door, we walked side by side for two blocks until we approached my house.

✝

I loved my little A-frame home. It reminded me of a ski chalet. It was only twelve hundred square feet, but the rustic nature suited my personality. A little rough around the edges, just like me, a socially awkward teen that'd turned into a recluse. I didn't have the spit and polish that Sydney had, or even something remotely close to it.

Gizmo, my cat, was peering through the front window. Although I couldn't hear her meowing a hello; as soon as I unlocked my front door, she scrambled to greet me. She was more like a dog than a cat.

Celeste followed me into the house and Gizmo gave her a greeting too, "Meow."

"Cat?" She leaned down and stroked Gizmo's silky fur.

I wished I were Gizmo right about now.

Celeste chuckled.

"Meet Gizmo, my cat. She's a little hussy. She'll cozy up to just about anyone if you keep petting her. Unlike most domestic cats, Gizmo never met a person she didn't like. I don't think she has a bit of independence or aloofness in any of her cells."

Celeste smiled. "She is a beautiful cat, like her mother."

No doubt my face was bright red again. I had to change the subject. "Um, do you have extra clothes or anything? Maybe a travel bag stashed somewhere?"

I noticed she carried a small backpack and I thought that was kind of odd because she definitely looked like a purse woman. Elegant women usually didn't add a backpack as a fashion accessory.

"I have limited Earth clothing, but…" She unzipped her backpack and pulled a wad of cash that would choke an elephant. Holding it out she said, "I believe I can use this paper to obtain more."

I hadn't really noticed her clothing before because I was too busy drooling over her lavender eyes. I scrutinized her outfit and quickly assessed how expensive her black pants and tailored silk shirt looked. The clothes fit her slim physique like a second skin. I admired a nice body as much as everyone else does, but it's always a person's eyes and their smile that sucks me in. In that respect, Celeste had pretty much everyone else beat.

"I'm sure we can get you more clothes tomorrow. I don't even want to know where you got the cash. Lucky for you I'm off on Saturdays and can take you shopping. My car's not much, but it will get us to the store and back." I recalled her *ship* comment. "I'm guessing, besides your ship, you don't really have a different mode of transportation."

I was proving to her that I could joke around just like everyone else. At least I preferred that notion to the other less acceptable one that I was feeding her delusion.

"Thank you, Bella. You are a kind and gracious host."

"I'm not much of a cook, but I can whip us up some dinner if you'd like." Actually, I am a pretty good cook, but no one likes a braggart so I chose not to share that fact.

Celeste tilted her head and frowned. "You have to whip your food before serving it?"

I laughed, thinking she was joking with me. "Funny. No I don't even eat red meat, so I hope you don't mind a vegetarian meal."

"I would love to try your plant varieties," she said.

"Okay spaghetti squash it is with a nice red sauce. I'll fix us some arugula salad with craisens and goat cheese. That should complete the meal. Would you like a glass of wine?" I asked.

"Oh yes. I am not supposed to try the wine, but I have wanted to taste this beverage ever since I read about it."

I put my finger to my lips. "Hmm, what should I choose? I'm sorry I'm not a huge wine connoisseur so I don't really pay attention to what wine pairs well with pasta. I don't really drink a lot of red wines, but I've read that Merlot goes well with red sauce so let's try that." I knew I was thinking out loud, but Celeste didn't seem to mind about my confession regarding wines.

I pulled a 2008 Merlot from Cave B out of my mini wine refrigerator and retrieved my birthday indulgence, an electric wine opener. I always seemed to get bits of cork inside the bottle whenever I tried using the more conventional wine openers—not that I had much experience. I saw this gadget in a kitchen store and had to have it. It was a ridiculous purchase because I rarely had company and almost never opened any of the bottles of wine I had stacked in my closet and in the special wine cooler. I'd opened maybe three bottles of wine in my lifetime, except for the occasional wine I opened while cooking, all for my family. I had hoped that one day I would have a reason to entertain, and now I did.

Zzzzzzzz

The electric corkscrew buzzed as the cork magically rose inside the gadget and then distended back down. I set the bottle on the center island in my kitchen to let the wine breathe because I'd read that's what you're supposed to do with reds. I never needed more than four wine glasses. I pulled two of them from the cabinet and set them beside the Merlot.

Celeste was standing in my kitchen watching me and I felt like an idiot because I hadn't even invited her to sit down and relax.

"Celeste, I'm sorry, why don't you take a load off?" I pointed to the bar stool next to the butcher-block island where the wine was breathing its way to an acceptable taste.

"What load would you like to me take and where would you like it?" she asked.

I chuckled. She really did have a good sense of humor. Maybe I could learn something from her. Yep, I continued my rationalization that her peculiar comments were all part of her incredible sense of humor.

"Go ahead and sit down," I directed.

She set her backpack next to the barstool, sat down, and watched me as I pulled out ingredients from my cupboards and clipped some herbs from the potted plants along my windowsill. The sauce was easy enough. All I needed to do was open up some canned tomatoes, crush some garlic, and add the wine and other fresh herbs. I tossed the ingredients into a large sauté pan and filled up a large pot with hot water. After placing the water and sauce on the stove to heat them both up, I turned to look at my guest.

I started getting a little nervous because she seemed to scrutinize my every move. I wondered why she appeared so focused on me. I normally fade into the background and the only time anyone ever bothered with me was to engage in a little all-American bullying. As an adult I'm now universally ignored, but as an adolescent I was the perfect lightning rod for teenage taunting with my coke bottle glasses, and braces complete with full headgear. Around the age of fifteen, I finally convinced my mom to let me wear contacts and my braces were also history, but that didn't matter to those who'd already pegged me as the enemy.

It was never a good idea to handle a large knife when I was nervous. I tend to slice things not meant to be sliced—like my fingers. I would have to be extra careful about cutting up the spaghetti squash lest I carve up my hand. I carefully quartered the winter vegetable and then tossed it into the water without bothering to wait for it to boil.

I figured the wine had *breathed* enough and, if it hadn't, I hoped Celeste wouldn't notice. I needed a drink to calm my nerves. I poured the wine into our glasses, handed her a glass, and held mine up to meet hers.

"Cheers," I said.

She tilted her head, but didn't bring her glass up to mine. "Is there a competition we are cheering for?" she asked.

I chuckled. "Come on, just touch your glass to mine so I can finally gulp this wine down. You're making me nervous, you know."

She brought her glass to mine, tapped it, and then watched as I took a big swallow. She followed my lead and took an extra-large swig and then immediately starting coughing.

I reached around to pat her back gently. "Are you all right? I don't think Merlot is meant to be guzzled. Try sipping it. I know I'm a terrible role model, but I tend to consume alcohol more rapidly whenever I'm uncomfortable."

Celeste touched my arm and that sense of peace I was beginning to attribute to her touch flooded me again. She sipped her wine and nodded. "This has a nice flavor. I think I will like trying more wine. There are many varieties, yes?"

"Oh yes, there are. It all depends on the type of grapes used, where they are grown, and who the winemaker is. The results are dramatically different. Making wine is a little bit art and a little bit science. Excuse me while I finish making dinner. Why don't you take your wine and relax in the living room." I pointed to the couch several feet away.

"I cannot assist you in any way? If you demonstrate a task, I am able to replicate the movements."

"No, please, go sit on the couch and relax. I'll let you know when it's ready."

She nodded and headed to the couch.

While I finished making dinner, I stole a few glances and saw how Gizmo, the little hussy, crawled into Celeste's lap and made herself comfortable. I could hear her loud purr from several feet away. I quickly tossed some arugula, blueberries, craisens, goat cheese, and cashews into a large bowl and grabbed my homemade salad dressing. My nephew always joked that it was like liquid gold because it was the best he'd ever tasted. I usually traveled to Leavenworth, Washington, to buy the special balsamic vinegar and olive oil. This particular batch was a combination of cranberry walnut balsamic vinegar and blood orange olive oil. It was by far my favorite. I wanted to impress Celeste.

Celeste was humming and I swear, combined with Gizmo's purr, it almost sounded like they were in harmony. I hated to interrupt, but dinner was finally ready.

"Okay it's ready, but don't let Gizmo con you into feeding her. She's a squash addict and she loves my red sauce. We can eat here in my tiny dining room."

Celeste approached the table and glanced at the two place settings. "You don't let Gizmo eat with you?"

I laughed. "Well, I don't set a plate at the table for her, but I guess she does kind of wiggle her way onto my lap at dinnertime, and I relent a little as I feed her table scraps. I know I shouldn't, but she's just so darned cute. I try not to feed her too much people food because it's really not good for her."

"She is a lovely companion. Her spirit is pure and she is very fond of you."

I waited until she sat down and then I brought over the salad, sauce, bowl of squash, and grated Romano cheese. I'd already placed the bottle of wine on the table. I pointed to the food. "Dig in. I'm not very formal, so you don't need to follow any strict ceremony here."

"Do I need to dig under there to harvest the food?" she asked as she pointed to the bowl of squash.

She was such a jokester. I laughed again. "Here, I'll dish it up for you."

We finished the bottle of wine and, because I wasn't used to entertaining anyone, my eyelids began to droop. I figured it was time to head off to bed. Besides, tomorrow would probably be a long day of shopping and touring Celeste around, and I wanted to be a good host.

I motioned for Celeste to follow me, pulled out a fresh towel, and dug in my guest bathroom drawer to find a new toothbrush for her to use. Fortunately, I had several in various drawers left over from my bi-annual visits to the dentist, along with multiple small tubes of toothpaste. I don't know why I kept them. I suppose I thought it would be wasteful to toss them out. I'd already located a t-shirt, some shorts, and a pair of extra sweats, which I laid out on the bed for her. I didn't know exactly what she had in her backpack, so I figured I'd better equip her with everything she might need.

Celeste seemed to be dragging as well. I don't think she was used to drinking alcohol and was probably a bigger lightweight than I was. It's not like she was drunk or anything, but I could tell that it affected her. She got a dopey look on her face and giggled a lot during and after dinner. We talked mostly about nerdy things like the Earth's geology and ancient myths, but she added her unique sense of humor to the discussion and that caused me to giggle along with her.

I led her to the guest bedroom after showing her the bathroom. "If you need anything at all, my bedroom is just one door down. Sweet dreams, Celeste."

She smiled and bid me goodnight.

When I settled into my bed, I let my mind wander—fantasize actually—that Celeste would knock on my door in the middle of the night. Then one thing would lead to another, and we'd end up making mad, passionate love. Of course I knew that would never happen, but a girl can dream. I closed my eyes and I'm sure I sported a smile on my face all night long.

Chapter Three

The morning came too rapidly and I awoke to a rough tongue swiping my face. Two paws were furiously making bread on my bare chest. I'd discarded my t-shirt in the middle of the night because it got too warm. I suspect my erotic dreams were the culprit to my increased body temperature. This time, Celeste versus Sydney was the major star of my nighttime adventures.

I giggled. "Gizmo, stop. I told you not to try to French kiss me until I've brushed my teeth."

Gizmo had a bad habit of trying to stick her tongue inside my mouth, and I would have to tighten my lips in an attempt at avoiding her loving attack. She was by far the sweetest cat I'd ever owned, but that didn't mean I would let her stick her tongue in my mouth. I hadn't even had the pleasure of a woman doing that to me yet, so I certainly wasn't about to let my first experience be with my cat.

I heard stirring in the other room and wondered if Celeste was already up. I wanted to make coffee or tea—I didn't know which she preferred—and then whip up my famous stuffed French toast. I didn't have a whole lot going for me to impress a woman, but I could cook a gourmet breakfast. Maybe the fastest way to a woman's heart was through her stomach.

I gently plucked Gizmo from my chest and set her to the side. She gave my hand one last lick for good measure and settled in for a long nap curled up on my bed. I grabbed my t-shirt from the floor where I'd tossed it and pulled it quickly over my head.

I didn't think my wooing chance would increase by sauntering out into the living room with a bare chest. My body wasn't anything to write home about. I wasn't overweight or anything, and I religiously worked out every day, but my flat chest and slim physique didn't cause any heads to turn—male or female. No six pack graced my abs, and my curves were virtually non-existent.

I grabbed the brush off my dresser in an attempt to tame my wild curls. I'd worked all night on my hairdo and it showed. Pieces of my 'do stuck out every which way. It wasn't that just-laid look that is so sexy on some women—it was more like a scary Zombie look.

I peeked out to see where Celeste was and, sure enough, she was looking out my front window. She seemed contemplative. It didn't take long for her to swivel her piercing lavender eyes in my direction—almost as if she sensed me watching her. She looked adorable in my University of Washington sweats that I had laid out for her the night before.

I coughed in embarrassment and walked out to greet her. "Good morning, Celeste. Did you sleep well?"

She smiled. "Oh yes, your sleeping quarters are very comfortable, not at all what I am used to."

I wanted to ask what she was used to, but I let it slide. I hoped her normal *sleeping quarters* weren't some mental hospital. "Are you hungry?"

"Yes, I am eager to try another food option. I do not wish to have any more wine this morning. I believe it was the cause of the unpleasant feeling in my head."

I joked back with her because I was getting used to her sense of humor. "That's good because I don't think my stuffed French toast really pairs all that well with any of the wine I have in my closet. You must really be a lightweight. I can give you something for your headache if you want."

Celeste tilted her head and looked at me with a sort of puzzled expression on her face. "I am of average weight where I come from. Is that what you call the unpleasant feeling—a headache?" she asked.

I chuckled. "Headache, hangover, your choice. A couple of aspirin and some food should help."

"Do not worry, I healed myself and the *headache* has disappeared."

I shrugged. "Okay. Breakfast will be ready in a few minutes."

She looked like she was going to say something back, probably another joke, but instead she just closed her mouth.

After I made a heaping stack of French toast, I watched her devour nearly three quarters of the stack as she licked her lips and made humming noises while she ate. I took that as a good sign. I think she liked my cooking.

"Your food offerings are very good. I wish to try more, but I have an unpleasant feeling right here." Celeste patted her stomach.

Yeah, I'd probably have a stomachache too if I ate that much. I didn't want to be rude though, so I kept my unkind thoughts to myself.

She smiled at me, tilted her head again, and I got the distinct impression that she could read those unkind thoughts. I told myself I needed to do a better job of censoring myself around Celeste because she could clearly read my body language.

"I need to take a shower and get ready. Feel free to take a bath or shower, whichever you prefer. We can both get ready at the same time because, fortunately for me, there's plenty of water for both of us. You can use the guest bath that I showed you last night. Whenever you're ready, we can head out and do some shopping."

She nodded her head vigorously. "Yes, I am eager to try out this shower I have read about with the sweet smelling products. I turned the dials last night and discovered how to make the water flow from the dispenser. The square item for rubbing on your body had a very nice smell that I wish to transfer to my skin."

"You mean my lavender soap?"

"Ah yes, lavender soap." She nodded as if she were just remembering something she'd forgotten earlier.

"You can either wear the sweats you have on or I could loan you some jeans and a t-shirt. I'm pretty sure you would fit into my clothes."

"Whatever you advise. I do not wish to stand out."

Fat chance of that. Celeste would look beautiful in a potato sack, but I wanted to see her in some jeans. I thought she would fill them out nicely, so I went to my room and rummaged through my drawers until I found a pair of low-rise jeans that I thought would look sexy on her. Sydney had even said I looked hot in them one day, but I knew she was just saying that to try to get me to climb out of my shell. Sydney was like that, she was always saying nice things to me. Sometimes I even fooled myself into believing her.

I must have been doing some serious astro traveling thinking about Sydney because when I went back out to the living room, Celeste was gone and I heard the guest shower running. *Shit, what do I do now? I can't just barge into the bathroom and set the clothes on the counter, she'll think I'm some kind of perv.*

As I was pondering my dilemma, I heard the water in the shower turn off and shuffling sounds in the bathroom. I felt like a deer in front of headlights as my indecision froze me to the spot. A few minutes later, the door to the bathroom opened and Celeste casually strolled out wearing absolutely nothing, not even a towel. I knew I was being rude, but I couldn't help myself—I gawked at her. Celeste was a goddess. The fact that she showed absolutely no inhibitions when she walked toward me and took the clothes from my hands just increased the drool factor. I was too dumbfounded to say anything, and simply held the jeans and t-shirt in front of me like I was presenting gold to a Queen.

"Thank you, my sweet Bella."

I'd forgotten to bring her underwear and only realized this after she'd taken my offering. She didn't seem to notice and I hesitated again. I wasn't sure about loaning someone my boring, white, Hanes for women. Then I figured lots of people go commando and don't even give it a second thought. Besides, it was exciting to know that this exotic woman would be wearing my jeans and that just seemed so intimate—like our most private places would share the same space. God, I was going to go straight to hell—I just knew it.

As I was daydreaming about smelling my own jeans after she'd removed them, Celeste had departed to the guest bedroom to finish getting dressed. I hurried back to my own bathroom because I was running behind. Now I was having daytime sex dreams and that would surely get me into serious trouble.

It didn't take me long to take a shower and get dressed. I was anxious to get going, so I did something completely out of character for me. Instead of blow-drying my hair, I shook my curls out and hoped for the best. I rarely let my hair dry naturally because I am so self-conscious about how it might look when I don't straighten it. I don't usually wear make-up, so it only took me another couple of minutes to throw on a pair of well worn jeans and a soft cotton t-shirt.

I found Celeste in the living room flipping pages in a book so fast that it was impossible to imagine her actually reading the information. This was a good thing, since it appeared as though she'd found my lesbian erotica. Even though I thought she hadn't had enough time to read the book in her hands, I could feel the heat engulf my body until perspiration appeared. I felt a trickle of sweat between my breasts. I'm sure my face was an embarrassing shade of fuchsia.

She looked up at me and I swear she had a wolfish grin. "Bella, do you wish to lick my pussy, or would you rather I suck your tender bud until you scream my name in ecstasy?"

I choked out an unintelligent, "What?"

I swear she smirked at me. "This book of yours is quite educational. Perhaps we shall discuss this tonight under the moon and stars. Let us go shopping now."

Damn, this woman put unholy thoughts into my mind and, yes, I did want her to lick me like a lollipop. I shook my head to try to get that image out so I could concentrate on our shopping trip.

"Before we head to North Bend today, I'd like to stop at Pioneer Coffee and get my favorite beverage, a double vanilla, soy milk latte. Do you mind?"

"Is this a drink I might like to try?" she asked.

"Oh yeah, especially with cinnamon on top."

I was now focused on my chosen addiction—coffee. This would, hopefully, help me steer clear of a new craving I was developing—fantasizing about Celeste.

We piled into my old beater and I noticed that Celeste was scrutinizing me as I pulled the seat belt across my shoulder and buckled myself in. She placed her backpack between her knees and, as soon as she clicked her restraint in place, we headed to the coffee shop.

She watched me again as I unclipped my seat belt and seemed to struggle with the release button, so I reached over and pressed the button with my left hand while I guided the metal buckle and shoulder strap gently back into the release mechanism with my right hand. I'm not sure why I did this because Celeste was not a child who might be startled by the seatbelt rapidly retracting. Maybe I wanted some kind of physical connection to her. This was the most intimate interaction I'd ever had with a woman as my hand accidently brushed against her stomach. How pathetic is that? My sheltered life was causing me havoc as I started to experience too many firsts in a short time.

†

Pioneer Coffee was a local favorite of our sister city, Cle Elum. Not only did they serve the best coffee drinks, but they also sold local wines. In the winter, the fireplace was always roaring and patrons would stretch out and relax on the comfy sofa and chairs that were strategically placed next to the warmth of the fire. Since it wasn't winter, everyone sprawled out in every nook and cranny.

When I opened the front door, I groaned as I spied Sydney and her bitchy girlfriend, Hollie.

Hollie was an accomplished attorney and everyone's golden girl—well, everyone who shared her political views and social standing in the community. The rest of us nerds and common people got to see her decidedly less charming side. When Sydney wasn't looking, her non-verbal messages were clear—stay away, loser.

I never understood what Sydney saw in Hollie. Sure, her outward appearance was flawless, but she was a soulless she-devil and treated Sydney like shit. Sydney was no more than her loyal and devoted lap dog. As far as I could see, Sydney was not an equal partner, but rather eye candy that Hollie loved to show off.

Of course, Sydney saw us enter the shop right away and waved us over. I couldn't be rude, so I reluctantly made my way to their table. Celeste followed my lead and stood beside me as I approached my high school crush and *the enemy*.

"Hey, Sydney. You remember Celeste, right?"

Sydney smiled and nodded. "Of course, you're the one who wants to learn all about stuff that our resident librarian and expert on remote and interesting trivia knows absolutely everything about. You couldn't have found a better person to help you. Mabs is amazing with the amount of knowledge she has in that big brain of hers."

I noticed Hollie scowling when she said that, but Sydney was too busy motioning toward the empty seats to register her sourpuss expression. However, before glaring at me, she focused her penetrating gaze on Celeste and I could tell she liked what she saw. I was willing to bet my house that she would turn on the charm with Celeste.

"Celeste, right?" Sydney pointed to Hollie. "This is my girlfriend, Hollie."

Hollie directed her perfectly dazzling smile at Celeste. "It's wonderful to meet you. I'm not sure what information you were looking for, but I'd be happy to help in any way I can. I don't think Mabel knows that much about our legal system or politics. So… anytime you want to have lunch, my treat of course, I'll fill you in. It sounded like you aren't from the US and it can be complicated to understand our system of justice." Hollie placed a business card in Celeste's hand and held on just a bit longer than I thought necessary.

I grinned when Celeste's response was polite but distant.

"Thank you, Hollie. I shall consider your offer, but so far Bella has provided me with the information I need at this time. I choose to continue my education with her."

Hollie narrowed her eyes. "Bella?"

Sydney chuckled. "Yeah, Celeste decided that was an appropriate name for Mabs and I have to agree. I might start calling her that myself."

If Hollie's eyes had the ability to shoot daggers, I'd be dead.

She turned to Celeste and smiled. "Why don't you and *Mabel* join us for dinner tonight?"

Oh now, that was rich. I'd known Hollie for over ten years and she'd never invited me to dinner before. Even Sydney seemed shocked by the invitation as she looked at her girlfriend.

"Oh, I am so sorry. Tonight I will be fucking Bella until she screams my name in ecstasy under this lovely moon and stars. I will lap up her sweet nectar from the pulsing, plump lips surrounding her vagina," Celeste calmly remarked.

Sydney burst out laughing and I hastened to clarify. "She's kidding."

I remember thinking that Celeste had the driest sense of humor of anyone I'd ever met. Death Valley had nothing on Celeste. She could deliver a punchline with the straightest face I'd ever seen. Her guileless expression was unflappable.

Hollie just sat there with her mouth hanging open—too shocked to respond.

Celeste looked at me and crinkled her nose. "Bella, did I not give an accurate enough description? I replicated the words in your book." She turned to Sydney. "I do wish to try the things that I learned in the lesbian erotica book I found. Bella seems to be an eager participant in my experiment."

Sydney smacked the table and smiled in my direction. "I knew it. You're a big ole dyke just like me." She frowned and I imagined that she was perplexed about why I'd never told her before.

"She's joking," I protested weakly. I felt bad about not confiding in Sydney, and she was the last person in the world that I wanted to hurt.

Sydney seemed to recover quickly and smiled at me. I thought she was trying to make me feel okay. "Hey, no worries, Mabs, we won't tell anyone. Your secret is safe with us." Sydney looked over at her partner. "Right, Hollie?"

Hollie just sat there smirking while Sydney was waiting for her to respond. "Oh absolutely, but whenever you're ready, we'll be the first to have a big coming out party for you."

I could hear the sarcasm in her voice and, fortunately, so could Sydney.

"Hollie, be nice," she chastised. "Mabs is shy and everyone has to be comfortable with who they are before they're ready to announce anything to the world. I promise you have our support no matter what."

I thought it best that I just not answer—that way they could think whatever they wanted to—but I wasn't about to confirm anything. How could I explain anything without painting myself into a tiny corner? I was pretty sure that if I'd come out in high school, no one would have treated me like they treated Sydney or Hollie.

Celeste was watching our exchange with a curious expression. She appeared not to understand what was going on. I needed to have a serious talk with Celeste about the kind of joking that she ought to avoid.

I was so not ready to come out to anyone, even Sydney. It was bad enough that Celeste knew after flipping through my book. If I were honest with myself, I was even kind of glad she found out. I'd never actually said the words to anyone, and I wasn't sure if I ever would. I suppose it didn't matter, because even though I didn't confirm things with Sydney and Hollie, it was pretty much a given that they knew now.

I needed to get us on a different topic. I knew how much Hollie liked talking about herself, so I went there. "Hey, Hollie, I read in the paper that you're running for state Senate. I bet you'll win in a landslide."

Hollie clearly liked the new direction of our conversation because for the next half hour she talked non-stop about it. I was able to get a reprieve when I went to the counter to purchase a latte for Celeste and myself.

I don't know how Hollie manages to be charming and witty when all she does is talk about herself, but she's an expert at sharing funny little anecdotes and normally sucks everyone into her sphere.

Celeste remained quiet and sipped her coffee— humming softly. I was beginning to recognize her humming as an indication of her pleasure when tasting something new. I wondered what rock she came out from under not to have ever experienced a latte. There was a Starbucks on practically every corner in the larger cities. Coffee shops sprouted up like weeds in the smaller towns that dotted not only the Pacific Northwest, but every other state in the nation. Celeste was an odd one, that's for sure.

Sydney kept stealing glances in my direction. I was becoming increasingly uncomfortable, so I guzzled the rest of my drink and made an excuse to leave.

"Sorry Sydney." I refused to address Hollie, the bitch. "Celeste and I need to leave if we're going to North Bend and then get back at a decent hour." I hastened to clarify that we would *not* be joining them for dinner. "We have a lot of shopping to do, so maybe a rain check on dinner."

"Do we need to check for rain before going to dinner?" Celeste asked.

I gave her a nudge in the direction of the door. "She's such a jokester."

Celeste scrunched up her face in confusion, but followed me out the door.

I practically ran out of the coffee shop and only felt remotely calm when I reached the sanctuary of my car. Celeste followed more slowly and I was ready to peel out the minute she shut the door and buckled herself in. It's a damn good thing there weren't any cops around as I burned rubber in my haste to get as far away from Sydney as I could.

†

I didn't want to be angry with Celeste and I certainly wasn't prepared to confront her, so I just casually remarked, "Um I'm not exactly…"

I didn't know how to finish the sentence and Celeste finished for me. "It was not a good thing that I mentioned what I learned in your book, was it?"

"No. That kind of teasing and joking around isn't very helpful to someone like me."

"Is it forbidden?" she asked.

"Uh no, it's just that Sydney and Hollie can get away with being open about their relationship because they're so popular and attractive. I'd never hear the end of it and I'm not that interested in being harassed until my last dying day."

She tilted her head. "I have so much to learn. I do not understand yet, but perhaps I will in time."

I spent the next hour telling her trivia about Snoqualmie Pass and pointing out various landmarks.

She acted like a kid turning her head this way and that, remarking on the beauty of the mountains. "We do not have this where I come from. It is very beautiful. I think I would like to explore these mountains."

I wondered where she was from. I started thinking that maybe she'd led a very secluded life—never exposed to other parts of the US. I'd heard about people who were homeschooled and protected from the outside world. I wondered if her parents were nutcases and that's why she was so unusual. I'd read about people, called empaths, who were sensitive to others. Of course instead of getting accolades for their special skill, they were isolated and shunned. I would just consider it my moral obligation to introduce her to many varied experiences, starting with a refreshing trek in the mountains.

"Well, I'm not much of a hiker, but I do own a pair of hiking boots and I could probably handle an easy hike or two," I offered.

"I would like that."

I didn't want to jinx anything because I was really enjoying Celeste's company, so I carefully broached the subject. "Um, Celeste, how long are you planning on visiting this area?"

"As long as it takes," she responded.

Okay that was definitely not helpful. I quickly interjected, "Um, it's no problem for me. You can stay as long as you like." I added, "I want you to stay."

"I will stay at least until the next moon change and then I will decide the future."

So I had at least a month. I smiled at her.

✝

We reached the outlet complex. I figured they would have everything she would need for the next month. My favorite place to shop was Banana Republic so I parked close to there. After Celeste got out of the car, I was so excited I grabbed her hand and pulled her to the store. I just knew she would look great in their clothes. Since she was about my size, I started pulling out pants, shorts, and shirts in a size six. Before I could check myself, there was a mountain of clothes in my arms the size of Mount Rainer. I laughed and she giggled right along with me.

She pulled me into the dressing room with her and I tried not to look, but it was hard—really hard. She didn't seem to notice or care and never looked away as I gawked at her.

I was right, there wasn't one outfit that didn't look amazing on her, but she limited her purchases to three pair of jeans, shorts, long-sleeved and short-sleeved shirts. I wondered if she liked the number three.

She didn't grab any underwear or socks, so I pulled out seven of each in different colors to match her new clothes.

I was curious about what else she might have in her backpack, as she rummaged inside and pulled out her wad of cash. I was amazed at how much money she had. It didn't seem like she'd even made a dent in the roll. I hoped that Celeste wasn't some kind of criminal like a drug dealer with all that cash. She really didn't seem the type. I watched as she stuffed part of the money in her back pocket before placing the rest back in her backpack. I tried not to be too obvious about sneaking a peak, but she zipped it up before I had a chance to see what might be inside.

The sales clerk was one of those bored rebel types with an impressive amount of metal attached to her face. She was literally wearing a dog collar with spikes, and I wondered how she possibly kept her job. It's not like Banana Republic is some punk clothing store. I watched Celeste scrutinize the young woman who rang up her purchases.

"Bella, does she need to be walked like a human canine companion?" Celeste pointed to the dog collar.

The woman raised her eyebrow, but fortunately didn't seem offended.

I cringed at her question. "Um, no. I'm pretty sure that's how she likes to accessorize," I whispered.

"Accessorize?"

"Yes, dress up her outfit," I explained.

"Is the metal on her face an accessory?" Celeste asked.

I didn't want to offend the salesperson, so I was just about to lead us out the door when the young woman chuckled. I was whispering, but Celeste wasn't especially quiet with her questions. She stuck her tongue out at Celeste displaying a small silver ball that prominently sparkled under the store lights.

The young woman winked at us. "This little accessory serves a dual purpose. My girlfriend loves it. You might want to get one." She looked directly at me. "I guarantee she won't be disappointed," she added as she nodded in Celeste's direction.

I blushed and mumbled, "Thanks."

Recognition seemed to pass over Celeste's face. "Oh, the little silver ball can be used to stimulate the clit when licking someone."

The sales clerk laughed. "Yep, sure can."

I tugged at Celeste and made a beeline for the door.

After we left the Banana Republic, an electronics store caught her eye and she stood mesmerized in front of the flat screen TV you could see through the window. Like a homing pigeon, she made a beeline for the section of the store with the fancy home theater systems. I followed her in like a puppy dog.

Normally stores put in action movies or animation because they show off the sound and color so well, but for some reason, this one had a romantic comedy because there was a couple starting to get a little steamy.

Celeste pointed at the television. "I would like to buy this instructional device."

"That's just a DVD playing. We can rent a DVD tonight if you'd like."

"Will it instruct me on the things in your book?"

Okay, now I was starting to get a little worried. Maybe Celeste wasn't joking before. Maybe my previous assumptions were correct and she was even more sheltered than I was. I silently cursed her idiot parents. I let an evil thought cross my brain. It had been quite some time since I'd watched a lesbian movie and if Celeste wanted some exposure to the dark side, well then, who was I to deny her? I already had a few favorites including the whole *L Word* series on DVD. Yep, the education of Celeste would begin this evening.

"Come on, Celeste. I have a nice TV at home and several DVDs that you might enjoy. You don't need to buy that. We should get you a comfortable pair of boots for hiking, and maybe a pair of tennis shoes or something casual for kicking around."

"Kicking around? I don't wish to kick anything, I think that would cause harm," she stated.

I laughed. She was so quirky. "I recommend Sketchers. They are the best shoes to do a lot of walking in."

She nodded and we proceeded to purchase a pair of hiking boots, a pair of Sketchers, and some casual loafers.

✝

I was getting hungry again so I suggested we stop somewhere for lunch. The North Bend Bar and Grill was relatively close, so I made the executive decision to stop there for a late lunch.

Celeste was eager to eat again. She sure seemed to enjoy food. Every time she ate, I would hear that humming sound. I didn't know where she put it all. For such a petite woman, she could pack in the food. She ate with more gusto than I'd ever seen anyone do before.

Since it was well past lunchtime and the parking lot was nearly empty, I knew we wouldn't have to wait for a table.

I think Celeste was learning to pace herself because she took my suggestion on what to order, and after we finished our meal, when the waitress asked if we wanted dessert, she followed my lead and shook her head. I didn't know if she was a vegetarian or not, but I decided to suggest the Portobello mushroom sandwich with sweet potato fries. Of course, she hummed again and the tempo increased just a tad after she took a bite of one of the fries. They were my favorite, too.

Sometimes I thought I would be happy with just sweet potato fries for lunch, but I kept hearing my mom's voice in my head that I needed to eat better or I'd blow up like a balloon. I wasn't overweight anymore, but that didn't stop me from feeling guilty every time I ate something that was remotely fattening.

When the check came, she snaked her arm out so quickly and grabbed the check from the waitress. "I noticed that the treat this morning required the paper I carry, and I would like to supply this for the food we consumed."

She lifted her right cheek, pulled out her money, and glanced at the check. I wasn't sure if she knew how much to give to the waitress so I looked at the check, pulled two twenties from the roll, and set them on the table. "That will be plenty and give the waitress a very nice tip. Thank you for lunch, Celeste."

"You are most welcome, Bella."

I slid from the booth and grabbed her hand. I was proud of myself for being so bold. Her hand felt nice in mine and there was a sort of warm energy that traveled up my arm. I never wanted to let go. We climbed into my old beater and headed for home.

✝

I needed to go to the grocery store to pick up some food for the next couple of days. I was going to impress Celeste with my cooking and maybe she would stay even longer. I was getting used to her quirky sense of humor and, of course, it didn't hurt that she was drop dead gorgeous. I was convinced that shopping with Celeste would be another adventure.

Celeste continued to look out the window and seemed in awe of the scenery around her. I guess I'd taken the beauty of the Pacific Northwest and the mountains for granted because I'd lived here all my life. As I watched Celeste admire the beauty, I had a new appreciation for where I lived.

It was a rare day and the sun was shining not only on the east side of the Cascade Mountains, but on the west side as well. Seattle was infamous for their rainy days, but on the east side, it was almost like a different state. In some parts of the state, the towns and cities boasted having over three hundred days of sunshine. It was one of the things I really liked about Washington—the diversity of weather. Since there was still some residual snow on the mountaintops, I had to admit it was breathtaking. When the sun bounced off the snow, the twinkles of light created a unique show for all to see. The reservoir, which was fed from the mountain runoff, displayed a perfect reflection of the majestic snowcapped peaks.

I pulled into the perpetually busy Safeway parking lot and Celeste followed me into the store.

†

I grabbed one of the smaller carts because I didn't really need to pick up too many things. Celeste kept looking around at all of the items stacked up neatly in the aisles. When she got to the meat and seafood section, she seemed dazed. As she looked at the whole salmon laid out on ice with their dead eyes staring at nothing, I wondered if her sheltered life included exposure to seafood. She crinkled her nose at the fish and the ridiculously red meat on display. I noticed her focusing on a trickle of blood that seemed to escape from one of the rib roasts.

"You eat the flesh of animals?" she asked.

"I don't eat beef, pork, or lamb, but on occasion I do eat chicken and fish," I replied sheepishly. As I looked at her face, I suddenly felt guilty for not being a complete vegetarian. It felt wrong. I tried to shoo her away from what appeared to be the slaughter of helpless animals, birds, and fish.

"Are chicken and fish good to eat?" she inquired.

I nodded. "Yeah actually they are really tasty, especially on top of a salad. I even like fish raw. I feel bad about it, but sushi is one of my all-time favorite foods."

I figured, since she asked, I could get some salmon and let her decide for herself if she liked it. I pointed to a wild salmon fillet and the man behind the counter wrapped it for me. I pitched the treat into my cart and continued to the packaged meats section.

She followed me to the refrigerated foods section and looked at all the packages—scrutinizing everything closely. For some reason, she was particularly intrigued with the sausages and hot dogs.

She picked up a packet of chicken hot dogs and scrunched up her nose. "These do not look like chickens or dogs. Dogs are pets right? Surely you do not eat your pets."

I laughed. "No, they take parts from the chickens and grind them up. I don't even want to know what parts they actually take, but I have to admit to sometimes liking a grilled hotdog occasionally. No we don't eat dogs here, but I think they do in some countries." I grabbed the processed meat from her hands and tossed it into the cart like I was making a basketball shot.

I traversed over to the bread aisle looking for some whole-wheat buns for the hot dogs.

She looked into the cart and asked a question that I was sure was one of the most guarded mysteries of the world, but being the nerd I am, I'd looked up the answer and was ready for her inquiry.

"Why are there ten hotdogs and only eight bread covers?" she asked.

"Very good question and inquiring minds like my own wanted to know that very answer, so I looked it up many years ago. Meat packers like to sell their items by the pound and ten hotdogs weigh one pound. Bakers don't like to make anything in multiples of ten because it's harder to split dough into five pieces. I guess it's easier to divide the dough into two or three pieces, so they prefer multiples of either eight or twelve. Before you ask, a baker's dozen is usually the result of that little extra piece of dough."

She smiled at me and I got the distinct impression that my explanation wasn't particularly satisfying to her.

When we got to the checkout stand, she pulled out cash from her back pocket and tried to pay. We had our first argument in line because she was my guest and I thought it improper that she should pay for groceries.

"You can just put that away. I got this. You are my guest and I want to cook for you." I pushed her hand with the cash away from the grocery clerk.

"I was able to obtain plenty of this paper. I wish to contribute equally," she insisted.

I wanted to ask how she got the cash, but we were in the middle of an argument, and I'm kind of stubborn sometimes. "I let you pay for lunch, which by the way I wasn't that comfortable with, so put your money away. You're insulting me."

"I suggest we both contribute," she offered and looked at me with those beautiful lavender eyes.

I sighed. It wasn't what I really wanted, but I'd never been much of a fighter and she seemed adamant, so I gave in. "Okay, but really I can afford this. I'm not poor, you know."

The clerk just looked back and forth between the two of us and, when we finally decided, she held out her hand for the money, half from me and half from Celeste.

Our hands touched when we forked over the money to the clerk and I felt a tingle all the way to my toes. I had it bad and I was in trouble. I was interacting with a real live woman, not some fantasy woman in one of my books. Even though she was odd, she was sweet, and she had this ability to bring me out of my shell.

No one had ever even come close to that, except maybe Sydney. Although I had to admit that even Sydney hadn't been able to get me to come out as a lesbian. Celeste had discovered my secret and I didn't care. I was happy about it.

As the grocery clerk was making change from the cash we'd given her, I noticed Celeste looking at the tattoo on her neck. I inwardly groaned, anticipating what new question might come out of Celeste.

I wasn't surprised when she asked, "Bella, why did someone draw on her neck? Is that a tribal symbol?"

The clerk glared at us.

I grabbed the change from the dispenser and gently pushed Celeste toward the automatic doors. I whispered in her ear. "That's a tattoo from the tribe, *rebellious youth*, even though pretty much everyone has one now."

I heard the clerk express her displeasure. "Weirdos."

"I do not understand." Celeste looked confused.

"Never mind." I pushed her out the door before rotten tomatoes starting flying in our direction.

We left the grocery store unscathed with our bounty, and I drove us back to my cozy home.

†

I knew that Celeste didn't have any idea where the groceries went, so I told her to relax in the living room while I put everything away. Of course she made a beeline to the erotica and picked it up again, flipping quickly through the book. I think she found my hidden cache because she pulled out two more books and began flipping through those pages as well. I wondered if she'd taken some kind of Evelyn Wood speed-reading course.

After I'd put away all the food, I walked out to the back patio to turn on the grill. I didn't want to cook anything elaborate and ever since Celeste picked up the hotdogs, I was craving them. It would be a simple meal and I was due some junk food since I'd been so good all week. I could cut up some tomatoes, pull out the relish and, voila, insta-veggies. I know it's a stretch, but I wasn't in the mood for healthy. I wanted everything about tonight to be bad. Junk food and hot lesbian videos would definitely push me outside my comfort zone.

It wasn't a big surprise that Celeste enjoyed the hot dogs and the Tim's cascade chips I set out. We both had a side salad and I smiled at the hodgepodge meal that seemed to please Celeste. I was saving a pint of Ben and Jerry's Chocolate Chip Cookie Dough for later. I would have popped some corn, but I knew we were both too full from dinner.

I pondered which video I should pull from my collection and finally decided on *Desert Hearts*. This movie was a classic and one of the first movies I ever saw that elicited a physical reaction. I know I must have taken a breath during the sex scene, because it was pretty long, but I sure don't remember that. The beauty of the magic between the two women mesmerized me and after seeing that, I never questioned my sexuality again. I had other favorite movies, like *Fire*, but *Desert Hearts* remains my favorite to this day.

I motioned for Celeste to sit on the couch and popped the DVD into the player. After I grabbed the afghan, I snuggled next to Celeste and pulled it over our legs. I couldn't believe how comfortable I was with sitting close to Celeste. I boldly took her hand. Who was this alien who took over my brain? This was *not* something I would normally be brave enough to do, but it just felt right.

Celeste glued her eyes to the images dancing across the screen and when they kissed for the first time, her head tilted to the side as if she was trying to figure something out. I kept myself from squirming when the sex scene heated up my living room, and I could almost feel Celeste react to what she was seeing. From her hand, I could feel the warmth travel up and down my body. I imagined that Celeste was Cay and I was Vivian. I could almost feel her mouth on mine, and when Cay traveled down Vivian's body, I felt the feather light touch of her mouth on my body.

I finally took a big breath when the movie ended. Celeste looked at me and smiled. "Bella, I want to experience a kiss. Will you kiss me like the women in the movie?"

My heart was pounding so hard I thought I was going to have a heart attack. Could I actually do this? I'd never kissed a woman before. What if I disappointed her? "I…I…really…uh…want to, but I've never done it before. I don't know how."

"It looks easy enough to me to replicate."

She leaned in and gently brushed her lips against mine. It tickled and tingled. I wanted more, so I touched my mouth to hers and brazenly opened for her as she captured my bottom lip with her own and ran her tongue along the edges. I reciprocated and sought entry as we both deepened the kiss.

Oh my God. I never wanted this feeling to stop.

I was panting as she broke away from me. Her smile widened. "I like kissing," she said.

"So do I," I touched my forehead against hers.

Even though I desperately wanted to make love with this beautiful woman, I wasn't ready for that. I felt completely off kilter with just the kiss and I had to know more about Celeste before I let things go further. I never in a million years thought I would find myself in this position. I still believed that making love was only reserved for someone I wanted to spend my life with, and up until this point, I hadn't exactly put myself out there to find that person.

She seemed to understand without my having to say a word. "Maybe someday you will replicate for me the other things we saw in the movie. I would like to understand love."

I wanted to understand love too, but I needed to understand Celeste. I blurted out the question I should have asked when I first met Celeste, "Celeste, where are you from?"

"It is called Sisterna. My home planet is nearly one hundred light years from Earth."

She offered this explanation so nonchalantly, that at first I thought I'd misunderstood or that she was joking again. Yet, at this particular moment, I knew deep down inside, that every word she said was the truth. I didn't question my gut, that all came later.

I took a few seconds to process what she'd just told me. "You're not joking are you? I'm guessing that you're not of this world, are you?"

"No, Bella, I am what you would call an explorer. They sent me to explore the planet Earth and to learn everything I can about your world. I am sorry I could not bring you to my ship, but the rules are very limiting. We are allowed to reveal many things, but cannot share our technology. Our leaders fear that some of your species would abuse this knowledge. We are a peaceful race. I could mimic the expression I was told you understand, but I suspect this is another earthling joke."

"Wait, let me guess. Was it, *I come in peace*?"
She chuckled. "Yes that is the one."

I don't know why I just accepted her confession, but I did because it all made sense. It's like the puzzle pieces suddenly all clicked into place. I didn't have to make up stories in my head anymore about why Celeste always made these off-the-wall comments, although a small part of me still questioned my own sanity.

What didn't make sense to me was why, out of all the people on Earth, Celeste would come to me. "Why did you pick me? I'm nothing special."

"Your energy signal is compatible with mine."

"I don't understand."

Celeste took both of my hands in hers and I saw the purple light glow between us. "What do you feel right now?"

"I feel an incredible sense of peace and this warm tingly feeling. It's not sexual or anything, it's just nice," I responded.

"I feel the same. When I touched Sydney, I did not feel the peace like when I touched you. On my world, we seek out our other half, the one who shares the same energy signature. When we find our compatible signature, the feelings and experiences are the same, a sense of peace and warmth. In your world, you may call this love, but I do not believe it is the same. I believe this feeling of love is much more…how shall I describe it so you understand…more intense. I volunteered to travel to Earth to bring back the knowledge of love. The energy force brought me to your town and I was compelled to seek you out. We do not make distinctions between genders on my planet. Sometimes energy compatibility is between two male life forms, sometimes it is between two female life forms, and on occasion, it is between a male and a female life form. This is the rarest, but there is no shame or concern when this occurs. I am perplexed by your desire to hide that you are drawn to the female life form."

"Welcome to my world and the concept of discrimination. It's getting better, but there are still some people who assume I'm attracted to men and would be less than pleased to know I'm not. I believe this applies to almost everyone in my family. Don't you have someone on your world that you share a compatible signature with?" I asked.

"I did. She was a primary healer and the territorial dispute with another planet diminished her energy too quickly for her to re-charge."

I saw a tear leak from her eye. She wiped it away and looked at her finger where the moisture clung like a sock removed from a dryer without one of those handy dandy dryer sheets.

"What is this water that escaped from my eye?"

"Haven't you ever cried before?"

"I have read about crying, and how this human response is connected to sadness. Love and sadness are foreign concepts to us. We feel loss, but I do not believe it is the same emotion. I must be able to replicate human feelings when I am on your planet." She quirked her head. "That is an interesting revelation. My superiors will be anxious to receive a report on this. We lack passion and as a result, the invaders from the other planet were able to take over most of our world. Since I have been on your planet, I feel things I am not accustomed to feeling. Perhaps I will learn about passion and bring this back to help with our revolution."

"When you lose your energy mate—sorry I'm not sure what else to call it—do you look for a new one?" I was particularly curious about this.

"Most of the time, yes, but there are times when we are not able to find another energy mate. I like that name—energy mate—it fits. I am surprised you understand these concepts so quickly. You must have above average intelligence."

I blushed. "It's not that hard to understand. Good luck with understanding love though, I think that's a concept causing many people to scratch their heads in confusion. I don't think I can teach you much there. I know there have been gobs of books written on the subject, so I suppose you could start with that."

She pointed to the television. "I like watching the picture images. Will I be able to learn more about love from those?"

I shrugged. "I suppose so. There are a lot of movies devoted to the topic. Sometimes they depress me because it seems like I'm always on the outside looking in, but I never get to actually experience it for myself." I chuckled. "You'd never be able to tell from my collection of books and movies. I guess if I can't find the real thing, the next best alternative is to get lost in the fantasy."

I jumped up from the couch and put in my next favorite movie, *Fire*. It's a beautiful story about two Indian women who definitely sacrificed everything for love.

"Well, okay then, let's start researching love," I blurted out.

I wondered if it would be so wrong to let myself explore something with Celeste. I'd be helping her with her research. Maybe she would fall in love with me and I could fall for someone who wasn't taken like Sydney was. It was far from perfect. Maybe Celeste didn't have an energy mate, but she wasn't even from the same planet. I was setting myself up for heartbreak. I knew that, but I didn't care because I genuinely liked Celeste and I wanted to feel something more. I wanted what other people had, someone who would love me that I would love right back, even if it was short-lived.

After I popped in the DVD, I liberated the pint of ice cream from the freezer and set it down on the coffee table in front of Celeste. I grabbed two spoons and removed the top of the container. Celeste was about to experience another delicious treat. I was looking forward to hearing her hum again. It was cute and one of the things that seemed to set me at ease.

I wasn't disappointed. After watching me dig into the container of Chocolate Chip Cookie Dough, she followed my lead and the humming started almost immediately. When the video got beyond the opening credits, she focused back on the television and became one hundred percent invested in the story up until the explosive ending. She wiped another tear away and turned my face to hers so she could kiss me again.

Wow, was she a quick learner. I think she sensed my hesitancy to take things further, even though I was pretty sure she could replicate what she'd seen and read. However, that did not stop her from boldly asking, "Bella, can I rest tonight in the same location where you will be resting?"

"Um…yeah…I guess that would be all right, but I…uh…don't think I can…uh…you know…do those things in the book that you read about…"

"Sweet Bella, I will wait to learn more about that. I only wish to exchange energy with you and feel the closeness of someone who is compatible with me. I miss that most of all." Another tear slowly trickled down her cheek. For someone who'd never cried before, she was sure giving her tear ducts a workout. How could I possibly deny her request? I wanted to take her in my arms and make this newfound sadness go away. It nearly broke my heart to see her tears. Maybe she didn't exactly know about love, but I was willing to bet my house that energy compatibility was a concept that rivaled love, even if it had a different name.

I imagined that a curious onlooker might wonder why I wasn't asking Celeste question after question, keeping her up all night learning about her life on Sisterna, but I wasn't wired that way. When I was a kid, I would painstakingly unwrap my Christmas gifts while my older sister tore into hers at a record pace. I liked the anticipation as much as the actual prize inside.

I was never one to reveal too much about myself so I didn't mind a slow tantalizing pace. I thought about how much I enjoyed it when that tiny little corner of the blanket uncovered just a hint of the naked woman beneath, or when a shirt was unbuttoned just enough to let you peek at the cleavage below. That's how I thought of what Celeste had shared with me that evening. Although I wanted to learn so much more about this fascinating person, the reward would be much more if I delayed my gratification and let things trickle out. At this point, I absolutely believed her story.

In my mind, anything worth exploring took time. Brick by glorious brick we would build a foundation of trust and friendship as we learned all about each other. I suppose I was deluding myself that something might come of this and she could choose to stay on Earth. It was a fantasy worth keeping. Beautiful women had never before just dropped in my lap wanting to exchange anything.

I gently grasped her hand and led her to my bedroom. Shyness overtook me as I realized we needed to change into some type of sleeping attire. I dug in my drawer and plucked out two pairs of gym shorts and two tank tops. I was no fool, I gave the smaller of the two tank tops to her knowing full well how hot she would look in what I picked out for her. I didn't have to say anything to her when I retreated to my master bathroom to change. After I changed, I pulled out another new toothbrush for Celeste, rather than retrieve hers from the guest bathroom.

Celeste was sitting on my bed waiting patiently for me. She'd already changed into what I left on the bed for her.

I motioned for her to follow me into the bathroom. Even though I'd laid out a toothbrush for her the night before, I wasn't sure how much she knew about basic human grooming. I handed her the toothbrush and she started to brush her eyebrows.

I giggled. "I suppose that might appear to be a tiny brush engineered for small patches of hair, but…" I nearly doubled over with laughter as a sudden thought popped into my head. "Uh…you didn't brush any other hair with your toothbrush, did you?"

She cocked her head to the side. "I do not understand. Why do you brush your teeth, they do not contain hair?"

"Well, depending on what you were doing the night before, it sometimes feels like you have hair on your teeth in the morning." I put some Crest on my toothbrush and pointed to the paste. "This is called toothpaste and it helps clean our teeth. Here let me show you. It's refreshing to brush your teeth. Good dental hygiene is important to keep our teeth from rotting and falling out."

I demonstrated brushing my teeth while she watched me. After she got the general idea, she stuck the brush in her mouth and tentatively moved it around giggling like a young child trying something for the first time. I think she particularly enjoyed spitting out the extra paste before she grinned broadly at me, showing off her pristine white smile.

"I like the taste of toothpaste."

"How do you keep your teeth clean?" I asked.

"We have machines that brush our hair and teeth and cleanse our bodies through the use of special energy blasts. It does not quite feel the same as your rain machine or toothpaste."

It was oddly domestic as we stood side by side brushing our teeth like an old married couple. At that moment, no one would have ever guessed Celeste was from another planet. She looked so normal, so human.

After we finished this nighttime ritual, I began to get nervous. I'd never shared my bed with anyone before except my cat, Gizmo. I think Celeste sensed my trepidation and touched my arm. The soft purple light infiltrated my body and once again created that wonderful feeling of peace and warmth.

I pulled the covers back and waited for Celeste to climb beneath the sheets before walking around to the other side and gently moving Gizmo from her normal spot. She let me know how unhappy she was with a stilted meow as she meandered to the end of the bed to stake out a new spot.

Celeste stroked my shoulder before wrapping her arms around me. I snuggled up against her body and let my hand rest on the small of her back. I was amazed at how comfortable I felt in her embrace. If this was what exchanging energy was about, I was all for it.

Celeste seemed content as she kissed my forehead and said, "Thank you for sharing your energy with me. I do not feel so homesick anymore. Sleep well, Bella."

"Sweet dreams, Celeste."

I closed my eyes and before I knew it, I was fast asleep, basking in the glow of Celeste's energy. My dreams were definitely on the sexy side.

Chapter Four

Mmmm. That feels so good," I mumbled, half-asleep and half-awake. I was at the glorious place where you're not quite conscious and the dream is still fresh in your mind. I didn't really want to wake up, but I was basking in the feather light touch caressing the entire left side of my body. I wanted to return to my nighttime adventure where I met a beautiful alien and we were sharing energy. As the touch brought about more awareness, I yawned, turned over, and looked into Celeste's luminous eyes. Gizmo, that little hussy, had curled up between the two of us and snuggled tightly against Celeste with one paw wrapped around her neck.

The sudden realization that this was not a dream, and I did indeed have an exquisite alien in my bed, instantly shocked me into becoming wide awake. I started to panic as I looked at the clock on my nightstand. It was almost nine o'clock. *Crapola, my parents are going to be banging on my door any minute.*

I bolted from the bed at the same time I heard my mom knock twice and then open the front door. "Hello…Mabel…it's Mom. Where are you? We're going to be late for church. Your father is being such a cranky pants this morning."

I popped my head out of my bedroom. "Sorry, Mom, I overslept. You and Dad go on without me and I'll catch up with you at the café after church."

My mom scrunched up her face in what I call her disapproving mug. "Mabel, that's the third time this year you've missed church. What in the world can you be doing so late at night that you can't get up for church in the morning?" She started to crane her neck around my living room.

My mom never really snooped in my house, and so as long as my books were safely placed in my bookshelf, she wasn't aware of my reading preferences. Today, unfortunately, several erotica books were littered on the coffee table from the time Celeste had perused them. Both the *Fire* and *Desert Hearts* DVDs were also prominently displayed for anyone to see. I panicked and ran out to head off my mom from scrutinizing the items in my living room.

I decided I needed to distract her before she either found those incriminating items or Celeste decided to make her presence known. "Mom, you need to hurry if you're going to make it on time. You know how Dad hates to be late. I promise to meet you for breakfast."

She grunted, but left without saying anything more. *Thank God for small miracles.*

I rushed back into my bedroom. "Celeste, we need to hurry and get ready to join my parents for breakfast. I'm so sorry, but it's a Sunday ritual that I can't wiggle out of. My mom is the nosiest person on the planet, and I've never introduced her to anyone but Sydney, so I'm not really sure how I'll explain your presence today. I'll have to think of something."

I was opening my dresser drawers and pulling out clothes like a madwoman. I stopped suddenly and blanched at a thought of my family meeting Celeste.

"You can't tell her about yourself. I don't think it would go over too well with her. I know it's a lot to ask, but can you please limit your questions today in front of my parents."

She nodded at me and took a second to touch my arm. I think she knew I needed her calming touch. I was getting addicted to that energy transfer that left me feeling warm and cozy.

"Shall I put on any specific type of clothing?" she asked.

"Any of the outfits you bought yesterday will be fine." I grabbed a new towel and shoved it into her hands along with her toothbrush.

"Do you wish me to use the rain machine again and brush my teeth?" she asked.

"Yeah, most people take showers daily and brush their teeth both at night and in the morning. I'll take my shower after you're done."

✝

The Cottage Café was *the* place to be on Sunday mornings. Roslyn didn't have any good places for breakfast, so everyone tended to drive to Cle Elum on Sundays. I think nearly the whole town eventually made their way there after church. We arrived a little before ten thirty, which was a blessing because then we could grab a table before the rush. On most Sundays we would patiently wait a minimum of an hour for an open spot. I knew that when I missed church my dad was secretly grateful because he wouldn't have to linger in the front of the restaurant. My dad wasn't the most patient man in the world. He was always Mister Cranky Pants on church day.

I still hadn't come up with a plausible explanation for why Celeste was joining us for breakfast. I didn't want to lie to my parents so I thought the less I said the better. Sometimes my introversion worked in my favor. I never really offered up that much about my life or myself, which is why my mom was constantly giving me the third degree. I knew it was rude but sometimes I just wouldn't answer her when she asked a question. Eventually she gave up and stopped asking me things. She liked to talk, or rather gossip, about everyone in town and that was just fine with me.

When I glanced over at the table next to the pie display, I noticed that a strange man was sitting with Sydney and Hollie. I didn't see his face at first, but from the back he looked stiff like some kind of government representative. I could tell that his hair had a military type of buzz cut. I saw Hollie whisper in his ear and she seemed to be flirting with him. She was sitting next to him and Sydney appeared oblivious to her disgusting display of seduction. I scowled in response to the exhibition. I'd heard that Hollie was bisexual, and she and Sydney had an on-again off-again relationship with her need to routinely explore her attraction to men. I hated every time Sydney took her back after one of her diversions to the dark side.

I felt a shiver and focused back on Celeste who seemed to stiffen as her gaze fell on the man. Before I could stop her, she abruptly left the restaurant. I wanted to go after her, but Sydney saw me and waved me over. I didn't know what to do so I thought I could say hello to Sydney and then make a quick exit to find out where Celeste disappeared.

"Hey, Sydney."

"Hi Mabs. Wasn't that Celeste with you? Why'd she leave?" Sydney had an uncharacteristically sheepish look when she asked me about Celeste.

The man turned around and burrowed his eyes at me.

I shrugged. "I don't know. I was just about to find out when you waved me over."

Hollie turned completely around and smirked. "Your *friend*, Celeste, is a total nut case. I knew something had to be wrong with her to hang out with you. Her family hired Greg here to find her. The wacko left after the mandatory three-day hold."

Sydney glared at Hollie. "Shut up, Hollie. Mabs, I'm sorry. It sounds like Celeste may need some help. Her family is really worried about her. She's delusional and thinks she's from another planet and that people are out to get her. You should probably try to convince her to go with Greg and get back on her meds."

At this point I was torn. Of course it all made sense now since beautiful women never gave me the time of day, but something niggled at my subconscious. On the one hand, it would explain a lot about her quirkiness and it was a credible explanation of her strange behavior, but on the other hand, something told me that Greg was not who he claimed to be. I really wanted to believe Celeste, even if that meant that I was not firing on all four cylinders.

Regardless of this new information and even if Celeste did have a mental health condition, I wasn't about to hand her over to this guy who may or may not have her best interest at heart. I already cared about Celeste and she sure didn't appear to be a threat to herself or others. So if she wanted to check herself out of the hospital, I thought we ought to honor her wishes. Besides, how could I explain the purple light and how she made me feel every time she touched my arm? In the back of my mind, I still had some doubts about this new version of the truth. I didn't know what to believe.

"She's a grown woman and, if she isn't harming anyone, I don't think Greg here has any right to take her anywhere she doesn't want to go." I felt my chin jut out as I made this bold proclamation that was so out of character for me. I never got involved in anyone else's drama.

"She's a paranoid schizophrenic who does have violent tendencies if provoked, especially if you challenge her delusions." Greg said. "Why don't you tell me where you live and I'll bring her back to the hospital where she'll get the medical attention she needs."

At least Hollie hadn't spilled those beans yet. Thank God for small miracles, but it was only a matter of time before she would provide him with all the information he would need to take her against her will. I needed to buy some time, find Celeste, and figure out what to do.

"Can I see some kind of identification?" I asked.

Greg visibly bristled at my request. "I didn't bring my business card with me, but I have it back at the hotel."

"How convenient. How about you give me the phone number for her parents so I can confirm your story."

Sydney quirked her head. I surmised that she hadn't thought to check this guy out.

"This is a very private matter for them and they don't wish to involve others to the point of making this more public than it needs to be, so I'm afraid I cannot divulge their identity. Celeste comes from a prominent family who wish to remain anonymous," Greg explained.

I didn't like this one bit. Sure, it seemed to fit with that big wad of cash she carried around, but something stunk more than a dead skunk. Every hair on the back of my neck stood at attention. Something was definitely amiss. I had a negative reaction to Greg and I trusted my gut on this. I tried hard to telegraph this to Sydney. If I had any chance of helping Celeste out, I needed her on my side because Sydney was my only chance at controlling Hollie's inner bitch. I knew the minute I left the restaurant, Hollie would be eager to reveal everything about me.

"Well I doubt that Celeste is going to hang around now that she saw *you*, Greg. Maybe she's schizophrenic and maybe she's not, but I'll bet she's smart enough to disappear. I doubt that she'll find her way back to my house. I'll look for her, but I can't promise you anything. Sydney, can you please tell my mom and dad that I had an emergency."

Greg narrowed his eyes and glared at me. He couldn't easily follow me without making a scene because he was wedged against the wall. No doubt he would bide his time and wait for the right moment to continue his quest. Cle Elum and Roslyn are tiny towns so it wouldn't take him long to track her down if he really wanted to.

I couldn't wait to make my escape. Just being in Greg's general vicinity made me want to take a shower. "I'll go see if I can find her and let you know," I told them before I ran out of the café in search of Celeste.

†

I looked all around, but there was no trace of Celeste anywhere. I saw my dad's car turn the corner and knew that if I didn't vamoose quickly I'd be stuck having breakfast with my parents. *Shit, where are you Celeste?*

I ducked around the corner hoping that I might find her there, but at the very least, I needed to avoid a confrontation with my parents. I walked quickly around the block and waited until I knew it was safe to go to my car. My dad would be pissed that I hadn't stayed and gotten a table. My parents weren't the only ones parking their cars and entering the café. The Cottage Café was starting to get crowded and that was a very good thing because it would aid my rapid escape. I was hoping that Celeste would find her way back to my house and we could figure this mess out together.

I reached for the handle of my car door and felt her presence glide behind me. When I turned around, the frightened look she gave me was all it took for me to shove her in my car and screech off for parts unknown. I just drove because I wanted us to be as far away from Cle Elum as possible. Seattle was a big city—surely we could get lost there.

"Celeste, you got some 'splainin to do." I tried to joke using my best Ricky Ricardo imitation. I loved the show, *I Love Lucy*.

She tilted her head. Why did I think she would get that reference?

"Sorry, I just meant that you left in a hurry without explanation, and I just had a very interesting conversation with Sydney, Hollie, and some guy named Greg. Tell me you don't know that scary dude," I implored.

Celeste looked down.

My heart dropped to my stomach. I wasn't going to like whatever explanation she was about to give, but I had to ask. "Celeste, did you check yourself out of the hospital?"

She nodded.

I felt sick. What a naïve fool I was. How could I possibly for one minute believe she was some kind of alien from outer space? For one glorious night I felt worthy, maybe even a little bit beautiful. Now I just felt defeated. I was confused and couldn't decide what to do. Celeste looked so forlorn sitting next to me and I honestly had no idea what to do about this tragic woman I had come to care for. If I asked her about it, would I get a straight answer or would her delusions get in the way? Celeste was still a human being and even though I was completely out of my element, I decided, illness be damned, to ask her what she wanted.

"What do you want to do now?"

"Please do not take me back to the hospital. They give me chemicals that stifle my energy. I cannot fight back when they inject me," she responded.

She looked petrified. I certainly didn't have the heart to take her back and turn her over to Mr. Slime Bag.

"Okay, Celeste. Are you up for a little adventure?"

"Of course. I am here to learn as much as I can. I knew you were the correct choice." She smiled and appeared to lose her fear.

"Seattle, here we come. It's a great city to visit. Consider me your personal tour guide." I decided it didn't matter if Celeste was looney tunes. I liked her just the way she was. She was colorful and if she happened to have an overly expansive imagination, well then so be it. Everyone has their little faults. I could do far worse in a friend or a lover. It's not like I'd had a whole passel of friends to compare her to and I'd definitely never had a lover—so what the hell.

Celeste touched my arm again and I felt that immediate flood of warmth. I wondered if this is what people experienced when they were falling in love. "Bella, I know you have your doubts about me and I want you to know I understand. Everything will work out as it should. I will not let any harm come to you, I promise."

Okay this was an odd thing to say, but then I considered that her paranoia most likely extended to me. At least she was a protective paranoid schizophrenic and so far she'd not done anything remotely aggressive or violent. I shrugged and continued to concentrate on driving to Seattle.

Seattle is one of the worst cities to navigate because the traffic sucks at all times of the day or night. You'd think that Sunday morning would be clear sailing on the highway into the city, but you would be wrong. Traffic slowed to a whopping thirty-five miles per hour. Either there was an accident or maybe some big event was happening. I didn't have a social life so I rarely paid attention to the numerous entertainment options the city had to offer.

Finally, we cruised into the downtown area and I found one of those all day parking lots a couple of blocks from Pike Street Market. I was starving because we hadn't stayed for breakfast and it had taken us nearly two hours to get to Seattle because of the crappy traffic. We made a beeline to the market because it was one of the best places to graze for a scrumptious meal.

✝

Pike Street Market is a major tourist attraction and always a flurry of activity regardless of the day of the week, but Sunday was particularly busy.

Celeste and I got lost in the crowd as I led her to a row of market vendors selling fresh seafood, baked goods, and ethnic specialties from every possible nationality. One of my favorites was a vendor selling chicken gyros. Although fresh fish and Seattle are synonymous, I was hankering for some Greek food and politely declined offers from the fish vendors. I ordered two gyros and a large Greek salad for us to share. I was looking forward to hearing Celeste hum again.

"Everything smells so wonderful." Celeste was looking from side to side trying to take in all the activity around her. When she noticed the flower vendor across the way, she made a beeline for the vibrant display. The bouquets presented a visual burst of color and invaded the senses of both sight and smell. It was as if an artist had personally arranged the canvas to heighten our experience. I took a deep breath and inhaled the sweet scent of Asian starburst lilies.

Celeste stuck her nose inside one of the lilies and the pollen left a large streak of orange all over her face.

I knew it would be difficult to remove so I giggled at the absurdity of this beautiful woman with a ridiculous smudge on her nose and cheek. She looked like a child who had gotten into something she shouldn't have.

I took a napkin and tried to brush it off, but the pollen stubbornly refused my efforts.

The owner of the gyro stand called out my name to let us know the order was ready. I grabbed Celeste's hand, led her to an empty table, and then walked over to pick up our order. Placing the gyro in front of Celeste, I dramatically proclaimed, "Your food, m'lady."

Celeste giggled and took a nibble of the tasty treat.

"What is this food?" she asked.

"It's Greek food. Greece is this wonderful country by the Mediterranean Sea and the gyro is their version of the American hotdog. It's Greek junk food, except in Greece, they stick French fries in the middle. They don't make gyros like that here in the US."

Celeste just stared at me like I had two heads or something.

"Oh, you probably want to know what's inside. It's basically seasoned chicken with condiments."

She took another big bite and mumbled, "I like this gyro."

She started humming again and I grinned at her. I was getting used to her eccentricities. Except for the fact that I had to explain a lot of things to her and she insisted she was from another planet, you'd never know she was a nut case.

We gobbled down the salad and I tossed our garbage in the nearest trash can before venturing out into the rest of the market. On a whim, I stopped at the flower vendor and bought a bouquet of Asian lilies. I figured if Celeste was going to wear their mark of shame, the least I could do was introduce her to the way that the flowers permeate the air and take over whatever enclosed space they end up blessing.

Our next stop was the famed Pike Place Fish Market where the workers put on a show by throwing fish at each other, joking, and playing with the tourists. There was usually a large crowd around the booth since they have the freshest fish around.

This company had developed and produced a famous management training video around their propensity to have fun while working. They called it the Fish Philosophy and it was so simple that hordes of major companies began to adopt their four simple principles—be there or be present at work, play and have fun, make their day, and choose your attitude. These guys loved what they did and it showed.

One of the guys spotted Celeste and pulled her into the show right away. "Hey, what's your name, pretty lady?" The guy joked while opening and closing the fish's mouth as if the fish was asking.

Celeste grinned and answered, "Celeste."

"Well, come on over here, gorgeous, and show everyone how you catch a fish," the fish monger shouted out.

I pushed her in his direction, encouraging her to get the full experience of the market. These guys were a hoot. Celeste seemed to embrace this new adventure with gusto as she followed the fish guy behind the counter, ready to catch the king salmon his partner was playfully swinging around for all to see. As soon as we entered the market, Celeste had safely secured her pack on her back leaving both hands free.

"Okay, now you gotta reach your arms out. Don't be afraid of the fish. You gotta grab it, you know, get a good grab on it cause we're not gonna sell this one."

Celeste giggled. "I do not know if I can do this."

"Sure you can. Say 'I'm gonna catch this fish.' You can do it."

Celeste grinned. "I am going to catch this fish."

"Yeah, there you go. Okay, now lock your fingers and put that back hand a little higher," he coached.

Celeste imitated his stance.

"There you go. Now grab it. How about Celeste!" he yelled out.

"How about Celeste!" the crowd mimicked.

"Hey, yeah," he called out.

"Hey, yeah," the rest of the fish mongers repeated.

The fish went flying in the air and Celeste reached out and, just like a skilled football receiver, she grabbed for that fish with everything she had, plucking it perfectly from the air. The crowd cheered as Celeste held her prize up.

I burst out laughing as Celeste proudly displayed her fish.

"Can we buy this please?" she asked.

"Sure, why not. He said he wasn't going to sell it, but I bet he'll sell it to us," I responded.

"You betcha. Ten bucks and it's yours," the monger replied.

"Deal," I said. For a ten-pound salmon, ten dollars was a steal.

He wrapped up our fish, added ice, handed us our trophy, and we giggled like schoolchildren all the way to the bathroom. I thought Celeste might want to wash her hands after her fish catching adventure.

We strolled through the rest of the market and made a final stop at a bakery. I wanted to purchase some cinnamon pastries and a dozen cookies for the road or maybe for dessert later tonight.

I didn't have the foggiest idea what we would do after visiting the market, and decided I'd better broach the topic with Celeste. I knew we couldn't hide out in Seattle forever, but I didn't exactly have a plan in my back pocket.

We walked along in the swarm of people, and I felt like a cow herded into an enclosed area before being sent off to slaughter. I shivered at that thought. Suddenly I was claustrophobic.

"Celeste, I'm not really sure what to do now. I wish I could just skip work tomorrow and hide out in Seattle until things cool down."

"I do not wish to cause you distress," she whispered.

"The only friend I have is Sydney and she lives with Hollie..."

"Hollie does not have good energy," she responded.

"That is an understatement. She's a first class bitch."

Celeste cocked her head. "Bitch?"

"Bad energy," I replied. I didn't want to explain the nuances of profanity. She was certainly good at remaining in character and true to her delusion.

"We shall return to your residence. Now that I am aware of the danger, I will be able to defend myself by using my energy reserves and mind probes. I just need to avoid the chemical injections."

I cringed when she mentioned the chemical injections. They'd obviously felt the need to drug her and I wondered if she became combative. I wasn't so sure that returning to Roslyn was the best strategy, but I didn't have a better idea. I'd forgotten about my phone and decided it wouldn't hurt to at least try to get more information about Greg from Sydney. It was a long shot, but maybe she could help us out.

I pulled my phone from my bag and gasped as I saw twenty-seven texts—some from Sydney and some from my mom. I scrolled through quickly getting the general gist of my mom's messages, which essentially communicated *what the hell do you think you're doing going off with some mental patient*. The intensity of her tone increased as the messages went unanswered by me. Sydney's were definitely less judgmental, but just as insistent. She wanted to know if everything was okay and if I needed any help.

Celeste was watching me as I scrolled through my messages and she picked up that something was wrong.

I looked at her and gave her a sheepish smile. "Um, I have a few text messages, so I need to let my mom and Sydney know that everything is okay."

I sent my mom a quick text, Everything ok. Promise I'll explain later.

Sydney's text would be trickier. I needed information and help. My fingers flew over the keypad on the phone, *Need ur help. Call me.*

The response from Sydney was instantaneous as my phone buzzed in my hand. "Hey, Sydney. Thanks for calling… No, I'm okay… Can you give me the scoop on Greg?… Shit, okay… I'm sorry, Sydney, I didn't mean to drag you into this… Of course you can stay at my house… Yeah, the key's under the big rock to the right of the welcome mat… No, we'll be back in maybe two or three hours… Yeah, that would be great if you can throw him off for tonight… Thanks Sydney, I owe you."

I ended the call and then I realized that Sydney was going to have free reign to snoop around and there was no hope of remaining in that big ole closet I'd carefully erected around myself. *Crap.* I guess confirmation that I was a card-carrying lesbian was imminent. I wasn't sure how I felt about that. On the one hand, it was a relief because I'd been keeping this secret for my whole life and it was getting rather burdensome. However, I was sure to hurt Sydney's feelings and she was the one person who'd always stuck up for me. How could I explain to her why I wasn't honest? She would never understand. She was one of the beautiful people.

Celeste touched my arm and my distress dissipated like early morning fog after the sun made its appearance known. She sure was handy to have around. I reveled in her touch. Maybe if she went on medication, we could make a go of it. Of course, if she did take her meds, she probably wouldn't be interested in someone like me. It was a catch twenty-two. Either I could have the woman of my dreams whose elevator didn't exactly make it to the top floor, or she'd be gone from my life like the dreams that wisp away when you wake each morning.

I cleared my throat to explain my phone call. "Sydney and Hollie had a big fight and she asked if she could crash at my house. She told me she would help us. She doesn't trust Greg any more than I do. The jig's up for me now, because I didn't exactly hide um…the books…or um…the movies."

"I still do not understand what appears to be forbidden about sharing energy or the human concept of love between two females," she remarked.

"Fortunately it is becoming less and less *forbidden*, but I just wasn't quite ready to share this with anyone, even Sydney. Being teased and bullied all your life has a devastating effect on your confidence. The idea of Sydney knowing my secret is growing on me. I am surprised that she asked to stay with us. She's never done that before and it's not like she doesn't have another place to crash. They break up every week it seems."

"Sydney and Hollie are not energy mates. You and Sydney could be energy mates. Although she was not compatible with my energy signature, her signature was positive and strong and I sensed the syncopation with yours. She looks upon you fondly."

I knew I was fortunate to have Sydney as a friend and I didn't ever dig too deeply around the reasons she was always kind to me. I just accepted the blessed miracle, for that is what it was—a damned miracle.

†

"Come on, let's head back to my Podunk town." I grabbed her hand so we wouldn't lose ourselves in the throng of people pushing and shoving inside the market. We walked hand in hand and eventually emerged to the less crowded street outside of the bustling tourist attraction.

I was surprised when it only took us ten minutes to navigate the streets of Seattle and make it back out to highway ninety. Although we slid over easily into the commuter express lane, it wasn't necessary because the road was relatively clear. This was a true rarity, even on a Sunday afternoon. I wasn't sure if this was a good or bad omen for us.

I turned up the stereo in my car connected via Bluetooth to my iPhone and effectively stopped any conversation for the ride back. As an over-the-top introvert, I'd conversed more with Celeste than I normally did with anyone in an entire year. I was done, exhausted. I needed to re-charge my energy. When we got back I'd need to play host to not one, but two beautiful women. It was almost beyond the realm of my abilities, but I was sure this was a once in a lifetime chance for me.

One of my favorite songs from a relatively unknown singer, Marie Digby, came on and I began to hum softly to the tune. The song, *Miss Invisible*, paralleled my high school experience. I looked over at Celeste and thought how odd that this fragile woman came into my life just like the boy in the song—out of the blue. The lyrics reverberated in the car, *then one day, just the same as the last, just a day spent in counting the time, came a boy who sat under the bleachers, just a little bit further behind.*

Celeste just smiled at me and took my hand in hers. She didn't say a word. She didn't have to.

I felt cared for. I felt good. Someone had finally noticed me.

The time flew quickly, both of us humming to the music. My old car rolled up to my little cottage and I was oddly peaceful when I saw Sydney's car in the driveway. Since traffic was clear on the way back, it had taken us less than ninety minutes to return home. We would have several hours of daylight left. I loved living in the Pacific Northwest in the late spring and summer because daylight stayed well into the evening.

Sydney was a far better friend than I deserved. All through school whenever she saw someone picking on me, she stepped right in the middle of it. Most of the time she would dispel the confrontation without harm, but on a few occasions, she simply punched her way out of it, ending up with a black eye for her efforts. I always felt guilty when she got hurt on my behalf, but eventually the bullies learned to hassle me when she was nowhere in the vicinity. Hollie was the worst of them and I never had the heart to tell Sydney that her on-again off-again girlfriend was the leader of the pack. I never understood why Hollie would even bother with me. I was a nobody. It just never made sense to me.

I thought back to when we were eleven years old and Tommy Harris pushed me into a puddle of mud. I sat there in the pool of sludge, crying and afraid to go home to explain about my soiled dress to my mom…

"Mabel mudbutt, Mabel mudbutt," Tommy laughed.

Sydney barreled into Tommy, ramming him into a sister puddle much larger than the one he tossed me in.

"Shut up, Tommy butthole, before I shove your face into that pile of horse shit over there." Sydney pointed to the Olson's field where they rarely picked up after their horse.

I blinked once.

She extended her hand to me. "You okay, Mabs?"

Tommy jumped up with his two fists clenched, pushed Sydney, and popped her in the nose.

Blood poured from her nose, but that didn't stop her from doing exactly what she threatened to do. She pummeled his back while she shoved his face into a fresh pile of manure. He was crying by the time I pulled her off of him.

I put the sleeve of my dress up to her nose to try to stop the bleeding. "Aw, Sydney, look what he did to you. Why'd you do that? He hurt you."

Sydney shrugged, pulled my sleeve away, lifted her t-shirt to her nose to stop of the flow of blood, and put her arm around my shoulder. "You're my friend aren't you? Friends stand up for each other. I know you'd do the same for me."

That was the first black eye she received on my behalf. I never did come to her rescue. Mostly because she didn't need me to, but a bigger part of it was my fear. I tried to fly under the radar. Sometimes it worked, a lot of times it didn't. I tried to repay her kindness. I would offer homemade cookies and cakes that mom packed for me in my lunchbox. I saved all my desserts for Sydney. It was the least I could do. Most of the time she refused them, but on occasion the temptation was too great. Mom made the best desserts…

I shook my head and came back to the present. I saw someone part the blinds and peek out. I was on the verge of bolting, when Sydney opened the front door and waved at us with a smile on her face. I trusted Sydney so I figured the coast was clear for now.

✝

It's amazing what a false sense of security one has when barricaded in your comfortable space. My home was that comfortable space, even with the two guests that I felt I needed to entertain.

Celeste was carrying her prize possession from our daytime escapade—the ten dollar salmon she caught with her bare hands at the market. I pointed to the refrigerator and Celeste must have understood because she placed the fresh fish on the middle shelf where there was an empty space. I was looking forward to preparing a special dish that evening.

I still had the lilies in my hand so I reached for an empty vase that I had stored in a cabinet next to the stove. I didn't bother to cut the ends because, honestly, I didn't think it really made all that much difference. I filled the vase with water, plunked the flowers inside, and placed it on the kitchen island. I could already detect the sweet smell as I envisioned the flowers enveloping all of the stale air molecules hovering in the kitchen. I pulled the kitchen shears out of the junk drawer and proceeded to clip off the pollen so that Celeste wouldn't obtain another mark on her face. I giggled again when I realized she still had two yellow stains on her face from earlier.

Sydney sat on the soft, moss green, ultra suede recliner in the living room and patiently waited for us to put away our bounty from the trip to Seattle. Celeste and I joined her on the matching sofa. Celeste grabbed my hand and I didn't pull away. Sydney seemed to focus on our joined hands. Celeste had already dumped her ever present backpack next to the couch.

"Okay Sydney, what's the full story? I don't mean to be rude or anything, but you've never asked to stay here before when you and Hollie were fighting, so there must be something more you didn't tell me over the phone."

Sydney's eyes never shifted their focus from our joined hands as she ignored my question and asked one of her own. "So, are you two an item now?"

"Bella has compatible energy to my own," Celeste offered.

Okay that was not very helpful.

I knew I was directing my frustration at the wrong person, but I couldn't help myself because I felt protective of Celeste. "Sydney, try not to judge please. Celeste is not doing anything harmful, so why can't everyone leave her alone. I don't care if she checked herself out of the hospital. She doesn't want to go back and I want to help her, so either you help us or you can just get the hell out."

Direct hit. Sydney blanched at my words and whispered, "I'm not judging. Sorry."

I felt bad. She definitely never deserved my angry words. "No. I'm sorry, Sydney. That was uncalled for. Look, I don't really know what our relationship is. I simply care for her and want to help."

"Mabs, I'm on your side. I just don't want you to get hurt. Hollie is being Hollie and she's enamored with Greg. I'm fed up with her. This time I'm done. She didn't even try to hide her flirtations. She is hell bent on helping Greg track you down." Sydney offhandedly waved her hand at Celeste. "I don't really need to stay at your place, I just wanted to be here to take you to my cabin. We can all crash there while we figure out what to do next. I suspect Greg will be here any moment to try to drag Celeste back to the hospital. Hollie has been very helpful with information about where you live and where you work."

"Won't he just come to the cabin when he doesn't find us here?" I asked.

Sydney looked down. "Hollie doesn't know about the cabin. I bought it on the sly six months ago when we started fighting again. I needed a place to go where she wouldn't follow me and wear me down again. I've been fixing it up during the day when Hollie's at work."

"She is not your energy mate. Her energy is very negative. She will destroy your positive energy if you continue to try to be compatible," Celeste offered.

"Celeste, you're not helping." I sighed.

"I don't really know what you're talking about, but we need to get to the cabin fast before they realize you're back. I stalked off after I caught Hollie hanging all over Greg. She probably thought I was just taking one of my long hikes in the mountains, but when I headed back to the house, I saw a strange car in our driveway. I didn't want to catch them in bed so I took off again. After ruminating over what I suspected was happening between them, I called Hollie. She and I had a screaming match over the phone. I told her I wasn't coming home tonight. She had the nerve to say, 'fine, I'll just entertain our guest by myself then.' You called about thirty minutes later while I was at the grocery store. Hollie can be *entertaining* for several hours, but I get the impression that after Greg gets his rocks off he'll be heading straight here. Throw a travel bag together and we can head out. We can take my jeep. The roads are a bit rough up in the mountains and we'll need the four-wheel drive."

"What about work? I can't ask you to drive me to work and pick me up every day. Besides, won't Greg just follow me after work or something?" I shook my head. Our situation was hopeless. Greg was able to track Celeste all the way to Roslyn. Surely he would be able to find the location of Sydney's cabin.

"Can't you call in sick for a few days until we figure this out?" Sydney asked.

I'd never called in sick a day in my life. I came from healthy German stock and I had strict morals around work and reliability, but I'd never cared for anyone like I cared for Celeste. It was a dilemma, but I justified my deception because I was helping someone out.

"Okay." It was just one word, but it said everything. Celeste was more important to me than my self-proclaimed integrity.

Sydney just nodded and I thought I saw a bit of sadness surface in her expression. I wasn't sure what that was about, but I didn't have time to contemplate what was going on in Sydney's head.

I jogged back to my bedroom and pulled out a large overnight bag. I began tossing shirts, shorts, jeans, underwear, and my bag of toiletries that fortunately, due to my severe case of OCD, I'd amassed neatly in a clear plastic bag.

I had a thing about my shower case. I wanted all the things that made me clean arranged neatly in one location in case I ever needed to go out of town. I didn't want to forget anything. I would religiously put them back into their little plastic bag and zip them up tight after every use. The bag included an impressive list of items: a second toothbrush, tube of toothpaste, shampoo, conditioner, face and hand lotion, handmade soap, and chapstick. I didn't wear much make-up, but I also had a second plastic bag for that in an equally organized manner.

I silently apologized to my shower and make-up bags after tossing them unceremoniously into the overnight duffel.

Celeste was watching me and I almost forgot about needing to retrieve a bag for her. I rummaged in my closet until I found my second overnight duffel and tossed it in her direction.

"Put all your new clothes and your toothbrush in that bag and grab whatever books you want to read and toss them in," I directed.

She walked out of the room with the duffel in her hand.

A few minutes later, I was packed and ready to head out. I could hear noises in the guest bedroom and hoped that Celeste wouldn't need any help. She came out of the room about ten minutes later and the bag looked full, so I let out of sigh of relief. For someone suffering from paranoid delusions, she was remarkably calm.

Celeste walked calmly to my bookshelf, scanned the titles, and plucked four from their cozy home in the bookcase. She unzipped her bag and carefully placed them on top before closing it back up. She grabbed her backpack and slung it over her free shoulder.

Gizmo had a sixth sense for when her mommy's normal routine was different. She would weave in and out of my legs before stretching her paws up and meowing loudly. It was as if she were saying, *hey aren't you forgetting something.*

"Crud, what about Gizmo. I can't just leave her here all alone. She doesn't understand. She's not like other cats, you know, all aloof and snippy. She'll definitely miss the people contact."

"Um, I guess we can bring her along. I don't have any cat food or a litter box, so we'll have to grab those and bring them with us." Sydney touched her hand to my arm and gently retrieved my bag to carry it out to the jeep. It was such a Sydney thing to do and I let the sweet gesture wash over me like one of those beautiful rain showers I bathed in with my Aunt on one of our *adventures.*

I don't know why I always forgot about all the gentle, caring, gestures that Sydney did throughout the years of our friendship. You would think I would have tattooed each one directly to my brain, burning each and every kind deed into my memory, but I found myself unworthy of her kindness so I promptly dismissed them.

Sydney left with my bag and was back a few seconds later. I'd located my container of cat food and some extra litter holding one item in each hand. Sydney promptly grabbed both and once again exited my house where I presumed she was making a second trip to her jeep to load the additional items.

Celeste had followed Sydney out on the first trip and when she came back, she was minus the overnight bag and backpack so I assumed she had already stashed them in the jeep.

As I was heading to the mudroom where Gizmo's litter box was located, I turned around briefly to ask, "Celeste, would you mind picking up Gizmo while I get the litter box?"

Sydney followed me into the mudroom and grabbed the box before I even had a chance to pick it up. I thought to myself, *what a butch thing to do, like carrying all my books to class.* I chuckled at that random thought.

I grabbed my purse with my phone, credit cards, and a small amount of cash. Actually, it was more of a small bag because I didn't carry a purse, and I looked around one last time before I shut the door on my comfortable, safe life. I was about to start a new adventure and with one quick touch from Celeste using her free hand, the calm feeling swept over me. I eagerly stepped into the Jeep.

Chapter Five

Sydney's cabin was hidden so far into the woods that I doubted a first rate bloodhound would be able to find it without detailed directions. I remember thinking it was so like her, unpretentious, simple, and elegant, with fine angular lines in perfect symmetry. I imagined her cabin absorbing the essence of Sydney, just like when pets begin to take on the characteristics of their owners.

I'd always wondered how she could stand to live in Hollie's ostentatious home in the haughty gated community that undoubtedly Hollie's father picked out for her. Sydney seemed to stick out like one of those pictures in an IQ test where they ask *what doesn't belong here?*

The ginormous evergreen trees bunched up around the cabin provided a layer of protection against outsiders hoping to break into the inner circle. Ten different shades of green blended together creating a postcard picture of splendor. I imagined this was a favorite location for the local wildlife, and made a note to peek out the window to try to catch a glimpse of the magnificent elk that might make a brief appearance.

It was an overcast day again, which wasn't a big surprise for late spring. Dark gray clouds blanketed the sky, and I couldn't tell if the trees let any sunshine breach their protective barrier. I hoped they did so that I could raise my face to the sky and absorb the healing light that always seemed to brighten my mood.

Sydney grabbed my bag again and led us into her private world. The inside of the cabin was just as spectacular with its gleaming wood floors and hand-crafted stone fireplace. Polished granite and marble accented various parts in the cabin, creating the perfect blend of wood and stone.

Celeste followed us into the cabin carrying her backpack across her shoulder and, in her other arm, Gizmo rested calmly as if going to a new place was the most natural thing in the world. She'd left the borrowed overnight bag in the Jeep, presumably determining her pack and Gizmo were her first priorities.

There was a slight hesitation from Sydney before she ambled down to what I assumed was the guest bedroom and gently placed my bag on the bed. She looked up quickly at Celeste who placed her own duffel next to mine on the bed. A frown replaced Sydney's usual quick smile, but she didn't say a word. Gizmo, the little harlot, was content to remain in Celeste's arms. Sydney quickly left the room and I momentarily forgot about getting the rest of our stuff, including Gizmo's litter box and food.

"I do not wish to offend, but I would enjoy sharing energy again," Celeste stated.

Fortunately, I knew this was not a euphemism for sex in her delusional world, because even if I was ready for that, I somehow didn't feel right having sex in Sydney's cabin. It almost felt like cheating. I knew that was ridiculous because Sydney and I were never anything more than friends, but I was still madly in love with her, even though I was starting to have very similar feelings for Celeste.

What a loser I was to fall in love with two completely unsuitable women. One was unobtainable and the other quite possibly might end up locked away in an institution.

I kissed Celeste's cheek to let her know I was okay with the sleeping arrangements. She smiled at me and my heart went pitter pat. One touch or one smile from her was enough to make my day. The only other person ever to have the same effect on me was Sydney.

Celeste sat on the bed petting my purring feline. I sat next to her and gave Gizmo a few scratches on her chin. She was adapting to the transition of a new place amazingly well. Celeste handed her to me as I hugged her closely to my body, absorbing the warmth and security of something familiar. After a few minutes, I set her gently on the bed.

I heard some rustling around in the living room and then I remembered about the rest of our shit and suspected that Sydney was probably hauling it all into her cabin. *I am the worst friend in the world sitting here relaxing on the bed while Sydney does all the work.*

My mind was jumping all over the place as I thought about where we would store the litter box because I didn't want to stink up her cabin. I should have thought to bring the flowers. That got me thinking about the fish that would undoubtedly rot in the refrigerator unless I called my mom to take care of it, but then she would ask a whole bunch of questions I was not prepared to answer. Maybe I could get Sydney to go back for it. God, what was I thinking?

I hopped up from the bed to help and started to think about some kind of plan to keep Greg from involuntarily committing Celeste to the mental hospital. Celeste was right on my heels as I entered the main living area.

Of course it was too late to help Sydney since she'd already finished bringing everything in. I felt like such a schmuck for not helping her. Now she was busy building a fire, and with one quick blow on the logs, the flames licked up the fuel and burst into a blaze of orange and yellow dancing lights. Rather than simply sit, she seemed to fall back on the chair a few feet away from the fireplace.

Sydney wasn't aware that we'd entered the cozy living room as she sat with her head in her hands. I'd never seen her so dejected. I wanted desperately to fix whatever made her so sad and to tell her how sorry I was for being so rude.

"Oh, God, Sydney. I'm so sorry that we left you to take care of all of our shit. I'm such an ingrate." I put my hand on her back to let her know I was there for her. "Sydney, what's wrong?"

She looked up and a quick smile returned to her face, but I noticed it didn't reach her eyes. "I'm just tired. This morning I came off my double shift."

Sydney was a Paramedic/Firefighter who worked forty-eight-hour shifts and then had a string of days off. I was thankful that she wasn't missing work on our behalf. It was bad enough that I had to lie to my boss. I was surprised she'd suggested I call in sick because Sydney was the most honest, straightforward person I knew. I don't think she had the constitution to lie to anyone.

Sydney gestured toward the couch and I took that as our cue to get down to business and try to figure things out. She looked directly at Celeste.

"Okay, if we're going to help you, I'd like to hear your side of the story. Something about Greg didn't ring true and I'm willing to keep an open mind," Sydney calmly stated.

"What would you like to know?" Celeste asked.

"For starters, did you check yourself out of the hospital like Greg claims?"

"Yes."

"Okay. Why?"

"I did not belong there."

"Did your family take you there?"

"No."

"Okay, maybe I'm going about this all wrong. Can you give me a little more information besides yes, no, and other cryptic responses?" Sydney shifted in her seat and I noted a touch of frustration in her voice.

"I fear you will not believe what I have to tell you. Initially, Bella accepted my story, but now I fear she was tainted by the information the government man, Greg, provided to you." Celeste tilted her head to the side and seemed to watch Sydney's reaction with interest.

I flinched when she casually revealed her perspective about me. She was spot on, I was influenced by what I'd learned at the Cottage Café, and it was reinforced when Celeste confirmed that she had indeed checked herself out of the mental hospital.

"I'm really trying here to be open to all possibilities. So please, give me a chance to weigh all the information before we proceed," Sydney pleaded.

"I misjudged the reaction of humans when I tried to find a human who was energy compatible. When I reached out to touch various women, one began to shriek and attracted the attention of a man in a uniform. I did try to explain I meant no harm, but he would not listen and when I tried to calm him by touching his arm, he used a burst of energy that caused momentary pain and left me without the ability to calm him or others. He placed shackles on my hands and led me to a busy building with humans bustling about. Some were injured and I wanted to help them. A nice woman came in to talk with me and I told her why I was here and tried to explain that I meant no harm. The shackles were uncomfortable and I tried to use my energy reserve to open them, but I did not have enough to break free. I was agitated and they stuck me with a large needle injecting a chemical substance that was very unpleasant. I woke up the next morning shackled to a bed and without energy to free myself. I needed the sun to recharge and the room was without light." Celeste gave her explanation calmly.

I groaned. I wasn't sure if Sydney would decide to yank her from her chair and escort her straight to the hospital. I tried to add a little levity to her explanation. "Well at least you learned your lesson and didn't approach Sydney or me that way."

She smiled. "Oh yes, I did learn. Sydney had an energy signature that did not appear to exhibit aggressiveness or an overactive response, so I just touched her arm to calm her. With you, I did a mind exploration to make sure you were not afraid. However, I did not need to touch you to determine compatibility. I knew right away that you were special, because your energy came off in strong waves before I made contact. This was how it was with my energy mate. It is a rare thing on my planet to determine compatibility prior to contact."

"How does Greg enter into this equation?" Sydney asked.

"I do not know who called Greg, but he showed up shortly after I became aware of my surroundings and he began questioning me. I sensed his motives were impure. He reminded me of the invaders. I refused to answer his questions. He became angry. I tried to touch his arm to calm him, but he slapped my hand away and then they stuck a needle in my arm again."

"How did you find your way here?" Sydney asked.

"I watched and listened. I learned what I needed to imitate to convince the lady doctor I was not a threat. I overheard them talking about releasing me to Greg. He told them he was a friend of the family. I'd convinced them to take me out to the garden so I could recharge under the Earth sun. I used a special energy burst and some minor mind manipulation on the lady doctor to get her to discharge me several hours early, and then I fled to this town."

Okay, so she had explained everything, but everything she said fit very nicely into Greg's story of her delusions. Sydney was still one step behind because she hadn't heard Celeste explain that she was from Sisterna and all the other stuff about energy mates and the quest to understand love.

Sydney stared wide-eyed at Celeste. "Um, I don't really understand your reference to 'energy compatibility' or using 'energy bursts'?"

"I could offer a demonstration, but it is forbidden to use our energy for superfluous reasons," Celeste responded.

"So you don't have family looking for you?"

"We do not have family on Sisterna. We have caretakers assigned to no more than three young ones. They teach us and provide the basis for our moral code of behavior. It is normal for us to want to be like our caretakers, and one of mine was an explorer so I naturally emulated her."

"Sisterna?" Sydney crinkled her nose.

"Yes, that is the planet I come from. My home world offers a different kind of beauty than Earth. Sisterna has three suns to your one, and although I am biased, I believe the result is a more spectacular sunrise and sunset. The additional energy assists with our recharging needs. It is difficult for me on Earth to achieve the same benefit."

"So you actually believe you are from another planet?" Sydney's eyebrow shot up.

"I warned that you would not believe." Celeste looked down and seemed to deflate right before my eyes.

I felt bad, but I had my own reasons for not supporting her. It was almost impossible to accept that this stunning woman would give me the time of day under normal circumstances. I didn't trust that anyone would want to spend time with boring, plain ole Mabel.

She looked directly at me. "You do not believe me," she stated. She didn't seem to care if Sydney believed her.

I couldn't lie to her. "I want to believe you, but you're so beautiful and I'm well...I guess it makes sense…um not that I think any less of you…oh shit, I'm just making you feel worse, aren't I?"

"This illness that you suspect me of is considered a substantial flaw?" she asked.

"Um yes, wait, no. I don't want you to think there is something wrong with you. Shit, this is all coming out wrong. I guess I just proved the enormous stigma attached to mental illness. I'm so sorry. I'm really not trying to judge you, but I guess that's hard to believe now."

"Bella, I do not know why you believe yourself to have insurmountable flaws making you unworthy of an energy mate, but on my world you would be highly sought after. Your energy signature is strong and vibrant. I think I now understand why you do not believe me. If I have this enormous imperfection, then it would make sense that I would choose you as my energy mate. You are not as flawed as your logic." She glanced at Sydney. "I am sorry, your energy signature is strong, but not compatible with mine. You would make a worthy energy mate."

"Okay, let's say for the sake of argument that I do believe you. Why don't you just take off in your ship and head back home if Earth is so dangerous and this Greg guy has nefarious motives?" Sydney asked.

"It is worth the risk to bring back the understanding of love and passion. We've been watching this planet and, while sometimes your passion leads to destructive fanaticism, it has an equal likelihood of generating what's needed on our planet to protect against the invaders. Love seems to be a powerful emotion and I must understand this before I leave."

"You know it doesn't really matter whether we believe her or not. I know you don't trust Greg and that should be enough to try to help her," I added.

Sydney sighed. "That's why I offered up my cabin in the first place. I'm just concerned that we're not the kind of help she really needs." Sydney looked directly at me. "I hope you know what you're doing, Mabs."

I looked over at Celeste and noticed for the first time that evening that she appeared a little pale and a bit sickly. I was worried about her. "Celeste, you look a little peaked. Why don't you take a nap while I help Sydney with dinner?" I looked over at Sydney. "I'm sorry, I don't want to be presumptuous and I promise I'll pay you for the food."

Sydney just waved her hand at me as if to say don't sweat it.

"Thank you. The sun did not shine enough today and my energy reserves are low. I do not know if sleeping will assist in the recharge process, but I know it does not harm me."

Celeste shuffled off to the guest bedroom and I got up to show Sydney that I was ready to help.

Sydney smiled at me. "I think I'm getting the better end of this deal. I know what a good cook you are and, frankly, I'm getting tired of eating out. A home-cooked meal sounds fabulous. When you called, I decided I should get more groceries to stock the cabin before heading back to your house to wait for you. I'm sorry I lied and told you I needed to stay with you, but I was afraid that Hollie would lead Greg to your house before I had a chance to take you to the cabin."

I tilted my head and bravely asked, "Why do you stay with her?"

Sydney shrugged. "I was immensely flattered when she first showed interest in me. I didn't think I had a chance with the person I really wanted to be with and Hollie was interested and attractive so I just accepted her advances. She isn't always such a bitch, you know. Sometimes, especially when it's just the two of us, she can be really sweet and loving. In her own way, I really believe she loves me as much as she can love anyone. We have history and it's hard to give that up. I've never had any incentive before to make a change."

"I'm sorry, but I think you can do way better than Hollie."

"Mabs, can I ask you something?"

I nodded and allowed her to change the subject.

"Why didn't you ever tell me you were a lesbian? I don't understand why you would keep that a secret from me. There were days that I suspected, but I figured if you were, you would have told me."

"Sydney, you saw maybe one tenth of the shit that people put me through in junior high and high school. I was convinced that if I so much as uttered a word about my preferences, it would get worse and I was barely hanging on. It was self-preservation pure and simple. After college, I just got used to the lie of omission."

"Hollie was one of the ring leaders, wasn't she?"

I didn't want to lie to Sydney so I nodded once.

"I'm so sorry. I should have known. She was so jealous of you and, when Hollie's jealous, she really acts out."

"Jealous of me," I remarked in astonishment. "What could she possibly be jealous of? I have a low paying job, no one special in my life, and just look at me." I waved my hands over my body.

Sydney looked at me. "Mabs, I am looking at you, and I've been looking at you for over ten years. Every year you get more beautiful. Sure, you went through an awkward stage in middle school just like we all did, but you seem to be stuck in the nineties and only see yourself as that awkward seventh grader. You're the whole package. You're kind and generous, incredibly smart, strong beyond belief, and more humble than anyone I know. Hollie absolutely hates the fact that you don't need make-up with your flawless complexion. She frets over every single traitorous wrinkle while noting that you have none."

I didn't know how to respond to what Sydney just said. Her generosity embarrassed me. I chalked it up to her personality. Sydney never said an unkind word about anyone and saw beauty in everyone. She was looking at me strangely and I got flustered so I looked away and couldn't meet her eyes.

"I'm sorry, I'm making you uncomfortable," she continued. "Celeste is very beautiful. I can see why you're drawn to her, even if she has some problems. She sounds so convincing. I can see why it would be easy to believe that she's telling the truth."

It was time to float out the thought that kept hovering at the surface. "Sydney, what if she really is telling the truth?" I held up my hand. "Wait, let me finish. I sensed something was different about her right from the start. When she first told me part of her story, I believed her because it fit with what I felt and saw when she touched me. Don't you remember that strange purple light that seems to emanate from her hand just before you feel this total calm overtake your body?"

I risked a quick glance in Sydney's direction and she didn't appear to discard what I was saying out of hand.

I continued. "Also, I could have sworn she talked to me in my mind. I know it sounds crazy, but I distinctly heard her ask me without really asking me out loud if I was frightened of her. Then I swear she whispered that I was beautiful in my head before deciding to call me Bella. The strange thing was I was thinking of that name right before she decided to call me that. I remember thinking about the movie, *Twilight,* and how I wanted a beautiful name like Bella instead of my crappy name."

"I don't know, Mabs, I've heard that some people who have mental illnesses can be quite convincing and you'd never know they were ill. I had this firefighter that I worked with once tell me that when he was visiting his sister, who was doing her medical residency at this mental institution, he struck up a conversation with a woman who convinced him that she was another doctor and a colleague of his sister's. He learned later that this patient was a master at imitating others."

"Can't we just consider it a remote possibility?"

"Sure, Mabs, anything for you. I promise to keep that possibility in the back of my mind so that she can pluck it from me when she finishes her nap. Come on, I'm starving and looking forward to whatever masterpiece you intend to put together for dinner."

I realized she was joking with me, but I also knew that she would actually do her darndest to keep an open mind for me. Sydney was a true blessing and it was nice to have such a good friend in my corner.

†

Sydney pulled a salmon fillet from her refrigerator and I noted that it was not only fresh, but wild caught. I guess it was national salmon shopping day. I would have to remember to ask Sydney to retrieve our whole fish and, unfortunately, we'd have to eat salmon two nights in a row. I spied the fruit bowl and noted there were several oranges and apples. I tossed Sydney a smile. It would be a delight to grill this fish in my garlic orange sauce. I know my mom is biased, but she always told me that my salmon was better than in any five star restaurant. Because of that, she would never order fresh fish when my dad took her out for a nice dinner.

"Can I just browse around your kitchen and see what else I can find to complement the salmon?" I asked.

"Absolutely, snoop away, and just tell me what you need me to do. I follow directions really well," she answered.

I was lucky enough to find red potatoes and I'd noticed a small garden earlier. I hoped I would be able to find some fresh herbs. Thyme grew like a weed and that would be a perfect addition to both the salmon and the potatoes. I nearly squealed with joy when I found arugula and goat cheese in the fridge and she even had some blueberry infused craisens in her pantry. A gourmet salad was definitely in our future.

"It won't take me long to prepare the salmon, but roasted potatoes will probably take at least an hour. I hope you don't mind having fish two days in a row because I forgot about our purchase at the market today, and was going to ask if you could go to my house tomorrow and get it for us before it rots in my fridge and leaves a smell I'll never be able to get out. Oh, and do you by any chance have some thyme in your garden?"

"Yep, sure do. I also have some basil, tarragon, mint, and oregano, but the thyme and mint are the only plants that are really big enough to get a decent harvest from right now."

I got the distinct impression that she was proud of her garden.

"Can you please pick some thyme for me? And if you have any basil or mint that is ready to cut, we can throw that on the salad," I directed.

She saluted me and pushed open the sliding glass door leading to her back yard.

I heard her cell phone go off and because she left the door slightly ajar, I could hear her end of the conversation. I wasn't really trying to eavesdrop, but when I heard her voice increase and become decidedly agitated, I admit I scooted over closer to the door to listen.

"Hello… No, I'm not ready to do that… I don't know. I have a lot of thinking to do… Don't, just don't… Leave Mabs out of this, she is not our problem… Stop it, just stop it right now. I'm not the one that fucked up… I know you do, it's just… Oh babe, please don't cry. I'm not trying to hurt you… Okay, tomorrow… Yes, I promise, but it's only coffee and a talk, I can't offer anything more at this point… Yeah, me too."

I heard Sydney sigh and peeked out the window to see her lean against the glass. She wiped her eyes and walked over to the patch of dirt with the tender green shoots. As she squatted down, I could tell she was crying just a little. I didn't want her to think I was spying on her, so I left her to her private moment. Maybe I should have gone to her, but if she was anything like me, she wouldn't want anyone seeing her at a vulnerable moment. I just hoped she wasn't going to cave and go back to that snake in the grass. I'd never hated anyone before, but I hated Hollie at that moment.

I had heard all our small town's rumors. Everyone thought Hollie first started seeing Sydney to rile her dad, but then she discovered she really was bisexual. She kept cheating on Sydney and swearing it was the last time. It never was. I didn't doubt that she loved Sydney, because who wouldn't love her, but she definitely did not deserve her.

Ten minutes later Sydney walked back into the cabin and, although I could tell she'd been crying, she acted like nothing was wrong. She managed to smile at me as she presented her bounty. "All for you m'lady."

I couldn't help myself and blurted out. "Hollie's a bitch and you deserve so much more. If you were mine, I'd never treat you like that. I'd thank God for every single moment I had you in my life."

"Oh Mabs, why couldn't you have told me you were gay…"

Celeste interrupted Sydney when she entered the kitchen and looked out the window. The sun was desperately trying to make an appearance and I could see blue skies on the horizon. She would only have maybe another hour or so before sunset, but maybe that would be enough to help.

"I could feel the Earth's sun ready to shine upon us this evening. May I step onto the patio to gather some much needed energy?" Celeste asked.

"Sure. Knock yourself out," Sydney replied.

Celeste tilted her head and I guessed that she didn't understand the phrase, "knock yourself out," but she didn't say a word. She still looked pale and unhealthy. I thought even if she was delusional, the power of suggestion might work in her favor like a self-fulfilling prophecy. If she was convinced that she could recharge herself through the sun, then maybe it would work and she would stop looking so ill.

I wanted to finish my conversation with Sydney because I thought I was missing something important, but the moment was lost. Sydney was looking at me as I was watching Celeste's every move.

"Are you in love with her?" Sydney asked.

I focused back on Sydney. "I care for her. There is something about her that is so compelling to me and it's not just about how she looks." I frowned.

"I know that already. Mabs, you are definitely not a shallow person, unlike the rest of the world that judges people by their outward appearance. She seems nice, a little eccentric maybe, but nice. You're more confident around her. That's a good thing. Someone needs to bring out the best in you. I wish…" Sydney's phone blared and interrupted what she was about to say. "Shit, sorry, I better take this."

This time Sydney walked out of the kitchen and took the call in the privacy of her bedroom. I wondered if Hollie was calling. Maybe she did love her, but I didn't think she respected her.

As I was preparing dinner, I looked out the window again and saw Celeste with her arms outstretched and her face lifted up to the sky. She was basking in the warmth of the evening now that our elusive sun was making an appearance. She looked so carefree and innocent soaking up the late evening rays, and I thought to myself, *this is how a Goddess must look*. An artist would take one look at her and want to create a masterpiece with Celeste at the center.

Sydney interrupted my thoughts as she emerged from her bedroom. "I might go out later tonight. I can get your salmon while I go back into town. Will you be okay here?"

I knew she was going to meet Hollie and that her resolve was wavering, so I made a final plea. "Don't do it Sydney. Don't run back to her. At least give yourself an evening to really think about what you want and what you deserve before meeting for coffee tomorrow."

She blinked at me and sighed. "She's really distraught. I've never heard her like this before. I just want to make sure she's okay." Her eyes focused on me and it felt like they were boring into me. "Wait, how did you know I was meeting her for coffee? Were you listening in before?" She didn't sound angry, more like perplexed.

I looked down at my feet and wouldn't meet her eyes. "I'm so sorry that I eavesdropped before. It's none of my business, just ignore everything I said. I don't know what's come over me lately. I never would have done anything like that before or butted into your business…it's just…"

She narrowed her eyes at me. "Just what, Mabs?"

I couldn't believe I was about to confess how I felt about her, but I caught myself just in time. "Nothing. It's nothing. Uh you go ahead and do what you need to do. I'll save some dinner for you, unless you want to wait just a bit and have dinner first."

Sydney glanced outside, watching Celeste before responding. "Yeah I'll do that, have dinner first because it smells amazing." She smiled at me, and this time it reached her eyes.

†

Dinner was a smashing success and I was proud of how well everything turned out. Sydney smiled as she listened to Celeste hum her pleasure with the meal. As if by some unspoken pact, we all decided to avoid any reference to Celeste's belief in her alien heritage.

It was a nice evening, so we decided to eat outside. It seemed like the sun really was helping Celeste because her rosy glow seemed to return with every minute we spent out in the final light of the day.

It was nice to receive their sincere admiration for my cooking skills. Celeste hummed while Sydney made satisfying *mmm* sounds. I shook my head as it wandered to thoughts about what kind of sounds either of them might make if we were making love. It was positively scandalous how I was thinking about both of them.

Sydney pushed herself from the table. "I better get going so that I can be back in time to deliver dessert. I won't be long and I'll bring us back a surprise."

"I hope everything goes the way you want it to, but if you need someone to talk to, I'll be here. All the times you had my back, it's the least I can do for you." I looked her straight in the eye. "This time I have your back, Sydney."

She chuckled and waved at me as she left the back patio.

I suppose it was ludicrous. Big strong firefighter Sydney needing mousy little me to have her back, but I meant it. I wanted her to know that no matter what happened I would support her. I was developing a bit of a backbone and I would go toe-to-toe with Hollie if she needed me to.

"Hollie is not well suited to Sydney. Their energy signatures do not match," Celeste stated.

I nodded. "I agree with you, but unfortunately Hollie has some kind of pull on her because she keeps going back no matter what that skank does."

"Skank?"

"Sorry, it's a very unkind description of someone."

"Can we watch the video box again?" she asked.

Her quick change of topics was starting to give me whiplash, but I was eager to talk about anything else but Hollie. I led her to the living room and when she was settled into Sydney's recliner, I showed her how to change the channels on the TV and pull the handle on the recliner so she could relax after dinner. Once she was involved in the TV, I picked up the dishes, brought them inside, started washing them, and got lost in my thoughts.

I would be sharing the room with Celeste again and I didn't know how I would get any sleep. My nighttime fantasies were suddenly coming to life and I was experiencing a brand new set of sensations that I wasn't sure how to handle.

I'd always told myself that I would wait to have sex with someone I was in love with, but that notion seemed incredibly old fashioned and somewhat unrealistic with each passing hour I spent with Celeste. Besides, maybe I was falling in love with this eccentric woman who, with the right drug cocktail, might be the perfect match for me. It was time to start living rather than existing.

As I let the warm sudsy water flow over my hands while cleaning the dinner dishes, I decided that if Celeste wanted to try out some of that stuff in my books, I would let her. I might even be brave enough to experiment with a few things I'd read about. I hoped it was as easy as the books described.

I wiped my hands on the dishtowel and slowly made my way to the living room to join Celeste.

She was watching some sappy Hallmark movie and seemed so engrossed that it was almost comical. It was like she was memorizing every word, every gesture. She looked up as I entered the room.

"I am learning about love from this video box," she stated.

I laughed. "I don't think you can really learn about love from the TV. That's just Hollywood's version of love. I think you have to experience it first hand before you know what love really is. I also think there are different kinds of love."

She tilted her head and looked at me. "Will you tell me of those different kinds of love?"

"Well, there is a mother's love…" I stopped because I suddenly remembered one of my favorite children's books and I wanted to share this with Celeste. I was glad I'd packed my iPad and could access the book on my Kindle app. I ran into the guest bedroom, pulled my e-reader from my overnight bag, and began scrolling through the Kindle library until I found the book, *Love You Forever*.

This book always made me cry. To me, this was the essence of love because no matter what the little boy did, his mother never stopped loving him. Of course it all came full circle when he rocked his mother and sang her the same words: *I'll love you forever, I'll like you for always, as long as I'm living, my mommy you will be.*

It was such a simple book, but captured the essence of unconditional love. As much as I liked to complain about my mom and her overwhelming need to try to stick her nose in my private affairs, I knew that she loved me. I don't know why I never gave her the chance to help me with my angst over growing up and learning about my preference for women. While she may not throw a celebration party, I knew deep down that it would never stop her from loving me. Someday soon I would have to let her in on that little secret and give her the opportunity to show me that love.

Of course, I started bawling the minute I began to read the book to Celeste, and she definitely did not understand.

"I do not understand why the water falls from your eyes. Is this not something that occurs when you feel loss or sadness?" she asked.

"Yes, we cry when we're sad or experience loss, but sometimes we cry for other reasons. It's hard to explain. Sometimes people cry when they experience great emotion, including love or happiness, or when something moves you like a magnificent piece of art or music. When something touches your soul in such a profound way, tears appear. Poems or books do that to me. I am moved by words. Words matter." I touched my chest where my heart lies. "I feel it here."

She quirked her head. "Love is very complicated."

"That, my friend, is an understatement. Besides a mother's love, there is love between friends. There is love between energy mates as you put it. There is brotherly or sisterly love. Humans love their pets, like children, and sometimes refer to them as fur children—especially lesbians. There is love of music, art, food, nature, and sport. I suppose love is synonymous with passion. We throw around the word 'love' so carelessly that it has lost its true meaning. True love means sacrifice and compromise. Sometimes love means pain. Some people say there is a fine line between love and hate. I'm not sure I subscribe to that philosophy, but love and hate are both the ultimate emotions. Love can also be destructive and addictive."

"I hope that I have enough time here on this planet to experience at least one of those types of love so that I may bring this concept back to Sisterna. What do you suggest I watch on the black box to learn about these different types of love?"

"Well I'm not so sure you can really learn about love from watching TV, but it can probably give you some rudimentary information. Like I said before, I think in order to really learn about something, you have to experience it firsthand. It might not be easy to explain, but everyone says you definitely know it when you feel it."

"I read about this passion you speak of in one of your books. I would like to experience this passion. Perhaps it will help me learn about love."

Okay this was it—the fork in the road. Would I be able to take the plunge? I decided to defer the decision until later. "Maybe, Celeste, but this will have to be experienced in private after we retire for the evening."

"Retire?"

"Yes after we go to the bed to rest like we've done in the previous evenings."

"This passion is experienced in the sleeping chambers?" she asked.

"Well not always, but for me, if it's going to happen at all, yes, it will have to be in the sleeping chambers behind closed doors. I'd rather my first experience be in a comfortable private place, so no back-seat make-out sessions or rapid kitchen table excursions for me."

She must have been satisfied with the answer because she turned her focus back on the television and continued to watch the movie.

†

Two hours later Sydney walked into the cabin with a cheesecake in one hand and our fish in the other.

I could tell she had been crying because her eyes had that puffy red-rimmed look about them.

I walked over to her, removed the dessert and salmon from her hands, placed them on the kitchen counter, and then did something uncharacteristic. I pulled her into my arms and hugged her. I stroked her cheek and then followed it with a kiss. "You okay?"

She pulled back and looked at me and I think she was in shock.

In all the years we'd been friends, I'd never had the nerve to hug her before, much less touch her so intimately. It was a chaste kiss, but I still kissed her on the lips versus her cheek.

She nodded, but didn't say anything about her visit with Hollie. "I called in a favor and got us a cheesecake from the bakery." She grinned.

I remembered the blueberries in her refrigerator and after I found a place to store the fish, I pulled them out to toss on top of the rich dessert.

"Excellent choice. They make the best cheesecake in the whole state."

This assertion seemed to rouse Celeste from her movie, as she stretched and gracefully moved toward the delectable treat laid out on the counter.

"Will I like this cheesecake, Bella?"

"Oh yeah, this will definitely have you humming."

"Sorry it's so late, but since none of us have to get up early tomorrow, we can enjoy the sugar rush. Coffee anyone?" Sydney offered.

"Sure why not. I might as well indulge since we can all stay up late and maybe I can experience a good old fashioned slumber party since I never got invited as a kid," I joked.

"You did too. I invited you all the time, but you never came," Sydney pointed out.

"That's because Hollie threatened to put super glue in my hair and other unspeakable cruelties. I didn't dare accept the invitation. Besides, your invitations didn't count."

I didn't really want to tell her all about the hideous, old-fashioned, night gear I had to wear as a further enhancement to my metal mouth. Mom had selected a positively ancient orthodontist who insisted on using the old techniques. I was beyond embarrassment about the additional accessories and would have never agreed to attend a slumber party even if Hollie didn't show.

"Why not? What am I, chopped liver?" Sydney asked.

Celeste was watching us banter back and forth like she was watching a tennis match, her eyes moving from one to the other.

"I thought your mom made you invite me."

"She did no such thing. I never understood why you always declined. Although, I must admit to wondering which creative excuse you would use. I looked forward to hearing them. My all-time favorite was that your cat had abandonment issues and would pee all over your shoes if you left her for one night." Sydney chuckled.

"Actually, at the time, that was true. Gizmo's not like that, but my cat at the time, Peaky, really did pee in a shoe when she thought I ignored her too much."

"Ew. What did you do with the shoe?"

"I threw it out, you doofus. What did you think I would do, wear it to the prom?"

Sydney shrugged. "I don't know. I only had two pair of shoes in high school, so I might have tried to rescue it."

"You did not. You had a different pair of shoes for every sport you played."

"Those don't count because I always left them in my locker."

"How come you only had two pair of shoes?" I couldn't fathom this at all. I admit to being a shoe worshiper.

"How many do you really need? I had one for casual dress and one for dress up. Black goes with everything, you know."

I laughed. "No it doesn't. That's ridiculous."

"Well it went with everything I owned."

I remembered back to high school and Sydney did seem to wear only black. That was her rebellious stage and I'm sure her parents were relieved when she grew out of it.

"Yeah, I guess it did go with everything you owned back then. Tell me you don't only have two pair of shoes now."

"Oh no, I've doubled my wardrobe. I now have four. Shoes aren't my thing."

"Someday you will have to let me take you shoe shopping. I don't think they'll kick you off the lesbian island for having more than four pair of shoes."

"Oh I know that. Hollie has hundreds." Sydney looked away when I frowned.

I definitely did not want her focused back on that she-devil so I took us down a different path. "How did we get on the topic of shoes anyway? Surely we have better subject matter to explore. How about if we talk about a plan of action for tomorrow?"

"I still have to meet Hollie for coffee. Nothing was settled tonight. It didn't go well." Sydney twirled her hair, which I knew was one of her nervous gestures.

Dang, that direction in our conversation backfired on me.

I reached for her hand and squeezed. Okay, now I was thinking that some kind of alien must have taken over my brain. I did not show anyone affection, except maybe my family, but that's what we did in our family, hugs for everything.

"We'll all take a hike when you get back. I seem to remember you enjoy all that nature crap. Maybe we can go camping or something. I know you were some kind of super girl scout."

"I would enjoy learning about the flora on this planet," Celeste interjected.

I had to hand it to her, she never broke from her belief in her alien origin.

"I think a hike is a perfect choice. I do my best thinking when I'm surrounded by the beauty of the mountains." Sydney looked at me. "You would agree to camping? You know there are no electrical outlets for your hairdryer."

"Everyone's a comedian," I grumbled. "That's what baseball caps were designed for."

Sydney slapped her hands together. "Perfect. I know just the spot."

"Hey, I'm only agreeing to one night. That's about as long as I'll be able to keep from having to dig a hole in the ground. I refuse to…you know…I'd rather hold it. No coffee for me tomorrow."

I did not camp, but if I wanted to cheer Sydney up, I knew I would have to agree to camping. However, there was no way I was going to defecate in the woods. That's where my compromise ended.

Celeste was staring at the cheesecake. "Will we be able to taste this dessert tonight?" She smiled at me. "Did I use the correct name?"

Sydney opened a drawer and pulled out a knife. "Oh sorry. I almost forgot about the cheesecake. Yes, I believe a little sugar therapy is in order." She cut the pie in thirds and reached into the cabinet directly above her head to pull out three plates. The slices were unusually large, but I wasn't about to complain about that. The bakery did make the best cheesecake in the state.

"I'll make the coffee if you show me where you keep the beans and the coffee pot." Sydney pointed to the cabinet on my left and I found a bag of Pioneer Coffee from the local coffee house, a grinder, and a large French press. The teakettle was already on the stove, so I filled it with water and plunked it back on the burner. I filled up the coffee grinder, pushed the button, and the smell of fresh beans wafted into my nostrils, eliciting a sigh from me. I loved the smell of fresh ground coffee.

Sydney opened another drawer and retrieved three forks that she unceremoniously distributed on each of the plates.

I took the blueberries hidden in the refrigerator and placed them on the island for everyone to use as the perfect topping for the cheesecake.

Sydney's eyes lit up while she pulled a large spoon out, dipping into the berries, and added a generous mound of the sweet fruit on top of each of our treats.

Neither of them waited for the coffee and plunged right into the creamy delight. Celeste's humming began almost immediately. Sydney was moaning in pleasure and I was having my own little reaction to their obvious pleasure. I decided to delay my own gratification because nothing went better with dessert that a fresh cup of coffee.

Sydney must have noticed that I wasn't eating and mumbled through a forkful of her dessert. "Mmm, aren't you going to eat that?"

I pulled my cheesecake closer to me and placed my arms around the plate. "Mine. Don't you even think about stealing a bite. I'm waiting to have this with my coffee."

Sydney laughed. "I wouldn't dream of it, Miss Possessive." She raised her eyebrow at me. "You know, Mabs, I don't know what's come over you, but I like this more playful side."

I blushed. "I kind of like it too."

"Her energy was hidden at first, but I recognized the potential," Celeste stated as a matter of fact.

"That's our Mabs, still waters run deep. I think there's a whole river of passion hidden inside her."

It didn't sound like she was joking and I blushed again.

"Is this the passion you described when you tried to explain love?" Celeste asked.

I shrugged. "Sydney's interpretation of love and passion may be completely different from mine." I grinned at Sydney. "Why don't you try to explain love to Celeste?"

Sydney's eyes bored into mine. "That's a tough one. I guess to me the ultimate love is putting someone else's needs above your own, and patiently waiting for the right time to tell the person you love how you feel. Even if you're not sure they feel the same way, you take that chance because it's worth the risk, but only when they're ready to hear it, because you love them enough to make sure they don't suffer any negative consequences from your confession."

"That's beautiful, Sydney, and brave." I felt my eyes water with emotion. "All right, enough of this mushy stuff. Let's get in our PJs and have an all night movie marathon or do whatever you do at a slumber party. I need to make a call to work telling them I won't be there tomorrow and then, let the party begin." I frowned because I still wasn't comfortable calling in sick. "You know I don't take nearly enough vacation and I don't think I can lie, so I'll just tell them I need to take a few days to take care of some personal issues."

"I knew it. You can't even tell a little white lie. I don't know how all that goodness fits into your compact little body."

I waved away Sydney's remark and made the call to my boss who didn't even ask any questions. I guess he figured since I never asked for much time off, it must be important to me. He told me to take a couple of weeks because I deserved a real vacation. I eagerly accepted his suggestion.

I knew our slumber party was just delaying the inevitable decision about what to do with Celeste and her desire to try out the stuff in my lesbian erotica. I still wasn't sure what I really wanted. I knew what my body wanted, but my mind was a completely different kettle of fish.

We ended up staying awake until about two a.m. and then one by one we dozed off. Sydney was the first to leave the party and retire to her bedroom. I woke up needing to go to the bathroom and found an afghan draped across Celeste and another one tucked around my feet and shoulders. I knew that Sydney had done this before she went off to bed. She was definitely the most thoughtful woman I'd ever met.

I gently shook Celeste awake. "Come on, Celeste, we should head off to bed because I don't think camping will be nearly as comfortable."

Saved by the slumber party. I knew I wouldn't be faced with any life altering decisions tonight. We were both groggy and shuffled off to bed. I did enjoy cuddling close to Celeste and, as she would put it, sharing positive energy. It didn't take her long to fall back to sleep with her arms wrapped snugly around my body. Although it took me a few minutes to join her in slumber, I followed her lead and was fast asleep before my body could react to our relative positions to one another.

Chapter Six

It was late the next morning when a noise wrested me from my dream. This time I was dreaming about Sydney. God, what a dream slut I was. One day I'm having sex dreams about Celeste and the next night it's Sydney.

At first I thought that Sydney was back from her *talk* with Hollie, but it didn't quite sound like her Jeep. The hairs on the back of my neck seemed to stiffen all at once and I got this sixth sense that something terrible was about to descend on us.

I gently nudged Celeste and whispered, "Celeste, wake up. Someone's here and I don't think it's Sydney."

I didn't even know why I thought we had uninvited company, I just felt all tingly like something was seriously wrong.

I heard the front door creak open and before I could rouse Celeste, the bedroom door flung open.

Greg was larger than life sneering at us from the doorway. "Well, look at what we have here. The little dyke librarian and her alien lover."

I noticed the gun in his hands and pulled the covers up even though we were both in shorts and t-shirts. It didn't take a rocket scientist to know that we were in deep shit and Greg was definitely not who he purported to be.

I called upon all the bravado I could muster. "What do you want, Greg? You can't just kidnap her against her will. She doesn't want to go with you, and unless I'm mistaken, you can't commit her without cause."

"I'm sorry, but my orders are to secure her using whatever means necessary. I'm afraid you are going to be collateral damage. I guess Celeste was violent after all. What a tragedy that she shot her friend during a psychotic break."

"Please do not hurt Bella. I will go with you if you leave her alone," Celeste pleaded. She scrambled out of bed.

"It's too late for that."

Although I am sure that what happened next only took a few seconds, it felt like everything was unfolding in slow motion. Greg raised the gun took aim and I felt a searing pain enter my chest. A dark purple blast of light shot out of Celeste's hand and knocked him back against the door as I heard the gun clatter to the floor. Sydney came barreling into the room and before I felt an overwhelming heat enter my body, I registered the wide-eyed look on her face.

Greg began to rise from the floor, so I shouted, "The gun, get the gun, Sydney."

Sydney had a moment of indecision, which was just enough time for Greg to retrieve his weapon from where it skittered across the floor. This time he took aim at Sydney.

I must have reacted to the scene unfolding before my eyes because Celeste calmly turned her head in Greg's direction and once again I witnessed a dark purple light shoot from her palm. Whatever the light was it had laser like accuracy, and the gun turned a bright red color.

"Fuck!" Greg shouted as he dropped the flaming red object.

I couldn't believe my eyes when the gun turned into a puddle of molten hot metal in the corner of the guest bedroom.

Greg started to move toward the bed and I could tell he was furious.

Finally, Sydney vaulted into action as she tackled him from behind and placed a well-executed elbow to his head as his nose met the floor with a sickening crunch. Sydney is a particularly adept fighter and, fortunately for us, her profession keeps her in tiptop shape. Using her knee to push him down again, she jumped up ready to do battle.

Greg was groaning on the floor and I took a second to look down at my chest. When I saw the spot of blood, I freaked out, and I imagine that my eyes rolled back into my head as I promptly passed out.

I don't think I was out for very long. I felt a soft touch on my face and looked into Celeste's beautiful lavender eyes. She looked concerned, but she also looked like she was ready to pass out herself. Her face was a ghostly white and her breathing was uneven. I looked around for Sydney and panicked when I didn't see her, but then I noticed Greg still on the floor and he looked like he was unconscious.

I sat up quickly and asked, "What happened? Where is Sydney?"

"She went to get something called a zip tie."

I touched my t-shirt where the stain still occupied a large section in a gruesome red hue. "I don't feel any pain, but I was shot, wasn't I?"

"I healed your wound because it was a mortal one. You should not feel any after-effects." She could only whisper.

Five seconds later Celeste slumped on the bed. Her face was devoid of color and I feared for her life.

I scrambled from the bed to search for Sydney. I had a moment of clarity as I realized that what Celeste needed was an energy recharge from the sun, and if we were not able to get her outside as soon as possible, she might actually die.

Sydney came back into the bedroom carrying a fistful of zip ties. I must have had a panicked expression on my face because she asked, "What's wrong?"

"It's Celeste. We have to help her. I think she's dying. We need to move her outside right now." I could feel the tears slip down my face. I was so thankful that the sun decided to make an appearance. I'd listened to the extended forecast so I expected the sunshine to last for another few days. Not that the weatherman or woman got it right all the time, but I looked out the window after Celeste passed out and saw the clear skies.

"I need to secure Greg first. Just give me thirty seconds."

Sydney was incredibly efficient as she rolled him over and secured his arms and his ankles together behind his back. I didn't imagine it would be very comfortable the way she trussed him up, but it served the bastard right. I wanted to kick him as I passed him to get back to Celeste, but I tempered my urge to do some damage to his already marred face.

"You take her head and I'll take her feet," Sydney directed. "I have a hammock out back that gets full sun from early morning until late afternoon. It should be comfortable enough."

"Okay," I answered.

Thank God Sydney was a take-charge kind of woman, because I was certainly way out of my element.

✝

111

In Sydney's rush to get inside she had left the patio door open so it was easy to maneuver outside and get Celeste settled in the hammock.

I looked down at Celeste. She still looked sickly, but her breathing seemed to even out a bit. She appeared to be resting comfortably and I wondered how long she would be asleep. I made a mental note to ask her if the energy charge works better when she's asleep. I didn't want to wake her up if that was the case, so I walked over to the sliding glass door and Sydney followed me.

Sydney pulled me into a hug and then looked at my shirt. "Are you okay?"

"Yeah, Celeste healed me. I think that's why she's sick. I think everything she did caused her to expend all her energy. You saw it all, didn't you? We're not crazy, are we?" I pleaded with her to tell me that I wasn't dreaming or seeing things.

She nodded. "Yeah, I saw it all, and if you're crazy, then so am I."

"She was telling us the truth all along. I never should have doubted her. I hope she forgives me. Thank God it's a sunny day. She has to get better and then we have to help her, Sydney."

"We will, I promise, but right now we have more pressing problems." Sydney looked away.

I could feel the guilt roll off of her in waves.

"How did he find us?" I managed to squeak out.

"I'm so sorry, Mabs. As soon as I figured it out, I rushed back, but I was too late."

"Figured what out?"

"Hollie set us up. It's why she was so desperate to have me talk to her last night. She needed to get me to lead him back to the cabin and then Greg could do his thing while we had coffee this morning. Fortunately for us, Hollie had to gloat a bit about Celeste heading back to the looney bin this morning.”

“I swear I’m going to kill her. I’m done being her personal punching bag. Now she’s hurt two people I care about. She has to be stopped.”

“I know, I know. In her defense, I honestly believe she thought she was protecting me.”

“Bullshit,” I declared.

“Look, all I know is that my cabin is no longer a safe haven. We have to find somewhere else to hole up until I can call in a few favors. I know I joked about the camping thing, but at this point, it’s really our only option. I’m fairly certain that Greg kept his superiors informed and others will follow.”

“God, Sydney, I didn’t mean to get you involved in this mess. I’m so sorry.”

Sydney shrugged. “Eh, what are friends for if you can’t get them involved in your drama.”

“What are we going to do with Greg?”

“Good question. I know some particularly remote places that we can dump him, but I’d be afraid that the stupid bastard wouldn’t be able to find his way out. I don’t want his death on my conscience. For now, we can leave him tied up until Celeste is ready to travel. Maybe she has some alien trick she can use on him.”

“Maybe.” I smiled for the first time that morning. Celeste really was an alien and Sydney was on our side.

I thought about our discussion on love and it suddenly dawned on me that everything Sydney was doing demonstrated her love for me. Maybe she didn’t love me in the same way I loved her, but she was a true friend. I was lucky to have her in my life and I knew I needed to make some changes to let her in a lot more than I had in the past.

Sydney rewarded me with one of her dazzling smiles and touched me on arm. "Come on, let's go check on our prisoner."

"I can't believe boring ole me is in the middle of this impossible situation," I mumbled.

†

Greg was awake when we went back inside and he looked mighty pissed. He was pulling hard on the zip ties, but they looked like they were just cutting into his skin. The harder he struggled the more painful they became.

"You have no idea who you're dealing with. You should have stayed out of this. She is far too valuable to us for them to worry about who gets hurt in our attempt to retrieve her and bring her to the lab. They won't stop until they find her. You have to know how hopeless it is to try to hide that thing. We will find her." Greg was spitting.

Sydney smirked. "You know, keep talking and where we choose to drop you off will get more and more remote. Right now, I would be more concerned with what Celeste might choose to do to you. I'm not so sure the laws on our planet extend to her."

Greg's tone immediately became placating. "Look, if you cooperate with us right now, I'll see what I can do to get you some kind of deal."

"You must think we have stupid tattooed across our foreheads," I interjected. "In what dream world would you think we would have one single bit of trust in anything you have to say?"

"Why can't you realize how important this discovery is to us? This could mean access to advanced technology that would enable the United States to regain our status as the supreme world superpower."

"From what I gathered from Celeste, her people are a peaceful lot. I wouldn't expect any type of military advantage with their technology. Isn't there enough war and violence in the world without you exploiting any knowledge you might acquire from Celeste?" I shook my head.

Sydney touched my shoulder. "Mabs, why don't you check on how Celeste is doing while I watch this POS."

"Pose?" I scrunched up my face in confusion.

"Yeah, piece of shit."

"Oh, I'll have to remember that one. Is that internet or texting slang?" I asked.

"Both I think. I learned that one from my nephew. It could also mean, parent over shoulder." She laughed.

"Are you sure you'll be okay watching the POS?" I had to try out the new lingo. It was fun and it rolled off my tongue like I was some kind of expert at internet slang.

"Ooh, look at you, using internet abbreviations like a pro. Yep, I'll be fine. Zip ties are more secure than handcuffs and since I'm not really into—well you know, that kind of kink—they were also more available to me." One corner of Sydney's mouth lifted in a lopsided smile. It was endearing.

I didn't really know what Sydney was and wasn't into, but it didn't hurt to squirrel that little piece of information away.

"Okay. I'll check on Celeste and I hope she has a few tricks up her sleeve, because honestly, we're in kind of a pickle here and I don't like our odds."

I left Sydney with Greg and went to check on Celeste.

I'd forgotten about Gizmo. She must have hidden somewhere after she heard the gun go off. She hated loud noises and didn't particularly bond well with men, so I suspected she gave Greg a wide berth. Once I'd left the bedroom, I spotted her tail peeking out from beneath the couch. She must have slipped under the furniture in an attempt to hide from danger. What a pussy—pun intended.

I made kissing noises and attempted to coax her from her hiding place. "Come on out pretty girl. I won't let the bad man hurt you. Come on pun'kin. I'll bet Celeste would love to have you jump up and join her in the hammock."

Her tail swished back and forth once and then she turned around and her little nose peeked out from under the couch. I squatted down and gently rubbed her nose. That was enough to lure her from her hiding place. She crept out and I picked her up to cradle her in my arms. I knew that Celeste had bonded with her so I thought she would be a welcome surprise for when she woke up. Petting Gizmo was always very comforting and healing for me, so I'd hoped it would be for Celeste. Armed with my own brand of calming energy, I walked out to the back yard.

†

Celeste was still sleeping peacefully in the hammock and her color looked slightly better than before. However, that wasn't saying too much because earlier she looked like walking death, a zombie without the grotesque decaying face.

I gently placed Gizmo on the hammock and she promptly curled up next to her sleeping charge. Gizmo knew her role and wasn't about to wake her up.

She looked so beautiful and peaceful in sleep, but her frailty alarmed me. What if she wasn't able to get enough energy from the sun to recover fully? Had she sacrificed her life for me? I felt helpless to do anything but watch over her and make sure the POS didn't get his meat hooks in her. My stress-induced thoughts must have affected her because she began to stir.

Her lavender eyes blinked open and she focused on me. "Bella, are you not well?"

I stroked her arm. "Oh Celeste, I'm perfect thanks to you. You had me really worried. Are you feeling any better? We brought you out into the sunshine hoping that would help."

"Yes it has helped. I estimate that I am about ten percent charged. I was dangerously close to empty. I require at least four to six hours more in the sunshine to charge to an acceptable level, more if I am required to expend a lot more energy. What has become of Greg?"

"Sydney is watching him. We have a small problem because we're not really sure what to do with him. We were hoping you had some kind of power that we could use without killing him to get him off your track. I'm so sorry I doubted you. We don't doubt you anymore. You can read minds, right? Can you manipulate thoughts?" I asked.

"Sometimes I pick up words or random thoughts, but mostly I pick up on energy signatures. We are forbidden to exercise mind control."

Celeste seemed to go somewhere almost like she was visiting a fond memory as she smiled. "When we were younger we didn't always abide by the rules, and Zaria, my energy mate and I, would play mind games with each other. We grew up together and would try to get the other to do unconventional things through mind control. She was much better than I was. One time she got me to climb up Cernia Hill, remove my outerwear, and swing my naked backside back and forth in front of the gathering. My caretakers were not at all pleased with our games, especially when we tried them out on others. Later, Zaria's skill at mind control was very useful when helping our injured comrades endure the pain and pass to the other energy realm. I learned to refine my skill as well. It was another way to help her as the primary healer."

"So, let me get this straight. You pulled pranks, she made you moon a bunch of people, and you helped with hospice care."

"I am not familiar with the things you have cited," she replied.

I was liking Celeste more and more and it seemed that her species was not that much different than ours. I suppose youthful indiscretions happened throughout the galaxy. I lamented about a time in my life that I would never get back. I'd never had the opportunity to goof around or play pranks when I was younger because I was almost entirely a loner. I vowed to change that and to start to live a life I'd never allowed myself to do before. I wanted laughter, playfulness, and yes, even trouble in my life. No matter what happened with Celeste, I pledged to myself that I would start living, not just existing anymore.

I shook my head. "Never mind that. Do you think you could get Greg to call his superior and convince him that he wasn't able to find you, and that his sources revealed that you were on your way to…hmmm…how about Alaska?"

"Yes, I possess the skill to do this. I suppose this would be a special exemption similar to when the guiding council allowed us to use this skill with our fallen comrades."

"You wouldn't by any chance have the ability to wipe Greg's memory so that whatever information you plant in his head is all that will be revealed to his superiors?"

"That is a little more complicated, but yes we learned to enter the mind to not only alter thoughts and beliefs, but to remove them entirely. This is a difficult process and not guaranteed to succeed. It will require more energy than I currently possess. I am able to exercise minor mind control to resolve the immediate issue. I will be able to misdirect information."

"When do you think you would be able to safely do this? I'm worried that someone else may be on their way and we don't have a lot of time to send them in a different direction."

"It would be best if I absorbed at least fifteen more Earth minutes of your sun's energy. That should be sufficient."

"I'll get Sydney to bring him out here so you can continue to recharge in the sun."

She nodded and cuddled up with Gizmo as she stroked her head in a loving gesture. Lucky cat.

I ran back into the cabin to update Sydney on the plan.

I was feeling more confident that things would turn out okay. I didn't really think beyond this particular moment of tribulation. I wasn't some master spy or anything and neither was Sydney, so I didn't really appreciate the seriousness of our dilemma. The only thing on our side was an alien with a set of particularly useful skills. At least Sydney knew how to survive in the wilderness. My only contribution would be a plethora of useless trivia. Useless facts were my specialty and they weren't even that interesting. It's not like I ever mesmerized anyone with my witty knowledge at a social gathering. I wasn't even handy to have around for game night because *Trivial Pursuit* was so passé. On the other hand, I was getting pretty good with *Words with Friends*. Internet games were right up my alley because I didn't have to interact with live people. Maybe the meek or at least the introverts would inherit the Earth because it seemed like face-to-face interaction was becoming obsolete.

Chapter Seven

Sydney was leaning against the wall with her arms crossed over her chest. Her outward appearance was casual, but I sensed that she was nervous. She fixed her eyes on Greg, but the minute she heard me enter the room, she looked up and started scanning all around her until her gaze landed on me. I could see her eyes relax when they met mine and it had the same effect on me.

I slowly approached and got close enough to talk to her without Greg listening in.

"Do you think it's okay to leave him for a few minutes. I need to talk to you," I whispered in her ear.

She seemed to shiver for a few seconds, nodded, and walked out to the main living area.

I kept my voice low so Greg wouldn't be able to overhear. "Celeste is a little better, but she needs a lot more time in the sun, so we're going to have to buy a little time. She has the ability to do some minor mind control. I think it works like hypnosis, but maybe a little stronger. We need to bring him to her because she doesn't have a whole lot of excess energy right now."

"Well, that could be a bit of a challenge. In case you haven't noticed he's a big guy, and I don't think he's going to just let us move him without some resistance."

"Can't you just knock him out or something, like you did before?"

Sydney scowled at me. "What do you think I am, Rambo or something? I didn't necessarily plan on knocking him out before, it just happened. I got lucky and probably hit him in just the right spot."

"Can't you activate one of those pressure points? There are at least three that I know of—pushing against the windpipe, pressure to the vagus nerve, and pinching someone's carotid artery."

"Mabs, this isn't Hollywood, you know, and I'm not Jackie Chan. I don't think that stuff really works in real life, and I don't want to do something that would permanently harm him."

"The guy shot me and you're worried about hurting him," I shouted.

I heard Greg grunt so he must have heard that last comment. Oh well, so much for not alerting him.

"Good point, but I'm not an assassin you know."

"Listen, Sydney, you know I read a lot right?"

"Yeah."

"Well trust me, I have a lot of useless information floating around in my brain and there really are these pressure points that I'm sure would work. Pick one and I'll tell you exactly where it is and what to do based on what I read."

"Why in the world would you read about something like that, and how can you possibly remember everything you read?"

I shrugged my shoulders, "Photographic memory. It comes in handy sometimes. I get bored and it's amazing the stuff you can learn when you read unconventional material. I suggest the vagus nerve because it's probably the most vulnerable pressure point. It connects the brain and the heart and a quick blow causes unconsciousness really fast. It's also not one little spot, but rather a long nerve that runs down the neck starting about one inch below a person's ear. I think you either have to put pressure on the nerve with your palm or forearm and bounce a few times, or a quick karate chop should do the trick. Don't hit him too hard though or you can kill him. If his eyes roll up right after you hit him, then I'm pretty sure you did it right. Even if he comes to after a few seconds, he'll be lightheaded and won't have the necessary motor skills to fight. Not that I'm sadistic or anything, but he'll also feel pretty shitty and I have to admit that I won't feel bad about that. I'd watch out for vomit though, cause I read that it's a pretty common side effect."

"Remind me never to piss you off." She grinned at me.

I blushed. "I could never get mad at you."

"Okay, I guess I better give this a try then. Maybe you can hold his head or something so I don't miss. I suppose a chop to both sides of his neck would increase my chances of getting it right the first time."

I nodded and stood up straight ready to help her out. I didn't even recognize this person I was turning into. If I really took the time to think about it, I probably would have retreated to my cozy little home and never come out. I was about to hold some guy's head while my friend Sydney karate chopped him. Real life was stranger than fiction, you can't make this stuff up. It was beyond absurd.

Sydney brushed by me and I felt my breath hitch as her body brushed against mine. I couldn't help myself, she still seems to affect me.

She looked down at me and our eyes met. I couldn't tell if she noticed my reaction or not, but when her pupils dilated, it seemed to convey something I didn't think I'd ever seen before. Was it possible that Sydney had a similar reaction? I shook my head at what a ridiculous notion that was.

I started to laugh when I saw Greg squirming around on the bedroom floor, like the snake he was, trying to find a way free. He snarled at us when we entered the room.

"Okay Mabs, grab his head for me," Sydney directed.

I was tempted to yank his head up using his hair, but he didn't have enough hair to hang onto. He was putting up a good struggle as I got behind him and tried to hold his head still. "I'd rather not hurt you, even though you did shoot me, you poser, but if you keep struggling I'll suggest a less humane way to deal with you." I boxed his ears as a warning.

That seemed to stop his struggles and gave Sydney enough time to execute a perfect blow to each side of his head in the exact spot I'd described. I was so proud of her. She was a quick learner that's for sure.

He slumped forward immediately.

"I'll take his head if you get his feet," I pronounced.

"Okay. Let's hurry and get him outside before he wakes up," she agreed.

We wasted no time in transporting him to the back yard. God, he was heavy. I noted that he could do with a few less desserts.

✝

We unceremoniously dumped Greg on the ground next to the hammock. He hadn't woken up yet and I took several paces back in case he started tossing his cookies all over my new shoes. I knew it was shallow of me to be thinking about my shoes, but in my defense, they were really expensive Mephisto's. Sydney took a page from my book and took several steps back herself.

Celeste looked even better than when I'd left her ten minutes earlier. She was starting to get a little color back in her face. I suspected after she performed her little mind manipulation, she might revert to her ghostlike appearance, but at least more time in the sun seemed to make a big difference.

"You temporarily interrupted his energy flow," Celeste stated.

"Uh yeah, he wasn't exactly in a cooperating kind of mood."

"We will need to wait until he is more alert and has recovered fully before I attempt mind control," Celeste explained.

"Will you be able to tell when he's ready?" Sydney asked.

"Yes, I will be able to determine the appropriate time frame," Celeste answered.

Sydney walked over to her back patio, grabbed two folding chairs, and brought them closer to the hammock. "Here, we might as well relax until sleeping beauty gets his energy groove back. I'd offer you a beer or some hard lemonade, but I think we should avoid drinking anything that might impair our reasoning until we can figure out how to handle this adventure we've all decided to take."

"Would I like this beer or hard lemonade?" Celeste asked.

"Probably," I giggled. "But I think that experience ought to wait for a little while."

"Ahhhh," Greg groaned, opened his eyes and promptly vomited in the grass. "What the fuck did you do to me?"

"Ew, I should get some of Gizmo's kitty litter because that," Sydney pointed to the fresh pool of vomit, "is definitely gonna stink."

"We should let him settle for a bit before we get Celeste to do her thing."

Greg got a wide-eyed look, and for the first time, I thought I saw fear in his eyes.

"Wha…what is she going to do to me?" he stuttered.

"Relax. It's not like she's gonna eat your face off or anything. Not that you don't deserve it, you douche bag," Sydney answered.

I looked down at Greg and noticed the burn mark on his clothes, probably from when Celeste blasted him with her energy burst. I hadn't spotted that before. No wonder he was nervous. I pointed at the scorch mark.

"Oh," Sydney muttered.

Greg looked down at his shirt and I swear I thought he was going to cry. Men can be such babies. I smirked at him. Served him right for shooting me. I wasn't above letting him sweat a tiny bit. What had come over me? All of a sudden I had this little evil streak running through me.

Sydney glanced at me and I thought that maybe she could read my mind or something because she laughed and blurted out, "Well, I don't think she's gonna have to eat your face, but I'm not sure exactly what she might have planned for you. She has become rather fond of Mabs here and you did shoot her. I suppose another burn mark is not out of the realm of possibility."

Celeste gracefully repositioned herself on the hammock so that she was sitting rather than lying down and cocked her head to the side. "You mentioned something called a prank, Bella. Is this what you are doing now?"

"Not really," I hedged, "and I suppose I should stop being mean. This is what you might call a cruel joke, letting

Greg believe that you are planning to hurt him in some way." I looked down. I felt ashamed of myself. All the times the bullies joked around at my expense should have taught me to be a bit more sensitive. Greg was, after all, another human being.

I glanced at Greg. "Sorry. Fortunately for you, Celeste is a gentle and pure soul and doesn't have it in her to intentionally hurt you. Violence is your thing, not ours."

"Can you please direct me in what specifically you would like to plant in his mind?" Celeste asked.

"Well we briefly talked about leading Greg to genuinely believe that he couldn't find you here in Cle Elum, but was able to determine that you were headed to Alaska. It's a state that's pretty far away from here up North. You're going to have to really make him trust something different from what he experienced because he'll be talking to his supervisor and he'll need to sound believable. Maybe you can throw in some facts, like he tracked you here after he got credible information from Hollie that led him to the cabin, but he lost you, and then had to track down more information to determine where you were headed. You can suggest that Sydney gave him the new information."

I glanced over at Sydney who frowned at this suggestion. "Sorry, Sydney, but I don't think it's believable that I would give him information if he's already made a report to his boss."

"Yeah, you're probably right about that. I was initially sympathetic to his story," Sydney acknowledged.

I thought of something. "Can you get him to be calm while we search his pockets for a cell phone to hold up to his ear? In case this doesn't work too well, we need to keep him restrained."

Celeste stood up and walked over to where Greg was half sitting, half slouched on the ground. She touched his arm and I saw the purple light leak out again. The lines on his face showing his stress and discomfort immediately evened out. He almost looked like he was in a drug-induced state.

Sydney, bless her heart, went searching in his pockets for his cell phone. Once she located it, she held it in the air for us to see.

Celeste continued her contact with Greg and his eyes began to flutter and twitch. I wondered if she was giving him instructions telepathically.

She nodded at me as if answering my question.

"You may put the phone to his ear after you select whatever button will retrieve the last call made," Celeste directed.

"Will you be able to hear who is on the other end, so you can direct the conversation?" I asked.

"I am able to decipher what he is hearing as I probe his brain while I simultaneously suggest the correct response," Celeste answered.

Sydney hit the button on the iPhone, swiped the screen, and frowned. "Damn, it requires a code."

Celeste seemed to narrow her gaze at Greg as he blurted out, "Four, one, two, six."

Sydney swiped the screen again and punched in those numbers. "Voila and presto. Time to do your thing, Celeste." She held the phone up to his ear after punching a few buttons on the phone.

Celeste tilted her head and I hurried to clarify what 'do your thing' meant. "She means do the mind control thing and give him the right instructions."

Sydney shrugged. "Sorry."

I put my finger to my lips to gesture that we should all be quiet while Greg talked with his boss.

"No, I don't have her yet… Yeah, she was here in Cle Elum until a few hours ago… No, it was credible information… Don't worry, I got another lead… Alaska… Yeah, you heard right, for some reason she's headed to Alaska… the other dyke gave me that information… No, I'm sure she was telling me the truth. It was confirmed by another source… Don't worry, I'm on it. They only have a two or three hour head start… No, you don't need to send anyone else, I can handle it… Give me two days and I'll have her secured for pick up… No, we don't want to cause anyone to ask too many questions and if you send up more people, it will be overly suspicious. With her odd behavior, the cover story is working… Just let me do my job. I'll be in touch."

"You may stop the communication device now," Celeste informed.

Sydney punched the end button and I relaxed a bit. The mind control appeared to work. Celeste swayed a bit and I jumped to her side to lead her back to the hammock. She had that pasty white complexion again and I worried that all the gains she'd made in the sun were once again depleted.

Greg seemed to be in a kind of trance like state and I hoped he would stay that way until we had a bona fide plan for keeping Celeste safe.

"Why don't you rest for a little while longer while Sydney and I figure out what to do with Greg."

It was still relatively early in the day, with plenty of sunshine left for Celeste to be able to recharge. I worried that every time she appeared to perk up a bit, we had another task for her that depleted her energies. I didn't think Earth's sun was as effective as the three suns on her planet and we were definitely taxing her body.

I glanced back at Greg while Sydney and I started walking back into the cabin. I wanted to make sure he was still out of it and wouldn't be causing us any problems. Sydney followed my eyes and nodded, appearing to agree with my assessment that we could leave him on the grass. I wasn't too keen on trying to drag him back into the cabin with us.

✝

My stomach growled loudly and I realized that I hadn't eaten since the night before with all the drama of the morning. I also hadn't taken a shower, brushed my teeth, or washed my hair yet. Ew, gross. I probably looked a lot like Bozo the Clown with my hair sticking out every which way.

Sydney grinned at me. "I hear your tummy talking. You haven't eaten anything today, have you?"

I shook my head. "No, been kind of busy, you know. Celeste hasn't either, but I think rest in the sun might be more important than food right now." I wondered how I would slip away for some personal grooming without appearing rude. I quickly smoothed my hair down in an attempt to look somewhat presentable in front of Sydney.

"Well, I'm not a fabulous cook like you, but I think I can handle a couple of turkey sandwiches with a side of Tim's Cascade chips."

"Um, Sydney, do you mind if I at least use your bathroom to brush my teeth?" I ran my tongue across my pearly whites. "They feel pretty grungy right now. I hate to leave all the work for you, but can you make one for Celeste and we can give it to her when she's done resting?"

"Of course." She waved her hand at me like it was no big deal.

While Sydney started making the sandwiches, I ran to the bathroom and quickly brushed my teeth. I didn't have time to do a thorough job like I normally would. Usually, I made sure I brushed for at least two minutes because that's what my dental hygienist always recommended. I didn't want to impose on Sydney's hospitality too much, so I just settled for having minty fresh breath after a cursory brush. I took one look at myself in the mirror and cringed. I found a brush in one of the drawers and tried to tame my bedhead. I didn't even bother to change my blood-soaked shirt because I didn't want to leave Sydney all alone in the kitchen.

I walked back into the kitchen and watched Sydney lay out the lunchmeat, mayonnaise, mustard, and tomato on the counter.

"Anything I can do to help?" I asked.

She shook her head and grabbed a loaf of whole wheat bread from her small pantry. She turned around and gave me a strange look like she had a question on the tip of her tongue, but didn't quite know how to ask.

"Go ahead, I know you're just dying to ask me something." I grabbed a knife and started to slice the tomato.

"I know it's not really my business, but do you see any kind of future with Celeste? I mean, she's not from our world and eventually she'll leave."

I know Sydney didn't point this out to me to be cruel, it was a fact I hadn't exactly absorbed. I frowned and felt like the elevator just dropped from a high rise. The knot in the pit of my stomach was probably as big as my fist. I knew at that moment that when Celeste left she would leave a huge hole in my heart. All the joy I'd been feeling over the last couple of days had an expiration date. I slumped on the stool in the kitchen. The balloon of happiness just whooshed right out.

"I haven't exactly been thinking too much about that. I was trying to live in the moment I guess. I'll take whatever time I can get. It's not like I'll ever have an opportunity for this kind of happiness again in my lifetime."

"What do you mean, you won't have an opportunity for this kind of happiness again?"

"Oh, you know, someone who thinks I'm beautiful and wants to, uh, you know…"

Sydney's face scrunched up. "Are you crazy or something? Women would have been lining up in droves if they'd only known that you played for our team."

I waved her away. "Thanks, Sydney. You are a true friend and I appreciate what you're trying to do, but I know what I am and what I'm not."

"You really don't know, do you? God, Mabs, I've had the biggest crush on you since the first day I ever laid eyes on you. Why in the world do you think I got in all those fights? Hollie's always known that. That's the biggest reason why she hates you so much. She never lets me forget it either. Now that she knows you're a lesbian she's doubly dangerous. Before, she would just remind me how straight you were, but I guess I always sensed that you were gay and just not ready to come out to the world yet. I never knew how much she actually picked on you or I would have put a stop to it. She's convinced that you are the reason we broke up this time. I'll admit it was a factor, but this has been coming for a very long time."

I imagined that a hundred flies would make the inside of my mouth their permanent residence as it hung open in shock.

Sydney gently took her index finger and placed it under my chin to close my mouth. The corners of her lips turned up and formed the sexiest smile I'd ever seen.

"Wha…what?" I stuttered.

Sydney didn't even bother to respond she just took a step closer to me and brushed her fingers against my cheek as she leaned in. I was about to be kissed by Sydney O'Donnell and I swear at that moment fireworks were going off in my head and she hadn't even pressed her lips to mine yet. I was glad I'd brushed earlier because I couldn't imagine kissing Sydney with morning breath and I was really dying to kiss her.

Am I a slut for wanting this to happen? Maybe I'm a home wrecker too, because everyone was going to blame me for breaking up Cle Elum's golden couple. What about Celeste? Was I cheating on her? I didn't get a chance to fixate on my thoughts because Sydney's lips pressed against mine and a party exploded in my nether regions.

I opened my mouth a little and her tongue explored my lips and darted inside. Our tongues danced the tango—sensuous and exciting—as she deepened the kiss. I was lost in a world of ecstasy as we continued to explore one another for what seemed like forever, but was probably less than a minute.

I was panting as she broke away from me. She looked into my eyes and I was sure I saw desire and maybe even something deeper.

"Amazing. I knew it would feel like that. I just had to do it, Mabs. I never thought I'd ever get the chance. It was worth the risk of you slapping me silly."

I sighed. Could I confess to her how I was desperately in love with her and always had been? She'd only told me she had a crush. That was about ten levels below love. "I would never slap you, Syd. I…I…"

"You called me Syd." She raised her eyebrow. "Is that all I had to do was kiss you to get you to finally call me Syd?"

I was still stunned from the kiss. "I called you Syd?"

"You sure did." She looked directly into my eyes. "Just tell me I have a chance and I'll be the happiest woman on this planet. I know you care for Celeste and I'm happy to wait until you work that out, but I've been waiting for this moment for a very long time."

I gulped. Celeste. God, suddenly everything was confusing and complicated, but I wanted Sydney like I'd never wanted anyone. Maybe I was just a rebound girl for Sydney. I'd seen with my own two eyes how upset Sydney got over her break-up with Hollie. Even though they were on-again off-again, they still had a lot of history between the two of them and Sydney always went back to Hollie. No one spends ten years with someone they don't love. I didn't want to be the rebound relationship, and then there was Celeste to think about. I started to answer her. "Uh, Sydney…"

She placed her finger over my lips. "I don't need an answer right now. You take whatever time you need to work things out in your head. I'll be waiting. I promise."

She turned and pulled a knife from the drawer and began making our sandwiches. When she pointed to the mustard, I shook my head. The light switch suddenly flipped off and the conversation was over.

"Is mayonnaise and tomato okay?" she asked.

I nodded.

"That's the way I like it, too. That's at least one thing we have in common." She grinned.

Two beautiful women wanted to be intimate with me. I had a lot to think about, and at least I wouldn't die a virgin.

I figured I better start a different conversation—a safer one—like what in the heck we were going to do about Greg. We would have to ask Celeste if her mind manipulation was permanent or only lasted while connected to him. He still seemed in a trancelike state, but maybe this was another alien trick that would allow her to recharge and get some much-needed rest. I wanted to get Sydney's opinion on this.

"So, what do you think we ought to do about Greg?"

Sydney gave the question some thought. "Hmmm, good question. Do you think that if we dumped him in his car and Celeste put the whammy on him again, he would start driving to Alaska to track her down?"

"Maybe. We better ask Celeste how long her mind trick works. At least we're safe for now."

Sydney looked pensive. She grabbed a plate from one of her cabinets, placed the newly made sandwich on top, yanked a paper towel from the dispenser, and handed me my lunch.

I nodded in thanks, took a big bite, and grunted my pleasure.

"I'm kind of worried. Hollie was really pissed when I stalked off after learning about her deception. I know she had to go back to work, so she wasn't about to follow me to my Jeep, but if Greg told her where the cabin is located, I'd bet my last dollar she'll show up after work tonight."

"That leaves us about five more hours to figure this mess out," I remarked through a mouth full of food from my second bite. It tasted really good and I was hungry.

Sydney seemed to ignore my bad manners. "Uh, Mabs, Celeste hasn't been looking so good lately. I think we have to get her somewhere that will allow her to fully charge her energy without having to use it for any reason. Don't get me wrong, I will be eternally grateful to her for saving your life, but it certainly took its toll on her."

"I know, I know. Were you serious about taking us somewhere remote to camp?" I asked.

"Hell yeah. First, I love camping, and second, I know where to go where no one would ever find us. At least it will give us a little breathing room to figure out what to do next. I've got enough supplies to last at least two weeks if necessary. You know, they've come a long way with freeze dried meals."

I was not looking forward to this camping adventure, but I didn't think we had a choice. "I can't wait," I deadpanned.

Sydney chuckled. "Hey, your boss gave you two weeks off, right?"

"Yeah." I hesitantly answered. I wasn't sure I could make it in the woods for two whole weeks.

"I'll just get someone to cover my shifts and we'll have two weeks to figure things out." She sounded way too excited about this.

"Um, I'm not going anywhere I can't take a shower. One night without a shower is one thing, but two weeks…" I knew I was being a princess and yet I couldn't help myself.

Sydney finished making the other two sandwiches and turned around to grab a bag of chips from her pantry. She ripped open the bag and laid them on the counter equidistance from both of us. "Mabs, there are guys with guns chasing down Celeste. I don't think we are going to solve this in one day. I'll bring my solar shower. You'll be fine. I've got the perfect baseball cap for you. You'll look adorable in it."

The guys with guns comment sobered me enough to realize she was right.

"Okay, but you better have a warm sleeping bag and a heavily padded air mattress for me to sleep on. Oh, and if I'm going to have to eat freeze dried slop out of a foil bag, I want to grill that salmon over an open fire that you're gonna build for our first night. So, you better have a huge ice chest for that and any other food I can manage to scrounge up. Besides, you don't want to leave that fish in your frig for two weeks. You'll never get the smell out." I grabbed a few chips and stuffed them into my mouth.

Sydney saluted me. "Yes, ma'am."

"I want fresh water to brush my teeth with too."

"Speaking of water, I forgot to offer you something to drink. As you can tell, I'm a pretty casual host. You don't have to worry. I'll bring plenty of fresh water for coffee, tea, and our instafood. I even have a French press specially designed for camping. I've got everything you need for our glamping trip."

"Glamping?" I inquired.

"Yep, glamorous camping is called glamping. Prisses like you don't camp, they glamp." She opened the fridge and pointed to the water, juice, and diet Dr. Pepper she had stored inside.

I stuck my tongue out at her. "If there was such a thing as a solar powered hair dryer, I'd make you bring that. I'll take some water, please." I grinned at her.

She handed me a bottle of water. "Sorry, I don't have that, a solar hair dryer, but I do have solar powered chargers for cell phones, iPads, and Kindle readers."

I jumped up and down with enthusiasm. "Oh please bring those. I can download some books for Celeste to read and she can learn more about Earth while we camp." I opened the water and gulped down nearly one quarter of the bottle.

"Done. Your wish is my command." Sydney took a bite of her sandwich and smiled at me.

I couldn't believe I was getting excited about camping. My first camping trip ever. Maybe it would be more fun than I thought. Then I thought about sleeping arrangements and I became nervous. Would Sydney arrange for us all to sleep in the same tent? Would we each have our own tent? I didn't really want to go there, but I had to know.

"Um, Sydney…do you have more than one tent and enough sleeping bags and pads for all of us?" There, I'd bravely blurted out the question, but was afraid of the answer. All the options would have a certain level of discomfort for me. I wasn't even sure which option I hoped for.

Sydney narrowed her gaze at me and I suspected she was trying to read my expression.

"I have a tent large enough for all three of us and plenty of sleeping bags and pads to ensure we sleep comfortably. Is it okay for us all to share the same tent?" she softly asked.

I wondered who would sleep next to whom. Would I be in the middle like a love sandwich? I chuckled to myself as a vivid picture of both women cuddled close to me while I basked in their attention. *Stop that. Stop that right now*, I mentally chastised myself. I could not even fathom what a *ménage a trois* would be like and, if I was really honest with myself, I wouldn't want one anyway.

"One tent is fine."

"You know, if I didn't know any better, I'd swear you had a little mini fantasy going on in your head," she teased.

I blushed and promptly changed the subject. "Should we see if Celeste is ready to eat something?"

Sydney graciously let me off the hook. "Sure, let's see if her color has improved any. If it hasn't, we should just wrap this up and put it in the fridge for her to eat later."

✝

I shoved the last bite of the sandwich in my mouth and grabbed a handful of chips as I followed her to the back yard. We'd both been devouring our food while we discussed our upcoming adventure. Sydney had the sandwich for Celeste wrapped in a paper towel.

I was happy to see Gizmo curled up again in Celeste's arms as she rested on the hammock. My little pumpkin was such a good girl. She always knew who needed her.

Greg was calmly sitting on the ground with an eerily vacant look and I worried that whatever Celeste did to him may have caused permanent damage. I hoped it didn't, but it was too late now to change anything. Besides, he didn't really leave us many options. I spied the pile of puke next to him and gagged. I have a particularly sensitive gag reflex, so I quickly looked away.

Thankfully, some color had returned to Celeste's cheeks and I thought we would be able to wake her up enough for her to have something to eat. I was craving salt again so I was glad to see that Sydney had also grabbed the bag of chips.

Celeste must have heard us approach because before we got to her she stirred and sat up to greet us. "I am much improved. Thank you for allowing me to recharge in the Earth's sun." She caught my eyes and then looked at Sydney. "Bella, your energy signature is changed."

When she made this observation, it seemed like a cloud of sadness enveloped her. She didn't exactly frown, but the joy that almost always surrounded Celeste had suddenly disappeared. It reminded me of when she told me about her energy mate.

I didn't want her to be sad so I went to her side and touched her arm. "Is something wrong, Celeste? Are you still not recovered? We can let you rest longer if you need to."

Sydney appeared to have a contemplative look on her face as she watched me go to Celeste and comfort her.

Celeste smiled at me, but it was kind of a sad smile. "No, sweet Bella, I am rested enough. Sydney, I see you have brought me another Earth delicacy."

"Well I wouldn't exactly call it a delicacy, but it'll do in a pinch. Sorry, I didn't know what you might like on your sandwich, so I just made it with tomatoes and mayonnaise. Most people like it like that,"

Sydney handed her the sandwich and Celeste took a huge bite. As usual, the humming began.

"Earth's food is something I will miss. The food on my planet is mainly for sustenance and survival, not pleasure. Perhaps I will bring a new perspective back to alter our view of food." She spoke around a bite of the sandwich.

It was good to know that all three of us exercised poor manners when we were hungry.

Sydney held out the bag of chips and Celeste selected a few.

Celeste popped one of the chips in her mouth and asked, "What do you call these? They are very tasty. I like them even better than this other food item."

"Yeah, junk food is quite popular on Earth," I responded. "I'm not so sure that is something that would be valuable to take back to your planet."

"Junk?" Celeste asked.

"Just a figure of speech. It's not really garbage. Well, I guess some people might call it garbage food, but…oh hell, do you know how hard it is to explain slang? You probably don't even understand the term *figure of speech*. We have funny ways of referring to things here. I wonder if I can download a slang dictionary or something that compiles all the strange figures of speech. There must be something out there to help you understand."

Celeste smiled. "I would like to read this on the communication device you call the Kindle." She looked at Sydney. "You have questions."

Sydney glanced at the trance-induced Greg. "Um, yeah, we were wondering if the mind trick you placed on Greg is permanent or just temporary."

"I do not quite understand."

"Well, if we were to place him in his car right now, would he speed off to Alaska in an attempt to track you down and find the fake license plate you suggested?" Sydney asked.

"Yes, he would do that after I activated that thought again and removed the block on his current energy state."

"So then he's okay to remain like he is for now until we're ready to take off, and then we can send him on his merry little snipe hunt?" I asked.

"If you are wondering if I have damaged him, then no, his current energy depleted state is only temporary. I do not know what a snipe hunt is, but I suspect it may mean that his travels will be as a result of the false thoughts I injected into his mind. Yes, whenever you are ready I can release the block and it will immediately send him on this snipe hunt."

"How will you be able to activate him without him seeing you?" Sydney asked.

Celeste furrowed her brow. "I will have to send the energy through the Earth's air molecules from a distance of no greater than one hundred paces. Perhaps we can use his car to drive to the nearest well-traveled road that has a bit of forest to hide in as I activate the new thoughts from afar. I am afraid this is more difficult and will expend much of my re-charged energy again."

"Does it matter how you capture the sun's energy? I mean could you get it while we're driving if I pop the top of my jeep off?" Sydney asked.

"Direct sun is best. As long as there are no barriers, I am able to re-charge."

"Okay, then let's get this show on the road. Mabs, I can drive the POS to the road while you and Celeste follow behind. Make sure you park far enough away from us so that he won't see you. Come get me when you're ready and we can find a place to hide while Celeste does her thing. First, let me take off the top to the jeep so Celeste can continue to catch those precious rays."

"Show on the road?" Celeste tilted her head. "Will you be performing for us, Bella?"

I doubled over in laughter. The thought of me doing some kind of performance was beyond absurd. In fact, I'd talked more with Celeste and Sydney in the past couple of days than I'd done in practically my whole lifetime. If there was a corner in a room, I would find it.

"Uh, no. More slang. You know, another figure of speech," I managed to say over my laughter.

Celeste nodded and Sydney jogged over to her Jeep and began removing the top. She climbed inside and appeared to be messing with her visor. I wondered what that had to do with removing the soft top. I couldn't quite tell what she was doing when she started rummaging around in her glove box. Whatever she did must have been necessary because then she hopped out, stuck something in her pocket, and grabbed the top pulling it up and folding it back. After it was folded back, she pulled out two pieces of Velcro and secured the top that she'd just folded back. She proceeded to unsnap and remove all the soft plastic windows, tossing them inside. She pushed a button that was holding the soft top frame and repeated this on the other side. Whew, I was getting dizzy with all she had to do to remove the blasted roof. Finally, she was finished and the roof was completely removed.

No wonder people rarely bothered with removing their soft tops. Note to self, *next car I buy, I want a sunroof that opens with a push of a button.*

Sydney walked back to us and grinned. "We can load all the camping gear after we send this poser on his way. Mabs, you want to take his head again?"

I walked over to Greg careful not to look at the vomit still puddled next to his body lest I puke right on top of it. While Sydney grabbed his feet, I held his head and we awkwardly crab walked to his car. Thankfully, he was as calm as a sleeping baby.

"Celeste, would you mind opening the door so we can toss him in the back seat?" Sydney directed.

Celeste opened the door and we callously threw him in the back like a sack of potatoes.

Sydney started to get in the front driver's side seat and then smacked her head. "Damn, I forgot to get his car keys. Shit, now I'm gonna have to rummage through his pockets." She crawled in the back seat and started searching his pants.

Greg blinked a couple of times, but never lost that unfocused look.

"Voila." She held the keys up in a triumphant gesture of victory. "Just follow me in the Jeep, and when I pull over, you need to find a place a safe distance away where we can hide and then quickly head in the opposite direction after Celeste flips the switch." She dug in her pocket and pulled out another set of keys, then tossed them in my direction.

I'm not very athletic, so I promptly squealed and they dropped at my feet.

Sydney chuckled. "I forgot that softball was never your forte, but you did look awfully cute in a baseball cap."

I stuck my tongue out at her. Sydney arched an eyebrow in response. I was beginning to like this more playful side of myself that had only recently made an appearance. I picked up the keys and gestured for Celeste to follow me. I was looking forward to driving Sydney's Jeep. I'd never had the chance to drive a *cool* car.

Celeste climbed into the passenger seat and lifted her face to the sun in a sensual movement that had me shamelessly staring. I jumped into the driver's seat with gusto.

Everything about these last few days was surreal to me. I had no idea what was around the corner for me and I loved it. I was on the precipice of a great expedition that blew to bits my entire, boring, ordered life.

Chapter Eight

The wind was whipping through my hair, alternately stinging and caressing my cheeks. I suppose I should have grabbed a baseball cap or tied back my hair, but I didn't care because I felt alive. The sun kissed my face and brought a warmth to my skin, creating a soft glow of excitement. Sydney led us down a winding, remote road near Snoqualmie Pass. The full majestic beauty of the mountains kept blinking on and off through the shadows of the mammoth evergreen trees as the sun alternately filtered through.

I would have been satisfied to continue driving, but all too soon Sydney stopped at a bend in the road. She provided us with the perfect opportunity to pull into a side road that would adequately hide our vehicle until Greg was safely on his way. I turned down the old logging road and pulled the Jeep over behind a massive pine tree that completely blocked the view of our car from the main road.

Celeste and I quickly scrambled out and hiked our way closer to Greg's car. We met Sydney in the densely wooded area.

"The car is about a hundred yards in that direction." Sydney pointed west. "I pulled his sorry ass out and dumped him in the driver's side. He should be ready to go after you do your mind thingy," she added.

"I will need to move a few paces closer until I feel the energy connection," Celeste explained.

Sydney and I followed Celeste as she walked closer to Greg. I was thankful when she stopped in an area with heavy vegetation. I didn't think anyone would detect any of us in the spot she'd chosen. The only thing I worried about was the purple light that emanated from her body. If anyone was around, their curiosity might compel them to check out the odd glow in the woods. I hoped that, since Greg was in the midst of the thought manipulation, he wouldn't register the strange purple light.

It only took Celeste about thirty seconds and then the light flickered out. She nodded to us and then slumped to the ground. This time I noticed her skin took on a sickly grayish hue. This was so not good.

I scrambled to her side and Sydney was right beside me as we lifted her together and moved her to an area where the sun peeked through the trees, creating a small patch of this essential lifeline.

Sydney placed her finger to her lips and we squatted beside Celeste until we saw Greg's car ease on down the road. Wanting to be sure he was well away from our location, we waited in the sunshine with Celeste for another ten minutes. I think we were both too scared to say anything, and the silence weighed on me like a heavy blanket of doom.

Finally, Sydney glanced at her watch and nodded. We each took one of Celeste's arms and draped them over our shoulders as we helped her to the Jeep.

Sydney was gentle when she lifted her and settled her comfortably in the back seat. We couldn't keep asking her to deplete her energy because at some point she wasn't going to be able to recover. The sacrifice she made for me was enormous and probably the beginning of the fragile state that she had not been quite able to fully recover from. I hoped that our camping trip would provide plenty of rest and relaxation that would give her the ability to fully recharge before permanent damage was done.

✝

It was late afternoon when we finally returned to the cabin. Sydney carried Celeste back to the hammock. She'd started to regain some of her color on the ride back. Thank God for the open air experience of the Jeep with the soft top removed.

I followed Sydney to a large shed in the back yard. When she opened the door, I was privy to her hidden chaos. Sydney must be one of those people who kept their house neat and clean, but allowed their garage or storage area to overflow with every imaginable item. I smiled to myself. Thank God, I had another closet pack rat I could commiserate with.

"Wow, I never would have expected this. What happened? Did Home Depot throw up in your shed?"

"Hardy, har, har, such a comedian. I could use your help, not your cryptic remarks on my organizational skills."

"Okay what would you like me to do?" I asked.

"Just grab as much of the camping equipment as you can and toss it in a heap. I'll go through it and decide what we should take. It's mostly located on that wall, although there might be a few items interspersed throughout."

I'd never been camping before, but I did recognize certain items, like the tent, sleeping bags, and Coleman stove. I decided to start with the usual suspects.

Sydney was a whirlwind of activity as she started to toss various items into the center of the shed, including water proof bags that weren't obviously camping gear.

I couldn't help myself as I nosed around and opened a few of those bags, curious about their contents.

"Ooh, looky here. These are so cute. I didn't realize there were special containers for bathroom items. Does that mean I'll be able to take a shower every day? This container is marked cream rinse. You take cream rinse while you're out camping and you tease me about glamping? I mean, who takes cream rinse on a camping trip, Princess Sydney." I doubled over laughing.

Sydney grabbed the container. "Gimme that." She tossed the hair product into the bag. "If you're not gonna help, just march back out and I'll take care of it."

"Sorry, I was only kidding."

It wasn't normal for Sydney to get testy. She was one of the most easygoing people I knew. "Hey, are you okay? You seem a little tense."

"No, I'm sorry. It's just I have a bad feeling. Hollie gets off work in a few hours and I want us to be far away from here."

I spied a huge cooler in the corner and dragged it into the middle. I was sure it would hold our salmon and a bunch of other items. I was excited to cook over a fire. I'd opened one of the other bags and had seen a bunch of those freeze dried camping meals, and they were definitely unappealing to me.

The mound in the middle of the floor was epic and I wondered how in the world we were going to fit everything into her Jeep. Sydney looked like she was surveying the pile and I imagined she had that same thought.

She slapped her hands together. "Okay, I think that's everything. Oh wait…" She turned around and grabbed three fold up camping chairs, the fancy ones with cup holders. I'd seen the same ones in Costco. "Now if I could only rip out the kitchen sink, we'd be set." She winked at me.

"Now what?" I asked.

"Now we drag this all out to the Jeep and let the master packer find a place for everything."

I must have had a skeptical look on my face.

"Oh ye of little faith," she added.

"Hey, why don't you move the Jeep closer so we don't have to lug the gear so far?" I asked.

"Good call. See that's why I need you in my life—to state the obvious."

While Sydney went to move the Jeep closer, I grabbed the tent and a sleeping bag and starting hauling it out to just outside the shed. I grinned as I glanced over at Celeste and saw Gizmo back in her favorite resting place, nestled on top of Celeste's chest. That stopped me dead in my tracks. Shit, what were we going to do with Gizmo. I couldn't leave her here to fend for herself. We were going to have to take her with us. Gizmo was a great cat and I thought she'd be just fine hanging around the campsite with us. She wouldn't even need a litter box because we would be in the great outdoors. I told myself that she would be just fine, but would Sydney be okay with taking her? Her food couldn't take up that much room and I'd be happy to hold her while we traveled to wherever we were going.

Sydney whipped the Jeep into an open grassy area next to the shed and climbed out. She immediately began retrieving the heavy items from the shed and started packing the gear.

"Um, Sydney…" I started to ask.

"Yeah." She turned her head to look at me as she was shoving the softer bags into corners.

"Can we please take Gizmo? She's very obedient, almost like a dog. I promise she won't roam."

"Sure, why not? I like the little furball," she replied.

We both headed back into the shed to grab some more stuff. The song, *Bitch,* by Meredith Brooks, blasted out of Sydney's back pocket. She pulled her phone from her pocket, glanced down, and placed a finger over her lips as she pushed one button and then another.

I wondered how pissed Hollie would be if she knew that Sydney was putting the call on speaker.

"Hi Hollie."

"Hey, baby. I'm assuming that by now Greg came and got that freakazoid and took her back to the looney bin so that we can get on with our lives. I know we can get past that little misunderstanding we had. Babe, you have to know that I did it for your own good. You're just too warm hearted. She could have hurt you, and don't get me started on that slut, Mabel, who put you in that vulnerable position." Hollie's voice oozed from the tiny iPhone speaker.

"Stop it right there. Don't you ever talk that way about Mabel again. I mean it. I also meant it when I told you we're done. You have to know this has been a long time coming. I just can't do it anymore."

"Aw, hon, you know they never mean anything and I always come home to you. Besides, I didn't even sleep with him. I only love you. I've always only loved you. You know that. Syd, I'll do anything you want. We can fix this. I'll even go to a couples counselor if that's what you want."

"Hollie, I wanted to do that five years ago when we may have had a chance to work this out."

"Look, I promise we can even talk about getting married, or kids, if that's what it takes. I know you still love me. I can't believe you bought us a romantic vacation getaway and didn't tell me. That was such a sweet thing to do, but I'm mad at you for not telling me. I had to find it out from Greg. Let's just talk this out like we always do." Hollie was pleading.

I didn't really understand why Sydney put Hollie on speaker phone or why she wanted me to hear everything. I was getting increasingly uncomfortable with the conversation, but maybe she needed my silent support. Whatever her reason for wanting me to hear all this, I decided I would stay and give her whatever she needed to stay the course. I nodded at her and heard an audible sigh.

"I didn't buy the cabin for us. I bought it for me. I needed a place to go to when I finally got the guts to end it with you. I don't want to hurt you, Hollie, but can't you see that we aren't going to work? You don't really want me. You just want something to rub in your old man's face."

"That's not true. Maybe at first I wanted to rub it in his face, but no one makes me feel like you do. You can't really blame me for stepping out. You leave me by myself for days in a row, especially when you pick up all those extra shifts. Lately, even when you're here, it's like I'm invisible. You have to take some responsibility here."

I couldn't stop myself and blurted out, "You gotta be effing kidding me. You're blaming Sydney for your infidelity?"

"What the fuck, Sydney? You have me on speaker phone and you're letting that bitch listen to our private conversation? What the fuck is she doing there anyway?"

"I warned you not to talk about Mabel like that. I've put up with enough of your shit over the years, but I'm done letting you trash Mabs. This conversation is over." Sydney was speaking through gritted teeth.

"Wait, please wait. I won't say anything more about Mabel. I promise. Babe, I love you. Can you just please tell Mabel to go home? I'm coming out there. Don't go anywhere because I'll be there by five-thirty with some takeout and a bottle of wine. I swear I'll do anything you want. Just give me a chance to change, and I promise I'll never cheat on you again. I'm really ready to commit now. Please, you can't want to throw away ten years just like that. I know we can make it work, please."

I could tell she was crying now and I almost felt sorry for her. Hollie's crying affected Sydney, but she took one look at me and I could almost feel the resolve build in her.

"I'm sorry, Hollie, it's too late. I won't be here when you come tonight, so don't bother. Goodbye." Sydney pressed the button, flipped the switch to silence mode, and placed the phone against her forehead. An errant tear rolled down her cheek.

I took a few tentative steps in her direction and then I felt compelled to pull her into my arms to comfort her. I really didn't intend to kiss her, but she was like a magnet and I closed the gap. It wasn't like our earlier kiss that had a respectable amount of passion attached to it. It was more like a commingling of two body parts. I just wanted to convey my support and love. I knew I shouldn't have done that to her because she had to be confused, but it just seemed right and I refused to feel guilty about it.

She smiled at me and lifted one eyebrow.

"Nope, if you're thinking I'm sorry I just did that, you would be wrong. I'm not about to apologize." After those words flew out of my mouth, I regretted them, because even though I wasn't sorry, I was still confused about what I was going to do about Celeste. We'd started something. I didn't know what that something was and she lived literally millions of miles away. It put a new perspective on long distance relationships.

Sydney interrupted my thoughts. "Good, because I wasn't asking for an apology and I'm not the least bit sorry you did that. I hate to break the mood, but our timetable just accelerated. We better be out of here in less than thirty minutes and be well on our way to our destination, or both of us are going to really be sorry when Hurricane Hollie arrives."

"I'll go get the salmon from the fridge and collect whatever else I might need to cook with. You don't mind if I scrounge around your kitchen, do you? We'll be able to get ice on the way, won't we?"

"Sure. I'll meet you at the Jeep in ten."

†

I was glad the cooler was super-sized because I ended up grabbing not only the salmon, but a bunch of other items she had in her freezer, including some steaks, apple chicken sausages, turkey hot dogs, and ground bison. The plastic bag I threw the items into was overflowing by the time I was done. I also raided her spice rack pulling out some dried thyme and old bay seasoning. I'd already seen the mini salt and pepper shakers in one of the camping bags, so I was sure I could make do with some minimal spices to add to the basic seasoning. Finally, I grabbed several bulbs of garlic because almost everything I ate had a liberal amount of garlic added to the recipe. I'd never had to worry much about garlic breath before. I made a mental note to pick up some chewing gum.

When I got to the Jeep, everything was already loaded up. Boy, was she fast. We would be far away from the cabin when Hurricane Hollie arrived since it was a quarter to five now. I lifted the cooler, which was the last item placed in the back and tossed all the perishables inside.

"Can I just grab our bags from the guest bedroom and toss them inside? I don't think I want to wear the same clothes for two weeks."

"Sure. I left some room on top of the cooler and in the back seat. It should all fit. I'll pack my bag and grab Gizmo's food, and then we can rouse Celeste and be on our way." Sydney was already heading back into the cabin as she replied.

We were like a well-oiled machine and, within ten minutes, we were ready to pack Celeste and Gizmo into the Jeep with the rest of our supplies and gear. I'd noticed that Celeste never went anywhere without her backpack, so I was sure to include that in the pile. I resisted the urge to snoop.

Sydney was scrutinizing me and I started to get self-conscious when she frowned.

"What?"

I looked down at the spot she seemed to be focusing on and noticed the rather large hole and red spot in my shirt. I'd neglected to remove the evidence when I'd brushed my teeth while Sydney was making the sandwiches.

"Um, you might want to change your shirt before we leave because we will want to make a stop to get some additional supplies and I don't think you want to explain that." She pointed at the place where Greg shot me.

"Oh yeah, right. My bag is already packed. Do you think I can borrow a T-shirt?" I asked.

"Sure, follow me."

I followed her back into the cabin and into her bedroom. She pawed through her drawers, pulled out a Seahawks shirt, and tossed it to me.

"Thanks."

"It's a little small for me, so it should fit you. I only wear it when I'm working out—by myself," she added. "The guys are such pigs and shamelessly ogled me when I wore it at the firehouse."

I gulped. She turned to leave me to change on my own. I quickly removed the stained shirt and replaced it with her T-shirt. Before I pulled it over my head, I brought the shirt to my nose and sniffed. I didn't know why I was doing that, because it's not like it would smell like Sydney after being washed, but the fresh lavender smell was heavenly. I didn't know what to do with the shirt so it remained clutched in my hands.

I knew we didn't have a lot of time, but I hadn't even showered yet today and I wasn't about to enter camping land with dirty hair, so I rushed into her bathroom and quickly washed and towel dried my hair. Of course I didn't have time to use a hair dryer, but at least I didn't have that itchy head feeling. I opened up her cabinets searching for an unopened toothbrush and got lucky when I found one in the drawer below the sink. I didn't think Sydney would mind if I helped myself. I wasn't about to be caught unawares if Sydney decided to bless me with another tongue tangle. I brushed quickly and was thankful for that minty fresh feeling. Even though I wasn't able to take a full shower, I felt human again. I chuckled to myself. I wondered if Celeste would feel icky not having the opportunity to clean herself, or would she just give herself a quick energy burst later on.

Sydney was patiently waiting for me when I emerged from her bedroom. *I was just in Sydney's bedroom. Oh my God.*

She took one look at my wet hair and shook her head. "I can't believe you just washed your hair."

"I've never gone a whole day without washing my hair. Sorry I had to. I hope you don't mind that I used the extra toothbrush I found in the drawer."

"Of course not. I keep collecting them every time I go to the dentist."

We left the cabin, walked over to Celeste, and before we reached the hammock she opened her eyes. "It is time for the next adventure," she stated.

"Yes, it certainly is. Can you make it to the Jeep on your own?" I asked.

Celeste handed me Gizmo and I pulled her close to me, still holding the gruesome shirt. I kissed her nose. "Hello, my little pun'kin. Are you ready to take a little trip with Auntie Celeste and Auntie Sydney?" She responded with a short meow and started purring on cue.

Celeste climbed into the back of the Jeep leaving me with the usually sought after shotgun spot. I stuffed the stained shirt on the floor of the Jeep. I could decide what I wanted to do with it later.

We were on our way in a flash and I felt both a sense of excitement along with a healthy dose of trepidation. I'd never been camping before, and I was sure that before the trip was over I would reveal my clumsy, awkward self to both Celeste and Sydney.

Sydney reached around to the back, pulled out her favorite Seahawks baseball cap, and gently placed it on my head. She grinned as I adjusted my hair, pulling it through the hole in the back. She lifted her fist to me and I bumped it with my own. I was turned sideways and noticed how Celeste watched us carefully, lifting her own fist. Sydney must have seen her in the rear view mirror. Sydney and I both laughed as we both reached around to bump her fist.

Even though I'd been shot, Hollie was surely going to kick my ass, and eventually I was convinced that Greg would come looking for us again, this was the most fun I'd had in my entire life. Sad, but true. Life was looking up for me.

Chapter Nine

The stereo on the Jeep was blaring as Sydney and I sang loudly while Celeste hummed to a wide variety of songs that Sydney had stored on her iPhone. I hadn't figured her for an oldies fan, but when *Magic Carpet Ride* filled the air, I smiled and joined in. Who knew?

Sydney wouldn't tell us where we were going as we headed in the direction of the mountains. I am directionally challenged, and even though I'd lived in the Pacific Northwest all my life, I had absolutely no idea where to camp. I hoped there was water available to bathe in, that was my only criteria. Sydney assured me that the crystal clear mountain lakes would provide clean water for my bathing needs, but she warned me how cold it might be.

I was glad that I'd raided Sydney's freezer because the meat doubled as temporary ice packs. They did an adequate job of keeping the salmon cold until Sydney located a safe place for us to stop and pick up some additional supplies, including fresh water and ice.

About forty minutes into our trip, Sydney pulled into a deserted lot at this remote mom-and-pop store.

I gently placed Gizmo on the passenger seat and she curled up into a ball and promptly fell asleep. She was such a good little traveler. We all piled out of the Jeep to check out the store.

Sydney pulled the weathered door open and a bell tinkled, announcing our presence.

"Hello, ladies, what can I help you with?" An old man with the stereotypical weathered face, wearing flannel and suspenders, greeted us.

Sydney glanced around the store and grumbled. "Damn, this is highway robbery."

"Um, sorry, we can just look around and I'm sure we'll find everything we need on our own." I directed my response to the old man. I smacked Sydney on her arm and pulled her off to the side out of earshot from the old man. "Oh, come on, considering the location, these prices are a bargain. Let's pick up whatever you think we need and I'll buy."

"Oh shit, I'm sorry, Mabs. I'm being grumpy. I don't mind covering the costs." Sydney grimaced. She looked a bit sheepish to me.

Celeste pulled out her trademark wad of cash, which I assume she'd retrieved from her backpack after I'd graciously set it beside her in the backseat. "Sydney, please let me purchase the necessary supplies."

Sydney's eyes opened wide. "God, Celeste, where did you get all that money. Please tell me you didn't do any mind manipulation to liberate some poor slob's hard earned cash."

"Don't be ridiculous. Celeste is not a criminal."

"I didn't say she was," Sydney hissed.

"I am able to perform a bit of alchemy with what you consider useless items. Your planet values gold and diamonds, and in exchange for those items I was presented with this paper currency. Although I have much to learn about your planet, the knowledge of the value of those items, and how to barter, was passed on to me prior to my journey."

Sydney blinked twice and nodded. "Okay, moneybags, I suppose it's your treat then."

Sydney grabbed a case of bottled water and three bags of ice. I walked down the junk food aisle and grabbed a couple of bags of Smartfood popcorn, Cheetos, a bag of marshmallows, several Hershey bars, and a box of graham crackers. What self-respecting campfire did not come with s'mores? At the counter, I spied an assortment of gum and candy, so I snatched several packs of Orbit White and tossed them on the pile of junk food. I'd prided myself on having super white teeth, so why not choose that particular brand. I didn't want my teeth to turn yellow, and now I could combine minty fresh breath with a whitening agent. Brilliant.

Sydney chuckled as she looked at my bounty. "Good call, Mabs."

Celeste was inspecting the Smartfood and Cheetos, and I wondered what crazy question would come out this time.

"Why did you buy more food for Gizmo?" She pointed to the bag of Cheetos. "Do you allow her to eat this kind of food?"

I must have look puzzled, so Celeste added, "The bag has a picture of a cat on it. It is what you would call junk food for a cat, is it not?"

The old man behind the counter laughed.

I shook my head. "The cheetah is kind of a mascot for the Cheetos, kind of like the Fritos bandit used to be, but Fritos is not exactly the preferred choice of junk food for thieves."

I smiled to myself when I remembered being lost in a book one night, eating a bag of Cheetos for dinner and distractedly waving one in the air. Gizmo grabbed it from my errant hand and I let her have it because she'd slobbered all over it already. Maybe Cheetos was a form of cat junk food, because Gizmo sure seemed to like the tasty treat she'd pilfered right out of my hand.

Celeste giggled to herself and pointed to the Smartfood popcorn. "I suppose that food is not what causes your increased intelligence."

I chucked. "If it were only that simple, I'd be a bona fide genius. I suspect that the amount of junk food I eat may be a disadvantage rather than a boon to my intellect, but I don't care. This stuff is addictive and if I have to suffer through camping, I want comfort food to tide me over."

The old man behind the counter was getting quite a kick out of Celeste. I hoped that the odd interchange would not give away the general direction we were heading for our camping adventure in case anyone happened to question him.

After Celeste peeled off a few twenties, we headed back out to the Jeep. Sydney showed more of her superior packing ability when she found yet another few cubbyholes to store the items we'd purchased for our adventure.

†

Finally, Sydney turned off the main road and proceeded to navigate her way up a gravel road with potholes the size of small lakes. I felt like a kernel of corn in an air popper as I bounced around in the Jeep even though I'd securely buckled myself in on the passenger seat. It reminded me of sitting in the back of the bus as a grade-schooler as we bumped along one of the less maintained roads in our small town. I remembered that as being a lot more fun than traveling along on this remote road.

Eventually the road turned into a dirt path with twice the number of dips and I felt the jarring all the way to my teeth. I was just about ready to call Uncle, when Sydney turned us into this flat patch of vegetation hidden by massive evergreen trees surrounding the area like quiet sentinels. Through the trees, I saw the most breathtaking lake I'd ever witnessed. The sun was still shining and the reflection of the mountains and various shades of green created a picture worthy of a postcard. I wanted to take off my sneakers and run down to the lake to dip my toes in the water.

Gizmo was fast asleep in my lap and, although I didn't want to disturb her, I needed to wake my little pun'kin up and get her acclimated to her temporary residence for the next two weeks.

"I'm sorry, baby, it's time to wake up and explore your new territory," I said.

"Meow." Gizmo looked up at me and yawned.

While Celeste and Sydney were stretching and walking around the campsite, I pulled out Gizmo's fleece blanket that Sydney had tightly rolled and stuffed into the corner on the floor in the back. Gizmo sniffed the ground and starting walking around like she owned the place, but when I laid out her blanket she sauntered over and curled back up to promptly resume her beauty rest. She's a cat after all, and God forbid we interrupt nap time.

I joined Sydney and Celeste who were looking out at the lake through the break in the trees. My eyes were glistening with excitement. "It's so beautiful."

"Yeah, it is, isn't it? I wanted to share this with you," Sydney whispered in reverence.

I was getting hungry again. I glanced at my watch and realized it was almost six o'clock. No wonder I was ready for food.

"So, can I get out of tent duty if I offer to get dinner started?" I tested.

"You got yourself a deal, but if we all unload it will take less time," Sydney answered.

Celeste had managed to sneak up behind us. "This is almost as beautiful as Rinder's Plateau."

I scrunched up my face in confusion. "Rinder's Plateau? What is that? I've never heard of it."

"It is a popular place on my planet to exchange energy," Celeste responded.

"So is that like a make out spot?" I was starting to understand Celeste.

"Make out?" Celeste asked.

"Yeah, like swap spit, tangle tongues, heavy petting, practice some of the stuff you read in that book that got me in trouble at the café. It's what our youth do when they want to get amorous with one another in a private place." I laughed.

"I think I need to read those books on slang and figures of speech soon so that I will understand what you and Sydney discuss."

"I can pull out my Kindle and download a few books for you." I smacked my head with the palm of my hand. "Oh crap, I forgot, no wireless service in the boonies."

"I will be able to pour energy into your reading device to allow you to download the books I require for better understanding of your planet," Celeste pronounced.

"Really. You can give us wireless internet access from here?" I pointed to our surroundings.

"Yes, it is quite simple really. I learned about your wireless system in the hospital from a fellow patient who they claimed was paranoid. He was very enlightening. He explained to me all about the wireless internet and how it was the government's way of spying on everyone. He was wearing a tin foil hat to attempt to block the wireless energy. I tried to explain that energy is all around us, and his hat was not efficient in preventing an energy signature from coming through. He was quite knowledgeable about this wireless phenomenon, and I was later able to create the correct energy frequency to duplicate the effects. Everything organic and inorganic has an energy signature that can be read and transmitted, including human emotions."

I was excited to see if she could produce the energy required for a wireless signature. I clapped my hands. "Well then, let's get that puppy unloaded, I mean the Jeep." I glanced at Celeste. "Puppy is just another figure of speech, we won't exactly be unloading a dog, you know."

Working together, we had the Jeep completely unloaded in less than thirty minutes. Of course, Sydney had to be the big tough butch and carry the large cooler all by herself leaving the lighter items for me and Celeste.

Sydney plopped down on the ground and began pulling out all the items in the tent bag and laying them out. She carefully unfolded the nylon tent concentrating so hard on undoing the shock-corded poles that her tongue was poking out of her mouth. She looked like a little kid concentrating hard on a complicated math problem.

I decided to wait to play with the Kindle until I had dinner well on its way. I didn't know a lot about camping, but I did think I could handle building a fire, and directed Celeste to gather kindling and larger hunks of wood. I'd noticed a circle of rocks that Sydney must have arranged on an earlier trip into the mountains. I was sure this was where we would build our fire.

I grabbed a large knife that was in one of the bags and began to prepare the fish. After chopping off the tail and head, I walked into the heavy vegetation and tossed them both a fair distance away from where Sydney was setting up the tent and where our main living area would be for the next couple of weeks. I hoped that they wouldn't smell too bad as they rotted. Maybe, if we got lucky, an eagle would swoop down and remove the discarded carcass. The old grill grate that Sydney packed would be perfect to place the fish on after I built a smoldering fire. I'd read a lot of lesbian adventure stories, so I was confident I could build a fire. I mean, how hard could it be?

Celeste was bringing over her bounty of wood and Sydney stopped what she was doing to cut up some of the larger pieces. She had an ax and knew just how to chop up the wood. She must have gotten hot because she removed her shirt and continued chopping the wood in her tight blue tank top. I watched her bulging muscles as she brought the ax down again and again. The sweat traveled down her chest into the perfect v of her breasts and hypnotized me.

In no time at all there was a pile of wood that I thought would last at least a few days. Sydney went back to her task of pitching the tent. She only needed to stake it down and add the rain tarp that would provide additional protection from the elements. I felt pretty proud of myself for even knowing the names for each of the tent parts. Who knew you could get a complete education on camping through a lesbian adventure novel.

I started making a little kindling teepee and then stuffed a bunch of pine needles underneath. I tossed a match into the middle and watched with fascination as the needles burned up quickly. Yeah, my first fire. Unfortunately, after only a few minutes, all the pine needles burned out and none of the kindling had even started to burn.

"Shit, what happened?" I muttered to myself.

Sydney walked over and I could tell she was trying not to laugh, but a semi-snort came out as she was covering her mouth. "Um, let me help you."

I pouted. "Why isn't this blazing already? It worked in the books."

"Mabs, it's a beautiful teepee, but the kindling is a little too high and the flames from the pine needles can't reach it enough to effectively start the fire. Let's try a more Lincoln log approach. You still need to ensure there is enough air between the kindling so the fire isn't smothered, but too much and the wood won't catch."

Sydney rearranged the kindling, grabbed some more pine needles and her fire was blazing in a matter of minutes. Show off.

While we were playing with the fire, Celeste had pulled out the camping chairs and arranged them around the circle of rocks. She'd found my Kindle and it looked like she was typing on the device with her index fingers, but her fingers were flowing so quickly, I wasn't sure. The soft purple light that I now associated with Celeste was glowing around her hands.

"Whatcha doing?" I asked.

"I found several possible choices of books that will explain slang and figures of speech. I did not wish to purchase those without your consent. I presume this one-click option will create an expense for you. May I offer you cash in exchange for the ability to download these books? I believe I understand your currency enough to be able to adequately compensate you for this electronic information."

"Sure, go ahead. Get whatever you want. I'm not worried about the money."

"Thank you, Bella. I think I will also procure some additional items that will help my education about this planet."

Her fingers flew over the keyboard on the device and she was swiping the pages so quickly that I wondered how much of the information she was retaining, but then I remembered how quickly she appeared to read my lesbian erotica. Considering that she had nearly recited the passages word for word in the café, I knew it wouldn't take her long to absorb the information.

While Celeste read on the Kindle, Sydney seemed to be fussing around the campsite, making sure everything was set up perfectly. I focused on dinner. Once the fire pit had a nice red glow going, I placed the prepped fish on top of the grate. We didn't really have any potatoes or other vegetables to go with the fish, so I guess my Smart Food popcorn would have to do. I laughed at the absurdity of combining fish with popcorn, but what the heck, maybe I'd start a new trend.

People always tend to overcook fish and ruin the flavor, but I pulled the fish off the grill before it had a chance to dry out. Sydney had all kinds of handy camping bags full of useful items, but a serving platter was not one of them. A piece of aluminum foil would have to do.

"Fish is ready," I called out. "Sorry I don't have any sides to go with it, but we do have popcorn." I grinned at my camping mates.

"Hmmm, popcorn with fish. An ingenious combination." Sydney laughed.

"Hey don't knock it until you try it."

Sydney held her hands up in mock surrender. "I mean that seriously. I'm looking forward to the meal."

"Me too," Celeste added.

The fish was delicious if I do say so myself. The popcorn was an interesting side and not entirely unappealing in combo with the main dish.

I saw Celeste sneaking little bits to Gizmo but I ignored the fact that she was spoiling my kitty rotten. I couldn't really fault her too much for that because I was notorious for slipping her table scraps. Feeding Gizmo small treats seemed to give Celeste such pleasure.

Sydney kept feeding the fire and kept it at a healthy glow because the sun was starting to sink lower on the horizon, and I could tell we might have a chilly night ahead. Even though we were experiencing an unusually warm spring, when the sun goes down in the Northwest, it can get downright cold. I wanted to stay up, toast marshmallows, and enjoy my very first campfire. I'd missed out on a lot as a kid, never going away to camp, and I wanted the whole experience including ghost stories around a raging fire.

"Sydney, will you tell us a ghost story?" I asked.

She chucked evilly. "Okay. About fifty years ago, right here in these mountains, there was a closeted lesbian couple who used to take a camping trip once a year away from their families. See, they were afraid to be together because they feared the reaction of their overbearing husbands, so they accepted their dreary existence, taking pleasure only once a year."

"Oh, that's so sad," I remarked.

"So anyway, they were spread out on their sleeping bags next to the fire and one thing led to another, and pretty soon the taller one was latched onto her partner sucking furiously on her, uh, sensitive bud. Just when she was about to hit the ultimate height of passion, their husbands crashed the campsite, and in a fit of anger grabbed the ax and chopped both women to pieces. Never reaching the pinnacle before her premature death, you can still hear one of the women screaming out in frustration. *Coitus interuptus* for all eternity. Not only does she haunt these woods and attack unsuspecting men, but she was so pissed at her lover for not getting her there quicker, she sometimes plays tricks on amorous lesbians by pushing them apart before they reach climax." Sydney shrugged. "That's why I've never taken a date up here. What would be the point?"

"Okay, that is the lamest ghost story I think I've ever heard."

"Maybe, but don't come crying to me if you ever find yourself in that position, and you feel an evil force come between you. I'd suggest that you and Celeste better not put yourself in that vulnerable position while you're up here in her old haunting ground." Sydney grinned.

I raised my eyebrow. "I don't think you have to worry about that."

Celeste was quiet most of the evening, satisfied with listening to our stories. Gizmo was curled up in her lap and Celeste was idly petting her. She was watching the interaction between Sydney and me very carefully. I wondered what she was thinking, but she never offered her perspective. Celeste yawned, and it was such a human thing to do that, for a moment, I forgot she was an alien.

Sydney noticed her yawn, stood, and stretched out like a cat. It was so sexy, I could almost feel the drool escape from my lips.

"I can see that at least one of us is ready for bed. I'm kind of tired myself. Why don't we hit the sack and get a fresh start in the morning. I'd love to show you some of my favorite spots." Sydney glanced at the blazing fire. "Before we retire for the evening, maybe you should toss your shirt in the fire. It might be hard to explain what happened. The Jeep's open."

I was glad for the diversion, because then I could let Sydney and Celeste figure out the sleeping accommodations. I was dreading that awkward moment. I suspected that neither Celeste nor Sydney had any issues about changing into sleeping clothes in front of each other, but I was thankful that I could put on my sweats and T-shirt in the jeep. I scrambled into the tent and pawed through my duffle bag to retrieve my sleeping clothes.

"Can Gizmo sleep with us?" Celeste asked.

"Yeah, there is plenty of room in the tent, and I don't want any wild animals getting any ideas about a late night snack," Sydney teased.

I didn't think anything about her comment because I assumed she was joking. Sure, I knew that there were coyotes and other animals out in the woods, but I assumed they steered clear of people.

I jogged over to the Jeep and retrieved my balled up shirt from the passenger floor mat. Shit, I was lucky to be alive. While I was in the Jeep, I changed into my sweats and T-shirt, and carefully rolled up my clothes to pack back into my duffle bag. I took a few minutes to center myself before heading back to the tent to face whatever sleeping arrangements Sydney and Celeste had decided on.

As I walked over to the fire and casually tossed the damaging evidence of my fallibility into the blaze, I experienced a mini panic attack. Everything that had happened in the last ten hours came crashing into my consciousness. This camping trip was merely a Band-Aid on a gaping wound. I knew that whoever was after Celeste wouldn't stop until they found her. I shivered.

"Hey, are you okay?" Sydney called from inside the tent.

"Yeah. I'll be right there. I'm just making sure it completely burns. I don't want any evidence of this morning to remain." As I was saying that, something niggled in my head. The memory of the melted gun in a blob on the guest bedroom floor flashed in my mind like a picture across a screen. I hadn't even bothered to check the bed to see if I'd left a bloodstain there. Oh well, too late now. I was sure that by now Hollie would have the entire National Guard out looking for us.

"Shit," I muttered.

Two heads poked out of the tent with identical looks of concern on their faces. Celeste was the first to speak. "You are worried, Bella. There is something wrong."

"I think we may have a problem, but I'd rather not worry about it tonight." I shuffled over to the tent and they both moved back as I entered. Celeste was on the right and Sydney was on the left. I guess they'd decided I would sleep in the middle. Part of me was relieved, but another part found this unsettling. I schooled my expression because I didn't want either of them to worry. It must have worked because I received stereo smiles from the two of them.

Gizmo, the little hussy, snuggled up inside Celeste's sleeping bag. She certainly seemed to bond with her. I was almost jealous, but wasn't sure which one I was jealous about.

We all crawled inside our sleeping bags. I laid there awake and anxious until I felt Celeste's gentle touch. The last thing I remembered before falling into a deep sleep was seeing that beautiful purple light.

Chapter Ten

I woke up in the middle of the night and noted the gentle snoring sounds of my two friends. I have the bladder of a gnat and can never make it through the night without having to visit the bathroom at least three times. I was glad I'd stuffed a pen light in my pocket, because I didn't relish stumbling around in the dark to look for a place to pee. I'd also managed to, on the sly, stuff some toilet paper in my sweats. I carefully unzipped my bag and crawled out, hoping not to disturb my companions. Sydney made a few snorting noises as she turned over. Celeste didn't even move.

Once outside I took a few steps before turning on the pen light. The moon was shining brightly through the trees, but I thought a little more light might help me find the perfect pee spot. I wanted to walk a fair distance away from the tent. First, I didn't want to wake them, but it really was because I had this anxiety about people listening to me pee. I won't even go to the bathroom in a public place unless I know it is deserted. I'd gotten really proficient at holding it during the day. I never could understand why I couldn't hold it all night. That never made sense to me, but if I ever tried, I'd be up all night squirming in bed until I gave in and visited the bathroom.

I was well away from the campsite when I pulled my sweats down clutching my hunk of toilet paper. I let her rip and felt the distinct sense of relief I always did when I peed.

"Ahhhhhh." I was mid-pee when I sensed I was not alone. I turned my head to see two glowing eyes. That is when I smelled the rotting fish. Shit, I'd walked to the very spot where I'd thrown the salmon fish parts, and now I had a big black bear staring at my exposed bottom.

I didn't know what to do. Should I finish peeing? Should I start running and let the pee splatter all over my sweats and shoes. I froze as the rest of my urine left my body before screaming and running—well, it was actually more like duck walking—back toward what I thought was the direction of the tent. The toilet paper went flying and the penlight was probably smack dab in the middle of my puddle of pee. I waddled as fast as I could with my sweats around my ankles. I could almost feel the breath of the bear as she followed me.

I'd chosen the right direction as I spied the golden glow of the tent. Two heads poked out of the tent, and I saw the panicked, wide-eyed look on Sydney.

Celeste tilted her head and I recognized the most glorious sight I could ever hope for—the rescuing purple light. "Do not be afraid, Bella. She is merely hungry and is worried about her two cubs that are a short distance away. You frightened her more than she startled you."

"Okaaay," I squeaked out.

"May I give her our leftover fish?" Celeste asked.

Sydney and I just nodded furiously while Celeste crawled out of the tent, walked over to the Jeep, and pulled out the leftover fish from the cooler. The light glowed softly around her as she unwrapped the fish and presented it to the bear. The bear sniffed the offering, grabbed it in her massive paw, and ambled off into the woods.

By this time, Sydney had managed to wriggle out of the tent and was standing beside Celeste with her mouth hanging open. She clamped her hand across her mouth in an attempt to stop the laughter, but she wasn't successful.

"What is so damn funny? I was almost the nighttime snack for a hungry bear," I barked.

"Um, sorry." Sydney pointed to my sweats circling my ankles.

I finally realized that I was standing in front of both Celeste and Sydney in my bare ass. I blushed and quickly pulled my sweats up to cover my naked bottom.

"I did not manipulate you into mooning us, Bella, I promise," Celeste remarked with a sly smile on her face.

Sydney starting laughing so hard I thought she might pee her pants, and Celeste joined in. What could I do, I laughed right along with them. Now that the danger was over, I realized how funny I must have looked. No doubt, this would be a story that would have to be told over and over.

"Next time, I don't care if I wake you up, I'm dragging one of your butts out of bed to accompany me in the woods. Sydney, it might have been helpful to warn us that there are bears in these parts."

"Sorry, I've never encountered one before. I thought we'd packed up the food sufficiently so that we wouldn't attract unwanted visitors. I've never had problems putting the cooler with all the food back in my vehicle. I wonder what enticed her?" Sydney sounded sheepish.

Now I felt guilty as I remembered the fish head and tail I'd dumped in the woods. "Um, I might have left something over there that attracted her." I pointed to my infamous pee spot.

Realization must have dawned on Sydney. "I wondered where you discarded the head." She chuckled.

"Perhaps we ought to be more careful with our food from now on."

I vigorously nodded. "I will, I swear I will. You just tell me what to do and I will follow your instructions to a T."

Sydney leered. "Although, I must say the show tonight was particularly revealing…"

"Can we please go back to bed," I pleaded.

The rest of the night was blessedly uneventful, and I got over my eccentric need to pee in private. Another phobia miraculously replaced my former fear of peeing in public—a hungry bear mauling me.

†

I loved living in the Pacific Northwest. You never knew what kind of weather you would get, but when the sunshine made an appearance in the spring, it was glorious. Sometimes we got a decent amount of sunshine, even in the famed Seattle area where we were legendary for our rain.

Sunrise came early, and even though it was a little chilly while we drank our coffee, the warmth of the fire was a welcome relief. Sydney got up early and had a roaring fire built before we even made our presence known. I'd smashed Sydney's baseball cap on my head to keep my unruly hair from sticking up all over the place. I would have to decide whether I could suffer the arctic cold of the lake while bathing and washing my hair. I could be deathly ill, sporting a one hundred and five fever, and still that never kept me from washing my hair every day. I wondered if there was a way to heat up some water and pour it over my body after soaping up. I shivered at the thought of jumping into the cold water, naked and unprotected.

Sydney must have seen me shiver. "Here, come stand by the fire, little princess. Oh, and don't worry your pretty little head about the equivalent of a cold shower. I hooked up the solar shower and added some boiling water until it was the perfect shower temperature." She pointed to a tarp wrapped around a couple of large trees creating a private space. "I've hung the shower over there, so feel free to wash your beautiful locks. I know you've been ruminating over how you might bathe without freezing your luscious ass off."

I looked at her with awe. She was the sweetest woman. I knew she'd done this especially for me, and that she probably never bothered when she was camping alone.

"Thank you." I kissed her cheek and ambled off to get a change of clothes, shampoo, soap, and the quick-dry camping towel I'd found in the bathroom bag. I hung the baseball cap on a broken branch just outside the tarp.

I was amazed at how well the solar shower worked and it was the perfect temperature. I dressed quickly and was in the process of rubbing the towel vigorously over my hair when I emerged from behind the tarp. I reached for the baseball cap not wanting anyone to see my mass of unruly curls. Without a hairdryer, I was afraid of what my hair would look like after it dried.

I was startled when Sydney said, "You should let your hair air dry. It's really beautiful. I never knew why you always tried to straighten it."

I blushed and placed the cap back on my makeshift hat rack, a broken stub protruding from the towering pine tree.

Celeste was sitting peacefully in one of the camp chairs arranged around the fire reading the Kindle. Big surprise, Gizmo was curled up in her lap again. I was beginning to wonder if she was still my cat. Celeste glanced up at us and smiled.

"I hope you do not mind, but I would prefer to read this morning while you take your walk in the woods. I will take a rain check on a hike." She grinned. "Did I use the slang figure of speech correctly, Bella?"

"You sure did," I responded.

"Reconstituted eggs or granola?" Sydney asked.

"Granola," I responded. "Reconstituted anything does not sound appealing to me."

"It's really not that bad. You're going to have to try some of these meals in a bag before too long."

"I can wait for the experience."

"I will try the reconstituted eggs," Celeste requested.

"Teacher's pet," I retorted.

Sydney poured boiling water into two pouches, stirred both, and then re-closed them by pressing the zip lock firmly on each bag. "It'll be a couple of minutes before they're ready." She handed me a bag of granola. "Sorry I don't have any milk, but it's pretty good dry."

"No worries, I don't like milk with cereal or granola anyway."

The coffee she handed me was surprisingly good. I noted the International Delight vanilla flavored creamer in a powder form sitting on the ground, and a warm and tingly feeling crept over my body knowing that she'd brought it just for me. I liked a little coffee with my cream and she knew vanilla was my favorite flavor.

"It's almost as good as the non-dairy creamer you overwhelm your coffee with," Sydney remarked.

I nodded. "Is this also flavored coffee? It's really good."

"Yep, French vanilla. I was going for a theme here. It's the next best thing to a vanilla latte. I even have some cinnamon to put on top if you'd like," Sydney offered.

"Really? Okay, why not?"

She pulled out the spice from a pocket in her sweatshirt and handed it to me.

"Mmmm. This is quite good."

"Can I try it?" Celeste asked.

"Sure." I handed her the cinnamon.

She sprinkled it on top and started humming.

Sydney shook her head. "What a way to ruin a decent cup of coffee. You two are ruining the taste of a rich cup of black coffee."

"Ick. I only started drinking coffee for the effect in college. When they invented these flavored creamers, I was in heaven."

"Perhaps I should try this black version," Celeste said.

Sydney handed her the cup she was drinking from. "Here, try this. Pure, untainted black gold."

Celeste took a sip and scrunched up her face like a little kid eating their first healthy, tasteless, pureed vegetable. "I am sorry, Sydney, I am aligned with Bella on this. I prefer her version."

"You are both traitors to the coffee gods," Sydney joked.

As Sydney was collecting and stuffing various items in her backpack for our hike, I walked over to Celeste to make sure she was okay. She looked a little melancholy to me and I wanted to cheer her up.

"Are you sure you don't want to come with us?" I asked.

She looked up and captured my eyes. "Sydney is your energy mate," she stated.

"Oh Celeste, I am so sorry. I…I…didn't mean to lead you on. I do care for you. Very much."

"We are energy compatible and I will admit to having this fantasy that you would return to my world and become my energy mate. You and your kind have so much to share with our world, but I cannot ignore what I observe. My offer will remain until I return to my world. If anything changes, perhaps you will consider this option. My world has a different kind of beauty that I think would be compatible with you and your energy signature. Besides, Dosnir would be green with jealousy, because you're hot." She grinned. She was proud about utilizing her newly acquired slang. I didn't know who Dosnir was, but I assumed he or she was a friend.

I touched her cheek and she leaned into my hand, closing her eyes for a second. I could feel the warmth between us, and I was grateful for the affection of this remarkable woman, alien or not.

Sydney cleared her throat and I turned around to see her patiently standing a few feet away. "Ready?"

"Absolutely. Lead the way, oh great explorer. Don't I get a backpack to carry?" I asked.

"Nope. I've got it all packed in here." She patted her pack. God, she was so sexy and so butch.

†

We hiked along the water at a leisurely pace until we came to an open area where we could see in the distance a waterfall cascading over the rocks and spilling into the lake. Sydney unrolled the foam pad and laid it on the grass. As she began pulling items from the backpack, it reminded me of when Mary Poppins kept pulling objects from her bag and you wondered how she could possibility fit everything inside. I hadn't seen her pack all the fruit so I was surprised when she began pulling out apples, grapes, strawberries, and various hunks of cheese. She fished a bottle of wine from her pack and laid it all out on the mat. I chuckled when she pulled out two plastic wine glasses.

I sat down on the mat in awe of the picnic spread. She'd obviously gone to a great deal of trouble to plan this little picnic lunch. My eyes sheened with unshed tears as her gesture bowled me over with emotion. I didn't really believe I deserved for someone to do such a romantic thing for me.

She jumped up and ran to a patch of wild flowers, hastily plucking them from amongst the abundant vegetation. Before she sat down on the mat, she presented the flowers to me with a flourish. "I didn't think I could safely pack a dozen roses for you, so these will have to do."

That did it. The tears did their little escape artist thing and fell freely down my cheeks. "Oh, Sydney…"

"Oh, Mabs, what's wrong? It's too soon, isn't it? I'm so sorry. I'm such an idiot. You don't feel the same way. Friends then. We can be friends. Please, I can't lose you as a friend. I swear it's enough. I promise I won't do anything to make you uncomfortable again…"

I placed my index finger over her mouth to stop her rambling. "I'm not uncomfortable. I'm just overcome with emotion that anyone would do something so special for me. God, Sydney, how could you not know that I've been madly in love with you since the fifth grade?" I blurted this out. What a time for my censorship to fail me.

She blinked once and then expelled the air she'd been holding. "And how could you not know that I've been madly in love with you since puberty when I realized I liked girls? By then you'd turned into this beautiful young woman. If you remember, I was a late bloomer. I always knew when you were in the same room as me. My eyes would follow your every movement, until you would look up, and then I'd quickly glance away. I was always afraid you would catch me and tell me to stop mooning over you because it was never gonna happen. I don't think Hollie would have been as much of a bitch if she hadn't realized my feelings for you."

"You really mean that?"

"I've never meant anything more in my entire life. I love you, Mabs, always have and always will." Sydney crushed her lips to mine and showed me just how serious she was. This time I could feel the emotion behind the kiss. This wasn't just a physical joining of our body parts to elicit a sexual response, it was something far deeper. I melted into her arms.

I was still basking in the glory of the kiss and didn't quite register Sydney carefully setting aside all the wonderful picnic items she'd pulled from her magic bag. After clearing the mat, she laid me down onto the comfortable foam and continued her attack on my lips. She was gently sucking and biting my bottom lip as her tongue snagged mine in the ancient dance of love. One or both of us groaned and the feelings washed over me like a ten-foot tidal wave. I was feeling way too good to panic yet, that would come later.

Her kisses traversed down to my neck and I discovered how much I enjoyed the exploration of this erogenous zone. "Oh my God, that feels heavenly," I managed to cry out.

What I was feeling was a hundred times more powerful than my first kiss with Celeste. I wanted to feel Sydney, all of her, on top of me and inside me. I didn't know how to tell her this.

"I want to make love to you, Mabs, but if we're rushing this then please tell me to stop, because pretty soon we are going to reach the point of no return."

"Don't stop," was all that I managed to get out.

Sydney snaked her hand under my T-shirt and brushed gently against the sides of my bra. The sensation went directly to the lower half of my body and I swear my brain told my vagina to start making lubricant because a flush of wetness landed inside my panties. Goodness knows,

I'd read about this particular reaction hundreds of times, but to actually feel it was indescribable.

Sydney lifted off of me and asked, "Can I take your top off?"

I immediately felt the loss of our connection and I wanted so badly to feel it again, but this time I wanted to feel flesh on flesh. I nodded and blushed as I boldly declared, "Only if you take yours off, too."

Her years as a Paramedic/Firefighter must have paid off, because she had her shirt and running bra off in a matter of seconds. I guess they have to change in a hurry when the call comes to respond to an emergency. Yet she took her time removing mine and I felt every part of her fingers as they caressed my skin when she removed my clothing.

I was really glad she was taking the lead, because despite my book knowledge there was nothing like direct practice to really become competent in a new skill. I was sure that Sydney had a whole lot of direct practice to ensure competence, because so far, she was playing my body like a rare violin.

Sydney lay back down on top of me and our naked breasts made contact with one another for the first time. It was electric and I felt like a river was now flowing between my legs. Her knee gently spread my legs and she began slowly rocking against me. I was quickly coming unglued and started panting.

"I can feel your wetness through our shorts. I don't want to rush you, but if I can't touch you or taste you in the next few minutes, I think I might die from anticipation. Can I please remove the rest of your clothes?" she pleaded.

"Yes, please," I begged.

Once again, she removed her shorts in record time and I noted she wasn't wearing underwear. She stroked my breasts as her hand traveled to my stomach and then the top button of my cargo shorts. Her fingers deftly undid the button and slowly pushed down the zipper.

I felt vulnerable with the shorts splayed open, almost like the filleted fish we had for dinner the previous night. When she caressed my panties, all thoughts of anything but her hands touching my body promptly flew from my brain.

My breath hitched.

"Is this still okay?"

"Oh, yes," I answered.

She slid my panties down and tossed them to the side. It would have been comical to look upon our nakedness with the exception of hiking boots and socks had I not been feeling everything so intensely. Maybe one day I would laugh about this, but for right now, I just wanted her to touch me.

She didn't disappoint me and was gliding her thumb through my wetness while she wasted no time entering me with her middle finger.

"Oh, God, yessss," I hissed, and I bucked to meet her hand.

As she simultaneously stroked my clit and pushed and in out with just one finger, I climbed rapidly to what I was sure would be a monumental crescendo. I was almost there when she abruptly stopped. I groaned in protest.

"Shhhh. I have to taste you and then I can die a happy woman," she whispered into my ear.

Her words brought goosebumps to my entire body. "Okay," I squeaked out.

She kissed and licked her way down my body. Her gentle hands parted my thighs as her tongue found its desired destination. She started to lick and suck gently on the hood and every time the tip of her tongue found my clit, it sent shockwaves through my body. When her thumb gently played with my opening before finding its way inside, beginning a slow tortuous rhythm, I was done for. My climax exploded all over her face and hand.

"Yesss, Sydney, Sydney, Sydney," I chanted. She was a Goddess and I was paying homage to her.

"I guess if you're not even going to call out Syd in the throes of passion, I better just accept that you'll never call me Syd again. I can live with that."

I lay there spent and exhausted by both the physical and emotional gift she'd given me. I opened one eye and looked at her exquisite body stretched out before me. I felt like she was an offering to me. Immediately recharged by the vision before me I stroked her breast and rolled one of her nipples between my fingers before clamping my mouth on top and sucking.

"Oh, God, don't stop," she moaned.

I gave myself a little pep talk. I can do this. How hard can it be? I'll just try to follow the instructions in my erotica books. Well they weren't exactly instructions, but close enough.

Sydney must have sensed my hesitation. "Mabs, you don't have to do this. I'm good."

That sweet declaration was all I needed to bolster my resolve that I could indeed do this.

"Yes you are good," I teased. "Oh Sydney, don't you realize how desperately I want to do this. You know I've never, uh, you know…"

"Just touch me. Everything feels good. There aren't any right or wrong ways, you know."

"I know. I just want to make you feel as good as you made me feel," I confessed.

Sydney grabbed my hand and placed it on her soft curls. "Feel how hot and wet I am. You did that. I can take more than one finger."

I began stroking her clit and her hips lifted off the mat to greet my fingers.

After less than a minute, she cried out, "Please go inside."

I tentatively entered her with two fingers and she reared up in an attempt to have me go deeper.

"More please," she begged.

I slipped in a third finger and pumped a little faster. She was panting now and I could feel her walls begin to close in around my fingers.

"Oh, God, Mabs, I'm coming. Don't stop, please don't stop."

Not on my life would I stop. Greg could have a gun to my head right now and I wouldn't stop what I was doing. I watched Sydney as she climaxed and it was the most glorious sight I'd ever seen. I wanted to spend an eternity making love with Sydney O'Donnell.

After she relaxed and the last quiver ended, I kissed her. "I love you."

"And I love you. I'm not just saying that because you just gave me the best orgasm of my entire puny existence." She looked at me with such love in her eyes that I knew she was telling me the truth.

I snuggled into her arms as she wrapped me in her protective cocoon. I felt safe and secure there. Everything felt right and I knew this as all the puzzle pieces of my life shifted into place. I was meant to be in her arms. Celeste knew this when she told me that Sydney was my energy mate. I wanted her to find that again with someone. I wanted her to feel what I felt.

I will now. Thank you, Bella. I can now take this feeling back to my home planet. The words resonated in my head, but instead of feeling violated, I was relieved that Celeste could experience what I was feeling through our connection. I now understood that we did have a connection, but it wasn't the same as my connection with Sydney.

I wondered if was wrong for me to keep this from Sydney. I didn't think she would want to share this with Celeste, but you weren't supposed to keep things from the person you loved. I had to figure out a way to tell her this without her feeling violated or angry. I couldn't imagine her getting mad, but this little revelation might hurt her.

She stirred and looked at me. I suppose she felt my unease with how to explain what just happened. "Please tell me you don't regret this. It will break my heart if you do."

"No, no, nothing like that, but I do have something I have to tell you and I'm not sure you're going to like it," I hedged.

"Mabs, you can tell me anything."

"Well, uh, what would you think about Celeste experiencing what just happened?" I asked tentatively.

"Oh, that. I thought I felt her energy or whatever it is. I can't really explain this, but I didn't mind really. I know that you have a connection with her. She calls it an energy connection, but somehow she's managed to make it agreeable. I don't feel like it's an intrusion or anything. I think she just wanted to experience love. Love is a beautiful thing. If that is how she needed to experience love to understand the concept so she can bring it back to her planet, I'm okay with it. It doesn't take anything away from my feelings or our connection. It's not like she was some kind of piggish male voyeur, looking to get his rocks off."

"Have I told you lately how much I love you?" I tightened my hold on her.

"Yep, but you can tell me again. I don't mind."

I gave her a peck on the lips and stretched as I sat up. I looked down at our hiking boots attached to our naked bodies and burst out laughing.

"What?" she asked.

I pointed to our boots.

She joined me and her body rocked with laughter. "I don't suppose this is a story we want to tell our kids about."

My eyes got wide. "You want kids?"

"Well sure. Don't you?"

"Uh, yeah, I guess," I stammered.

She frowned. "But not with me?"

"Oh, no, no, no. I can't think of anyone else I'd rather have kids with, but you really think that's our future?"

"No doubt in my mind. I'd have asked you to marry me at thirteen, but it wasn't legal back then."

"Um, can we date a little first? This is all a bit new for me. I'd prefer several more steamy months of sex before we settle into lesbian domesticity. Also shove me off a cliff if we ever experience lesbian bed death."

"Deal." She stuck out her hand and we shook. She looked up at the sky. "We should probably eat some of my carefully prepared picnic and head back before Celeste starts to worry." I helped her put the food back on the mat.

"Thanks, Sydney. If this was our first date, I must say it was definitely memorable."

Chapter Eleven

Sydney intertwined her fingers with mine as we walked through the woods. She would periodically stop to pick a wildflower and hand it to me. I had quite a collection. She would prattle on about each plant sharing her knowledge of the local fauna. I didn't have the heart to tell her that I already knew about most of the plants. As a librarian, I read everything I could get my hands on and this included all the nature field guides for the Pacific Northwest.

It was late afternoon as we came close to the campsite. I could still smell smoke from the fire so I knew we were close. I was glad that even though Celeste had stayed back to read, she'd been with me the whole time through whatever energy connection we had. I was just about to call out to her when someone clamped a hand over my mouth and I felt the cold steel against my temple. When I turned around, I locked eyes with a very pissed off Greg. At least that's the impression I distinctly got from his energy signature. I was picking up Celeste's lingo as much as she was assimilating ours.

Sydney's arm flailed as another man grabbed her from behind. He wasn't quick enough to stop her from yelling out, "Celeste, run…"

"That was incredibly stupid of you, and if you don't want to see your little girlfriend in a world of hurt, you'll get Celeste to come with us peaceably. If you help us, I promise you we won't kill you. No one would believe you if you tried to talk about this anyway, so our orders have changed and we're allowed to spare your lives. It's a win-win situation. You help us, we help you."

I should have told Sydney and Celeste about my uneasiness earlier, but I honestly thought we had more time. I'd underestimated Hurricane Hollie. I knew she would contact Greg the minute she got to the cabin and found it empty. If there was blood on the guest room bed sheets, that would have fueled her sense of panic. I was just guessing here, but I'd bet my house that's how they found us so quickly.

As they were leading us at gunpoint to the campsite, I heard the words in my head. Celeste was talking to me, Do not worry, Bella, they will not catch me unawares again. I felt your anxiety long before Sydney warned me. Just follow their instructions and I will take care of the rest.

As we entered the clearing, Celeste gently placed Gizmo on the ground and stood to face her attackers. She raised her face to the sun and spread her arms out. This time, the glow from her body was not a soft purple light, but an angry magenta, and as she directed the light in their direction, the guns glowed red hot in their hands before dropping in the grass and seeping into the ground after turning into a liquid. The men grabbed their heads and screamed in agony.

A third man rushed out from behind the massive tree with a Taser in his hands. I opened my mouth to warn Celeste, but it was too late just as Celeste whirled around and directed a burst of energy in his direction the Taser jolted her. The two energy blasts each hit their target, and as the

Taser went flying, following the same fate as the guns, Celeste twitched like a grotesque form of modern dance. The magenta light started to fade to the soft purple light I was more accustomed to, but not before the third man held his head and grimaced. All three men were now on their knees.

Celeste collapsed to the ground and I ran to her side cradling her head in my arms. Her eyes rolled back and her state of unconsciousness alarmed me. I tried to check for a pulse, but I didn't even know if aliens had a heart to pump blood to their life giving organs. She remained motionless in my arms.

All three men seemed to be in a trance-like state and they sat placidly on the ground.

"What the hell just happened?" Sydney called out.

"I don't know. I don't know. Celeste isn't moving and I can't feel her pulse. I don't know how to help her." I started crying.

"She's always gotten better after a few hours in the sun. Maybe if we just lay her out on a blanket in the sun, it will help."

"I don't think that's enough this time. Oh God, this is all my fault. I knew they would come looking for us," I blubbered.

Sydney came over and kneeled on the other side, picking up Celeste's hand and holding it while she caressed my cheek. "No, hon, it's not your fault. You have to trust that Celeste knew what she was doing. I don't think she could live with herself if something happened to you because of her."

Gizmo who had been crouched on the ground slithered over and jumped on top of Celeste while I cradled her in my arms. I was just about to gently remove my cat, when she started licking her face. I was openly weeping and

Sydney was crying right along with me, when Celeste opened her eyes.

"What is the big hairy deal, you crybabies?" Celeste asked with a smirk on her face. "I am particularly fond of that figure of speech."

I smacked her arm. "Jesus, don't ever scare me like that again."

Celeste sat up, and although she was still a little wobbly and her skin tone lacked that healthy glow, she was upright and talking.

"Damn, Celeste, I thought you were a goner for sure. What happened?" Sydney asked.

"As I explained before, everything has an energy signature that can be read and focused, even emotions like love and sadness. I did not realize this until I met you, sweet Bella. We are a dispassionate race and that will be our ultimate downfall unless I am able to bring back all I have learned. Your emotions, along with the emotions of Gizmo, flooded my system with life-giving energy. I absorbed the love from both of you and your furry friend, enough to continue my survival until I am able to properly recharge," Celeste explained.

"I don't think you're as dispassionate as you think. Don't forget, I've heard you talk about your energy mate. You may not have realized what it was, but it sure sounded like love to me with a side order of passion."

"Perhaps you are correct. My reaction to the demise of my energy mate was similar to this emotion you call anger. At the very least, the guardians were not pleased and considered it a rebellion. They gave me the choice of space exploration or temporary placement at a re-education center. I am sorry I did not confess the whole story earlier. I let you believe I followed in the footsteps of my caretaker rather than a forced option. The truth is that I refused to seek out another energy mate. It was an unacceptable reaction. On my world, they categorize those who do not seek out energy mates as mutants and outcasts. I was not a fully functioning member of society. It is unfortunate that I had to travel hundreds of light years away to open myself to another energy mate and, just my luck, your signature is more suitable with another. I will miss you, Bella."

We were still somehow connected and I could feel her anguish. It felt like my heart was breaking right along with hers. I don't know what Sydney was feeling, but she placed a protective hand on my back and started rubbing.

"You're going to leave us, aren't you?" I swiped away my tears.

"I cannot survive on your planet long term with only one sun and no energy mate. I would not last one of your Earth's years." She looked up at me and the tears in her eyes fell freely down her face.

"What about if we can find you an energy mate? I don't want you to leave. I just found you. We still have so much to learn from each other. You made me feel beautiful. I know I can't be your energy mate, but I can be your friend. Remember when I told you there were many different kinds of love. I love you, Celeste. Please stay."

"Oh, Bella, I will never forget what you taught me. I understand love now. I love you, too, but I don't think my love is the same as yours. Love hurts, but it is also the most wondrous feeling. I understand the saying, *it is better to have loved and lost than to never have loved at all*. I am twice blessed and twice cursed, but as your people would say, *three times is a charm*. I will search for love on my own planet and I will teach others." Celeste picked up two rocks and closed her hand as her purple light transformed them into two perfect diamonds. She opened her hand and offered them to us. "Use these for your ritual of love and remember me fondly when you recite your vows."

"I know I will never forget you. Thank you, Celeste." I took the offered diamonds. "We will cherish these gifts. I don't know if the Kindle will work on your planet, but it seems like you really are enjoying our slang. I'll load a bunch of other books about love on the reader for you."

"I would like that," she graciously responded.

Giving her my Kindle seemed like such a lame thing to do. I wanted to give her something more personal to remember us by, but I couldn't think fast enough to know what that might be. Nothing I owned was valuable or sentimental. Then I got an idea that might seem entirely outrageous and ridiculous to some, but ended up being the perfect gift in the end.

"Celeste, you asked me to go back with you, right?" I asked.

Her eyes brightened. "Oh yes, I did."

"Does that mean you could take Gizmo with you?"

Celeste smiled. "Yes, of course I could, but she is your special companion. Wouldn't you miss her?"

"More than you know. She's been my everything since I adopted her, but now I have Sydney and I won't feel so alone anymore. Gizmo is very friendly and usually gets along with almost everyone. I can tell she's really bonded with you—more than any other. She's fixed so she can't have any kittens or anything, but I think she can teach you about another kind of love." I picked up Gizmo and placed her in Celeste's arms.

Celeste brought Gizmo to her chest, hugging and kissing her. "Oh, Bella. I will take such good care of Gizmo and I will give her the energy needed to have baby kittens. This gift will not only be for me, but for my planet. I will treasure her always."

"Do you think that maybe you will be able to come back someday and visit?" Sydney asked. "Um, I don't really know how long it takes to travel from Sisterna to Earth," she added.

"I cannot promise anything, but it is not outside of the realm of possibility," Celeste answered.

"When will you have to leave?" I asked.

"I will need to fully recharge before attempting to make the journey back home. One more day under the sunshine should be sufficient."

Sydney glanced over to the three men who remained nearly catatonic. "What about the three stooges there?" She pointed at our attackers.

Celeste frowned. "I am sorry. I let my anger control my reaction to them. I do not know if the memory removal will be permanent or temporary. However, I would guess the current state they are in may last for several weeks."

"Hmmm. How ironic that Greg may end up in the very place he claimed to want to take you back to. Karmic justice is a bitch. Sydney, do you have any ideas about how we can get someone to take them to a hospital or something until they recover?" I asked.

"I suppose we could make an anonymous call about three strange guys roaming around in the mountains and provide the authorities with the general location after we pack up in a day or two. Will we at least be able to feed them until we're ready for the forest service to *find* them?"

"I believe they will be able to follow rudimentary commands," Celeste answered.

"I'm not giving up my sleeping bag, so I hope they like sleeping under the stars on whatever extra blanket or pad we have to offer. Too bad they're catatonic. I'd pay money to see the bear come back and scare the shit out of them." I giggled.

"You're evil, but I like it," Sydney stated.

I smacked my hands together. "Well now that we have everything settled, I do believe it's time to pull out the meat for dinner. I have a confession to make."

Sydney raised her eyebrow.

"I'm so glad tomorrow will be our last day camping because I don't think I can make it two whole weeks without you know…uh…taking care of my biological needs. I refuse to dig some hole in the ground and squat like a heathen over it while I do my business. It was touch and go this morning, but I managed to avoid the necessary evil after my coffee. I was trying to come up with some reason to take the Jeep and head to the nearest town."

It's amazing how our brain signals can convince our bodies of just about anything. My locked up tight sphincter muscles were obeying me. Nothing was coming out that I didn't want to release until I was good and ready. I giggled to myself because only a nerd would talk about their sphincter muscles, but no matter how much of a doofus I was, Sydney still loved me.

"You're kidding, right?" Sydney asked.

"Nope, I'm really not, so for future reference, two days is my limit," I said.

Chapter Twelve

The next day I woke up to a cloudless, brilliantly blue sky. Good fortune was shining down on us for the third day in a row and I celebrated Celeste's ability to soak up the sun's life-giving rays.

I stretched and crawled out of my cozy cocoon. Celeste was still lightly snoring, but Sydney's sleeping bag was empty. I poked my head out of the tent and watched as Sydney was brushing her teeth while stoking the fire that I assumed she'd just built. She was a multi-tasker. Good to know.

Greg and his buddies were mumbling to themselves using nonsensical words. If we hadn't recently experienced their wrath, it might have been comical. I noticed that their eyes still had a vacant, unfocused look. I wondered if Sydney led them all to the camping chairs in front of the fire this morning because they were sitting in a semi-circle and babbling like babies who haven't learned to talk yet. Was this some kind of side effect of the memory removal Celeste inflicted on them—taking away their most basic memories like rudimentary language skills? They reminded me of their Neanderthal ancestors who grunted in conversation as a mode of communication, but I wasn't sure whether they understood each other.

I wish I'd taken a picture of the trio when I braved the night chill and wild animals for my nightly pee, because they had been spooning each other like sardines in a can. I burst out laughing and Sydney looked at me to see what was so humorous. Like my bladder, I could hold my laughter in only so long before it exploded out of me. I pointed to the men and she chuckled. Too bad we couldn't show their bosses the touching picture.

Sydney pointed to the French press and I shook my head. I was serious about my vow not to get my system started this morning. She shrugged and I thought I saw her shaking with laughter as she turned around to rinse off her toothbrush.

It didn't take us long to get ready, and this time we insisted that Celeste accompany us on our hike. I wanted to spend as much time as I could with her before she had to return. Celeste readily agreed to our plans for the day.

"I will be happy to follow your *bootelicious* self," Celeste proclaimed.

I snorted and laughed out loud as Sydney smirked and mouthed *bootelicious* to me. "I bet you're pretty proud of yourself right now, using slang and all, but where in the world did you get that adjective. I've certainly never heard that one before."

Celeste grinned. "Your reading device is very informative, but I may have combined a few words to create my own slang."

✝

Sydney did a good job of leading us on a path that would allow Celeste to remain in the sunshine.

Celeste had an uncanny ability to find the beauty in not only the wildflowers, but also the weeds. In a way, I felt like that weed she noticed and pointed to, bringing out the beauty for others to see. She knew the names of most of the plants that Sydney drew our attention to. I could tell by her grin that she already knew what they were when Sydney would proudly point them out, but she never revealed her knowledge. She was content to let Sydney be her guide. When we came across a Purple Dead Nettle she asked about it.

"Oh that's just a weed." Sydney waved her hand away as if the weed was not worthy of a name.

"The weed is beautiful. Why do you wave it off with disdain?" Celeste asked.

Sydney squatted next to the purple flower. "You know, you're right, this Purple Dead Nettle is beautiful. I guess we are extremely arbitrary and capricious when determining which plants are beautiful flowers and which are noxious weeds."

"I like your saying, *beauty is in the eye of the beholder*. If a person on your planet is not considered beautiful, are they also considered unworthy?" Celeste asked.

"Wow, Celeste you've really hit the nail on the head. Our society does place far too much emphasis on appearances, so because I never felt beautiful before, I also never felt worthy."

Sydney tilted her head in my direction. "Did you really believe that? God, Mabs, you have the whole package because not only are you beautiful on the outside, but your soul is just as exquisite." Sydney got this look like she'd just figured out the meaning of life. "You know, I just realized that what I really fell in love with is who you are inside. Remember how I told you I fell in love with you the minute I reached puberty? Well, you've definitely blossomed since then. No offense, Mabs, but your coke bottle glasses and that extensive metal mouth weren't exactly the most attractive accessories, yet I still fell for you. I guess I'm not as shallow as I thought I was."

"Well too bad I can't say the same thing about myself. I am completely shallow because you, Sydney, are a complete hottie, and Celeste is out of this world gorgeous," I teased. "Seriously, Celeste, you just reinforced a very important lesson. Every living thing is worthy and should be treated as such. I'll never look at another weed in the same way. I always thought I was more accepting of people because of my own experience in high school, but you've taught me that even I have biases."

I wasn't in any hurry to get back to the campsite because I knew it would mark the end of Celeste's visit to our planet, so we meandered along the path in no particular hurry to end our hike. I avoided the topic like the plague, lest I turn into a sobbing ball of hysteria.

On our journey, we came across a black SUV and I assumed this was the vehicle Greg and his companions used to travel to our location. It wasn't too far from where we pitched our tent, definitely in walking distance. I thought it might not be a bad idea to walk the guys closer to their car so that when the authorities went looking for the *strange men* hanging out in the mountains, they would find the vehicle.

With each hour, Celeste improved and by the time we made it back to the campsite, her healthy glow had returned. I was pleased to see Gizmo curled up on the blanket I'd placed in front of the tent.

I didn't know how to suggest one last dinner before the impending goodbyes, so I didn't say anything. I felt like I would be suggesting something like the last supper. How depressing is that? It turns out that Celeste was on a similar wavelength.

"Do you think we could cook up another meal and have the s'mores for dessert again? I will miss the Earth food almost as much as I will miss you."

"I think those chicken apple sausages would be the perfect thing to roast over the fire. No prep needed," I replied.

There were so many things I would miss about Celeste. Her humming while enjoying a tasty meal was something I would never forget. It was a whole lot better than a loud belch when expressing your satisfaction over a meal. I'd read somewhere that in some cultures a burp or passing gas was a high compliment to the chef. I preferred not to receive that type of accolade. She didn't disappoint me this last evening as she starting humming almost immediately after a bite of the sausage.

We made the guys eat those awful reconstituted meals. No matter what Sydney said about them, she would never convince me that they were almost as good as a fresh meal.

Sydney licked her fingers after devouring her second s'more and stood as she stretched her long frame. "I better start tearing down the tent and packing up before it gets too late. I hate unpacking in the dark."

Celeste looked over at me and her mournful expression was my undoing as I burst into tears. "I am sorry, Bella, but it is time."

"I know," I sniffed.

Sydney busied herself with packing up our campsite and gave Celeste and me some privacy to say our goodbyes.

Gizmo could sense something monumental was about to happen and strolled over weaving her body in and out of our legs.

"How will you get back to your ship?" I asked.

"Do you know this show, *Star Trek*, that is on the black box?"

"Yeah, why?"

"We are able to use energy to transport ourselves from one place to the next. As long as I have Gizmo in my arms, I will be able to transport us both to my ship," she answered.

"What about food for Gizmo during the long journey home?" I asked.

"Some of our food comes in the form of pellets that are surprisingly similar to your cat food. I believe this food source will be sufficient for her needs."

"Yuck. No wonder you like our food. Maybe you should try to harvest the vegetation on your planet and have fresh food every once in a while. You never know what might be tasty."

Celeste decided to bypass the exploration of new food choices and went straight to a potentially controversial topic. "Will Sydney be upset if I kiss you goodbye? I will make it a chaste kiss. I must teach this energy exchange to my planet. It was quite enjoyable."

Sydney and I hadn't really talked much about monogamy or our relationship, but I got the distinct impression that was where we were heading. However, Sydney was the kind of person to understand things and I knew she recognized that Celeste was special to me, but not a threat.

"I think she would understand. You know, Celeste, under different circumstances, I might have seriously considered your offer, but you were right, Sydney is my energy mate. That in no way diminishes the depth of my feelings for you. You will always be the one who first made me feel worthy of love. I'll always love you." I let the tears fall freely.

Celeste brushed her fingers over my cheek, leaned in, and gently placed her lips on mine. She pulled me into her arms and hugged me before stepping back and picking up Gizmo. "I will do everything in my power to find an energy mate and bring her back to this wonderful planet where I learned about love. In the meantime…" She touched her hand to my heart. "I will remain right here. You will feel my energy and I will feel yours. That is what it is like to be energy compatible. If you had become my energy mate that feeling would have intensified by at least one hundred times."

I bent over and kissed my cat and I petted her head one last time. It was so hard to let her go, but I knew Celeste would take good care of her. "Bye little pun'kin." I stepped back to give Celeste enough room to do whatever she needed to do.

The soft purple light I now associated with Celeste surrounded her entire body, and as the light diminished, Celeste and Gizmo disappeared. I heard in my head: *Goodbye sweet Bella, take good care of Sydney. She is a good choice for any energy mate.*

I stood there for a few seconds as I let the grief flow over me inhabiting every corner of my soul. It wasn't long before I felt Sydney's protective arms wrap around me.

"Is there anything I can do to make this less painful?" she asked.

"You're already doing it. I just need you to hold me for a few moments."

In this whole ordeal, I'd lost something very precious, but I gained something even more treasured—Sydney's love. Maybe it would have happened eventually, but I didn't think so, because I was never in the right mindset before to believe in my self-worth before Celeste came along to show me.

After a few minutes of just soaking in Sydney's love, I was ready to get going. I wasn't naïve enough to believe that we didn't have more challenges ahead of us. Hurricane Hollie would be our first hurdle.

I wiped my eyes one last time. "I'll help you pack up the rest of the gear and then we better find a place to purchase a disposable phone to make that anonymous call. I don't think it's wise to use our cell phones. Besides, I don't have a signal."

"Wow, I feel like some kind of spy or something. I was rethinking the suggestion I made earlier about an anonymous call. I think I'd rather just use my phone when we get a signal. I have a buddy in the Forest Service. I'll call her and if someone asks any questions later on, we can admit to meeting Greg, but then tell them we didn't realize he was some nutcase. I think the closer we stick to the truth, the better it will be to keep our story straight. It's not a lie to say we don't exactly know where Celeste lives, but she went back home. Since she never gave us a last name, we don't have to make one up. We can just tell them we never asked."

After we packed everything up, we led the three goons down the path and sat them down close to their vehicle. They were remarkably compliant. They'd stopped their nonsensical chatter and just sat there in the weeds staring out at nothing in particular. They weren't quite catatonic, but they were minimally responsive.

I grabbed Sydney's baseball cap from the tree branch and smashed it on my head while pulling my hair through the back loop. I didn't want my hair whipping in my face on the ride back home. Sydney had a hair tie to keep her gorgeous locks from blowing around. We were finally ready to leave.

I had to admit, camping wasn't as bad as I thought, and I might be willing to come back again for a couple of days. This was the place where Sydney and I first made love, so coming back would be something special. Sentimentality would override comfort. I was, after all, a romantic at heart.

†

That damn road jiggled my innards again and I was glad when we finally made it to a smoother surface. I had to pee again because the road shook up my bladder, sending desperate signals to my brain. I was a pro now, so when Sydney stopped to make the phone call, I figured I could slip out and squat behind the closest tree.

Sydney kept checking her phone every few minutes, presumably waiting for enough bars on her phone to contact her friend in the forest service. It took us at least twenty minutes to travel into cell phone range. I was sure that my eyes were yellow because I had to pee so bad. I was squirming in my seat hoping I wouldn't embarrass myself too much with my desperate need to urinate.

Sydney smiled when she glanced at her phone again and pulled over to make the call. In her line of work, she saw all kinds of horrendous accidents that were the result of people messing with their phones while driving. She had a strict rule about texting and driving and that extended to talking on your cell phone. She always claimed it was too much of a distraction.

While she was making the call, I scurried out of the Jeep to do my thing. I looked around to make sure there weren't any hungry bears. I was never going to be caught with my pants down again—literally—unless something really good was happening while they were wrapped around my ankles. Sydney's gentle hands and mouth suddenly flashed in my head. I was daydreaming about how good that would feel, when Sydney startled me.

"Why, Mabel Butt, if I didn't know any better, I'd think you were thinking some very naughty thoughts, but I don't mind it one bit. You can moon me anytime you want."

I blushed and hurried to pull up my shorts. I didn't even bother to try to shake a little in an effort to enhance the drip-dry approach to bathroom breaks in the woods.

"Why is it you always catch me in an embarrassing position with my pants around my ankles? Just for once, I think it would only be fair to catch you in a compromising position."

Sydney just chuckled in response. I followed her back to the car.

"How'd the call go?" I asked.

"It was fine. She didn't ask too many questions. Apparently finding weirdoes in the mountains isn't really an unusual occurrence. She told me they'd had to dismantle a few meth labs over the last few years. I guess this pristine wilderness attracts all kinds."

I was rethinking my romantic notion of returning to what I thought was an unspoiled location if there was a high probability of running into some nasty characters. "Great, now you tell me."

"Oh don't worry, I've been coming up here for years and this is the first time I've ever run into anyone. If it makes you feel any better, next time we can carry some mace."

It didn't make me feel any better, but I nodded anyway. Love is compromise and I would brave the great outdoors again if it would make Sydney happy.

Everything suddenly came into sharp focus for me and I abruptly stopped. I'd just realized that me, Mabel Butt, the consummate misfit, was actually heading for a real relationship with Sydney O'Donnell, the town heartthrob.

She turned around when she noticed I wasn't getting into the Jeep. "What's wrong?"

I made a big show of pinching myself and she crinkled up her forehead.

"I'm just checking to make sure I'm not asleep, having some vivid dream where I'm about to get everything I've always fantasized about. You know that being with you is a dream come true for me."

"Well if you're dreaming, then it's playing right into my ultimate desire. I've never been more sure of anything else in my life. We were meant for each other and I'm not about to let anything or anyone come between us. I know you probably need to work a few things out, like telling your parents, but I'd shout it from the rooftops if I could."

Sydney jumped into the Jeep and stood on the seat poking her head up through the roof. "I finally captured the heart of Mabel Butt," she shouted.

"Oh shit, my parents," I groaned.

I didn't have the foggiest idea how they would react. I'd have to add that to the pile of challenges slowly forming a substantial mountain for us to climb.

"I wouldn't worry too much. They never treated me any different after I came out. Your mom stayed as sweet as apple pie. It's not like they don't know me or anything."

"It's one thing for your daughter's friends to be gay and quite another to learn one of your children is a lesbian. If you don't mind, I'd like to build up the courage to reveal this little tidbit."

I was rethinking this whole coming out thing. I'd lived my life so far in near obscurity and I kind of liked it. Now that I was Sydney's girlfriend, everything would change. I didn't know if I was ready for that, but I was determined to try, at least for her.

Sydney must have seen my indecision because she jumped down from her perch and pulled me into her strong embrace. She kissed my forehead. "Mabs, I'm not pushing you if you're not ready. We have plenty of time for you to do this at whatever pace is comfortable for you. I love you and that's never going to change."

I smiled and pecked her lips. "I love you too. I don't want to go back to my empty house. Can I stay with you for a while?"

"I'd be devastated if you didn't want to stay with me, and I'd be ecstatic if you wanted to make that a permanent arrangement. My cabin has plenty of space, not that your house isn't a good option too. Wherever you want to stay, I'll adapt. Just tell me where you want to go and we'll be there in no time. I have plans for you this evening."

I blushed. "I'd rather be in a more remote location tonight, so your cabin is probably the best choice. My mom has absolutely no boundaries and no compunction about dropping in unannounced anytime she feels like it. I'd rather not do the shock and awe approach to coming out if your plans mean clothing is optional."

Sydney wiggled her eyebrows. "Yep, something like that. Come on, Mabs, time's a wastin'."

I got a warm feeling all over just thinking about Sydney's plans for the evening. We hurried back into the Jeep, buckled up, and were on our way in two seconds flat. The drive home was uneventful and I was glad when Sydney suggested we unload everything but our overnight bags in the morning.

Chapter Thirteen

By the time we arrived at Sydney's cabin the sun was starting to set and blessed us with a kaleidoscope of colors. I interpreted that as a sign that God was pleased and laid out that beautiful rainbow just for us. I stood looking up at the canvas in the sky and wondered if Celeste ever witnessed this much beauty on her planet. I hoped that she did. I got a warm feeling from that thought and imagined Celeste sending energy my way as a thank you for thinking of her at that moment.

Sydney stood next to me and draped her arm around my shoulder. She didn't say anything as we stood there looking at the sky. I was thankful that she wasn't the kind of person to try to fill in the void with idle chatter. Sometimes silence is more powerful than words. She turned me around and her kiss started slow and steady, but soon turned into a passionate exploration of every part of my lips and tongue. I was panting in no time. We abandoned our bags at the doorstep as Sydney led me into the cabin.

Even though we were desperate to remove our clothes, Sydney had a way of undressing me quickly without the frantic fumbling normally associated with two people who are desperate to touch one another. As we removed each article of clothing, the path to the bedroom was like a trail of breadcrumbs. If anyone did happen upon the cabin tonight, there wouldn't be any doubt about what was happening this evening.

Sydney pushed the remote light switch button, holding it down until the dimmer created a soft glow in her bedroom. I glanced around the room and it was neat and tidy. She'd even made the bed before we left for our camping trip.

I didn't want to kill the mood, but my side trip to the woods to empty my bladder popped in my head and I wanted to take a shower before Sydney started devouring my body. I was a little self-conscious about how I might taste or smell after the drip-dry method. I didn't care if this little quirk of mine made me as crazy as my eccentric Aunt Marie.

"Um, Sydney, do you mind if I take a shower before we um, you know…"

"You are absolutely adorable. Mind if I join you?" she asked.

I'd never taken a shower with anyone before, but I'd sure fantasized about it enough. It was definitely on my bucket list. I was so pathetic that things most people considered pretty routine made it on my bucket list.

"I'd love that."

Sydney caressed my shoulder before taking my hand and leading me into her master bathroom. I thought I'd died and gone to heaven when I saw the enormous forest-green tiled shower with three showerheads. On the wall facing the sliding glass doors, in offsetting cream and black tiles, was a design of three orca whales that looked like they were dancing in a circle. It was the coolest thing I'd ever seen. She must have had the shower specially designed. It was beyond decadent.

By the time she pulled me into the water, the temperature was perfect. The way the water cascaded down her perfect body captivated me. She lifted her head up and slicked back her hair. I could see her muscles ripple under the stream of water.

I looked around for a washcloth or shower pouf, but all she had was some gel and a bar of lavender soap. I got excited when I realized that if she planned on soaping me up, she would be using her bare hands. That was perfectly all right with me. Even more appealing was the opportunity to slather her up with soap as I explored every inch of her body.

I pushed back my wet hair and reached for the bar of soap. After I produced a healthy amount of suds, I ran my hands over her breasts and down her taut stomach. She moaned in pleasure as I reached her soft pubic hair. It was hard for me to tell whether the slickness was as a result of the soap, or the special attention I was paying to this part of her body.

She abruptly turned my body around and pushed down the shower gel dispenser to acquire a handful of the sweet smelling liquid. She went straight for the patch of hair between my legs and the sensation traveled to every single nerve ending in my body. As she washed my most private parts, she stroked my clitoris thoroughly until I was calling out her name in the throes of ardor.

"Oh, yes, yes, right there. God, Sydney, what you do to me…"

My first orgasm in a shower, but hopefully not my last, built so quickly that I didn't have time to prepare for the overwhelming sensation. Once the aftershocks stopped, she turned me back around and kissed me so softly that it almost made me cry with emotion. I could feel every ounce of love that she poured into me with that kiss. I was a violin and she was the virtuoso.

It was time to return the favor. I wanted to try something I'd only read about in books. I wanted to taste her as the water flowed over my body and spilled onto my head.

I started kissing her neck and making my way down to her breasts. I took one nipple into my mouth and gently sucked until she starting squirming. It wasn't long until she was bucking in my direction and begging for me to arrive at my final destination.

"Please, Mabs, stop teasing. If I don't feel your tongue in the next few seconds I think I'm going to self-combust."

I looked up into her eyes and saw a look of pure lust. "I seriously doubt that," I giggled.

She groaned and I took pity on her as I continued kissing and licking my way to the treasure trove before me. It wouldn't take long for her to reach satisfaction. I started with a few flicks to her sensitive nub and then followed with some gentle sucking as I entered her with two fingers. The warm water felt glorious, but I knew that if we stayed in the shower much longer we'd run out of water and I didn't think Sydney would enjoy the shock to her system. I increased my rhythm and pretty soon I felt her contractions as she cried out in pleasure.

"So good, that felt so good." She pulled me up to her and captured my body in a warm embrace.

"We better finish washing our hair before the hot water runs out," I said.

"Good idea. I have no intention of cutting our time short tonight, so a cold shower is definitely not warranted." She kissed me on the tip of my nose before pouring out a generous amount of shampoo in both of our hands.

Even though I felt completely satiated after our shower, Sydney introduced me to a few very creative ways to give and receive pleasure and I was an eager pupil. After several hours of lovemaking, I fell asleep curled up in her arms as she stroked my head. The last thing I remember before plummeting into dreamland was her telling me again how much she loved me. I would never get tired of hearing that, especially from her.

✝

I woke up to Sydney's feather light touch and one thing lead to another. I was blissfully unaware of anything besides Sydney's talented tongue between my legs.

"Mmmm, that feels heavenly," I remarked.

The *click click click* didn't register until I heard Hollie's voice.

"What the fuck?" Hollie screamed.

I jumped so high that I must have banged Sydney's nose.

"Mmmph, my nobse," Sydney garbled as she popped up, held her nose, and scrambled out of bed.

I grabbed the sheet to cover my naked body and looked up at a very pissed ex-girlfriend. Sydney was still holding her nose and I was glad I didn't notice any blood pouring out from it. She was blinking her eyes rapidly as they teared up. I must have bumped her in just the right place.

"Oh, God, Sydney. I'm so sorry," I said.

Sydney didn't even bother to get dressed she just dragged Hollie out of the bedroom. Before she left she called out over her shoulder, "Stab in bed, it won't take me long to resolb dis." I guess she was still smarting from my unfortunate hip thrust.

"Okay," I mumbled.

The minute the door closed, I crawled out from under the sheets and made my way to the door to listen. I never said I was an angel or anything and I was desperate to hear their conversation. I placed my ear to the door, straining to eavesdrop on their private chat.

"And to think I was worried about you, only to find you fucking that loser. I thought that nutcase kidnapped you. How could you do this to us?" Hollie screeched.

Thankfully, Sydney's speech returned to normal and I didn't hear any impediment. I hoped that meant I hadn't done serious damage to her nose. I didn't think she would be able to explain to her co-workers. They'd never let her live it down. I mean what could she say. *Well, remember when I told you still waters runs deep with Mabel, she's quite the little animal in bed. Got this black eye after she bucked so hard while I was licking her pussy.* I shook my head. Sydney would never say that. I craned hard to hear her response.

"There is no 'us' and if you actually bothered to listen to me, you would know that. I never meant to hurt you, but I love her and if you ever talk negatively about her again, you and I are completely finished. I will have nothing to do with you, not even as friends." Sydney's voice was eerily calm, but I could hear the hard edge to it.

"Don't worry. After seeing you put your tongue on that disgusting piece of trash, I'd rather pluck my pubic hairs out one by one than have your hands or mouth on me again. You'll be sorry and when you're ready to come back, I'll have definitely moved on. Have fun with your mousy little librarian, Sydney. I bet she sucks in bed."

Sucks in bed, why that mean-spirited bitch. I didn't think that Sydney screaming my name meant I sucked in bed.

"Get out," Sydney ordered.

"I wonder what little Miss Goody Two Shoe's mom and dad will think of her walking over to the dark side." Hollie laughed.

I heard the door slam and hurried back to bed. Damn, I was going to have to make that call to my parents sooner rather than later. Could I get away with telling them over the phone? Probably not the best tactic. I sighed. It was time to call mom up and ask her if she wanted to have breakfast at the Cottage Café today.

Sydney opened the door and must have noticed my flushed face. She grinned at me. "You're such a little eavesdropper. I know you heard it all and I'm sorry Hollie was such a bitch. I know it's not right what she says about you and she can be really horrible, but I do think she is saying all that because she's hurt. I'm responsible for that, not you."

"It's okay, she's said and done far worse to me," I answered.

"I don't think she's done causing trouble. I'm really sorry, Mabs, but I think her parting comment was a warning that she's about to out you to everyone she knows. You know how small our town is and it won't take long to get back to your parents."

"Yeah, I know. I better call and arrange breakfast with my parents this morning," I replied.

"I can come with you if you need me to," Sydney offered.

"No, I think I'd better talk to them alone first. I'll call you as soon as I'm done. Can you take me back to my house so I can get my car?"

†

I paced the small parking lot of the Cottage Café. Since it was a weekday, the lot wasn't full like it normally was on the weekends. Dad would be happy to not have to circle the block, looking for a parking space. He'd also be happy there wasn't a line a mile long waiting for a seat inside the café.

My dad's Kia came careening into the parking lot and it wasn't long before he was walking over to where I stood waiting for them. He gave me a big smile and hugged me.

"What a pleasant surprise, Mabel. We missed having breakfast with you on Sunday. It was an absolute madhouse in here. Where is your friend from out of town? We didn't get a chance to meet her. You know I take everything that Hollie says with a grain of salt. I know my little girl wouldn't befriend some nutcase."

Mom stood silently by his side. Her expression was grim and I wondered what she'd heard already.

"Hi, Mom." I gave her a quick hug.

She hugged me back, but I could tell something was wrong.

"Come on, let's get a booth. I'm eager to buy my two favorite girls breakfast." Dad led us into the café and we slid into an open booth.

†

I kept thinking it would be best to just come out with it. *Rip the Band-Aid off* was the mantra going through my head.

"You know, Mabel, whatever it is you have to tell us, it will all be okay. We love you unconditionally," my dad pronounced.

So I went for it. "I'm gay, always have been, and I'm in love with Sydney O'Donnell," I blurted out.

"Oh thank goodness for that. I thought you'd never figure it out. I take it that Sydney finally dumped her girlfriend?" Mom asked.

"What? You're not disappointed?" I asked.

213

"Why on earth would we be disappointed? Sydney is a lovely girl. We're not some redneck homophobes, you know. Your father and I were wondering when you would finally tell us. We've known ever since middle school when you starting bringing Sydney around. God, how you mooned over her. *Sydney did this, Sydney did that, oh isn't Sydney just the best.*" Mom chuckled.

This conversation was not exactly going as I thought it would, but I still didn't understand the frosty reception I'd gotten from my mom.

"So if my being a lesbian is not an issue, why do I get the feeling that something is wrong, Mom?" I asked.

"Oh that. We heard something about some new girl that you were hanging out with and I just assumed she was your girlfriend. We heard she was a mental health patient and I didn't want you getting mixed up with someone unsuitable for you."

"I'm sorry, Mom. Celeste was just a woman who came into town and we became friends. She's a really nice person, but had to go back home. She had some stalker after her and he was telling a bunch of lies about her being in a mental hospital. That's what you probably heard from Hollie. There was something really off about him and, if you ask me, he's the one who probably escaped from the looney bin. Sydney met her and we all decided to go camping because she had never been and neither have I. It's actually fun. I might consider doing it again sometime." I grinned and thought back on our picnic in the woods and my first time making love.

"Yes, Harry, your boss, told us you were finally taking a vacation. We were surprised to hear that. I went by your place to see if Gizmo was being taken care of, but you must have taken her with you," Mom answered.

Shit, that was a detail I hadn't thought about. I would have to sort of tell the truth and hope I didn't get too many questions.

"Um, I gave Gizmo to Celeste. They really bonded and she needed her more than I do. Celeste hasn't had it easy and, even though I'll miss Gizmo like crazy, I just knew it was the right thing to do."

There were genuine tears in my eyes as I explained this to my parents.

"Oh honey, I know how much you loved that little cat. She was such a wonderful companion to you. I suppose now that you have Sydney, you won't be so alone anymore. You are such a wonderful friend and if you gave this woman your cat, she must be special." My dad was very understanding.

I swiped the tears from my face and smiled at my parents. "Celeste is special. Hey, can I call Sydney now? She's probably wearing a groove in her cabin about now wondering how you'll take this new revelation."

"You tell Sydney that we expect to have dinner with both of you very soon. We want to hear all about how the two of you finally got together. I just love a good romance. It reminds me of how your father and I got together." Mom likes to reminisce.

My dad turned to face my mom. "Honey, leave the poor girl alone and please don't bore her with that old story."

"I don't mind. I love that old story." Dad was such a romantic, just like Sydney.

✝

I'd called Sydney to give her the good news and to tell her that I would drop by my place to gather up some

215

things before coming back over. I mentioned that I'd bring a pizza from Village Pizza and she whooped in gratitude.

When I reached the cabin, Sydney was waiting for me outside.

"Close your eyes. I have a surprise for you."

"What about all my stuff and the pizza?" I asked.

"We can get your things later. Here let me take the pizza and I'll lead you inside," she answered.

I handed her the pizza. "Okay."

Sydney took my arm and led me inside. I stepped on her wood floor and heard a soft mewling. I felt soft fur brush against my ankle. My eyes popped open as a tiny ball of fluff circled my legs. I picked up the kitten who looked exactly like Gizmo when she was young. I held the kitten on my shoulder and she snuggled into my neck. The purring was instantaneous.

"Oh my God, she's precious. It is a she, isn't it?" I asked.

"Yep, sure is and the best part about this is that I rescued her from the pound. My friend called when she heard I was looking for a kitten."

"How did you possibly have time to arrange this?" I asked as I looked around and saw a mound of toys for the new kitten piled up next to the couch. Sydney had purchased toys, a bed, a deluxe scratching post, pet carrier, and several bags of kitten food—the good stuff.

"I have my connections. You mean the world to me, Mabs. I would do anything to see that lovely smile. Is this okay? It's not too soon, is it? I wanted to make sure you had a friend to hang with when I have to do my two twenty-four hour shifts. I don't want you to ever feel lonely again."

"Have I told you lately how much I love you?"

"Well you have been gone for a while, so not for a few hours," she answered.

"Well I love and adore you. You're helping me raise this little ball of fur, so I'll be sure to have you in my life for at least another fifteen to twenty years."

"Oh, Mabs, if you'll have me, I hope it's a lot longer than that."

Epilogue

It was exactly one month later from the fateful night when Celeste returned to her home. I was relaxing on the couch reading a book while Sydney played with our new kitten, Yazdi. She'd bought a laser light and was torturing poor Yazdi, who would chase the light to the point of exhaustion. Sydney would laugh hysterically as Yazdi ran in circles chasing the red light.

Sydney wanted to change the kitten's name to Parrot because she had a habit of scaling up Sydney's pants to perch on top of her shoulder. I didn't think we should encourage that behavior because, when she got older it wouldn't be so cute, but Sydney would just laugh and kiss her furry head. I had to admit that it was adorable.

Sydney's cell phone startled me and I looked up to see her pull Yazdi into her lap at the same time she grabbed her phone to answer it.

"Hello," Sydney answered. She caught my eye and I motioned for her to turn on the speaker. She nodded as she pulled the phone from her ear and pushed the button.

"This guy, Greg, insists that some alien was the cause of his nearly catatonic state," the woman on the other end stated.

"Well that's ironic," Sydney responded.

"How so?" the woman asked.

"Well, when Greg came to town he claimed that the woman Mabel befriended was some nutcase who thought she was an alien, and had checked herself out of the mental health facility she was admitted to. Mabel kind of challenged him and started asking questions. He seemed to bristle at that. To be honest with you, I spent time with Celeste and she seemed perfectly sane to me."

"The psychiatrist mentioned he'd never seen anything like it before. He'd heard about a kind of mass hysteria, but never experienced more than one person having the exact same delusion. Apparently, their stories are eerily similar. They claim to be able to prove it. Greg insists that there is a melted gun on the floor of your guest bedroom."

Sydney started laughing.

Fortunately, Sydney is an incredibly handy-fix it person and had managed to rip up the old wood with the melted metal, replacing it with extra pieces from when she originally put in the floor. It was impossible to detect the difference between the original and the new section.

"That's pretty funny. Anytime someone wants to check out our floor is fine with me. I put the floor in myself and I'm very proud of my craftsmanship, but I certainly don't have any extra art welded to the floor. He did come by about a month ago, and I told him to get the hell off my property or I'd call the police for trespassing." Sydney winked at me as I held my hand over my mouth to keep from laughing.

"Hey, don't worry, Syd, the doc didn't believe him, especially when they called the number of the guy he claimed was his boss. They insisted this phantom person could verify their credentials. Doc called the number given to him and it was a disconnected number. I just thought I would tell you about it. Greg was pretty pissed and after his angry reaction, the hospital decided to keep them all for an indeterminate time. Doc doesn't believe it would be safe to release them as a result of the threats they were making. I just wanted to warn you that this guy, Greg, has a real sick obsession with you and Mabel. Watch your back."

"Thanks for the heads up, Janie. Let me know when you're out our way and we'll have you over for dinner. I can't cook worth a damn, but Mabel is an artist in the kitchen."

"You got yourself a deal. Later, dude."

Sydney pushed the button to end the call.

I didn't like what I'd just heard, but Sydney didn't seem too fazed by it.

"It sounds like we have an enemy," I said.

Sydney waved her hand at me. "Don't worry, Mabs. I have friends at that hospital, on the police force, and with the forest service. The minute they discharge those bozos, if they actually end up ever discharging them, I'll hear about it. My buddies in the police will watch out for us. If Greg so much as puts one foot in Roslyn or Cle Elum he'll find a big blue wall. Police and fire always have each other's backs." She shot me her confident cocky grin I loved so much.

Sydney was always so confident about everything. I had to admit that things were working out very nicely for us. I thought back to the day after Celeste left.

When we unpacked the bags after the camping trip, we found Celeste's huge wad of cash and it amounted to a little over one hundred thousand dollars.

With everything that had happened after we returned to Sydney's cabin, we'd forgotten all about unpacking our bags. I found Celeste's backpack and could finally satisfy my curiosity.

"God, I've been dying to find out what Celeste hid in this pack. Hey, maybe she left us some cool alien technology. Although, I wouldn't have the foggiest idea how to use it." I unzipped the mysterious bag.

"Okay, so what's in the bag?" Sydney asked.

I peeked inside. "Holy shit." I started pulling out bundle after bundle of rolled up balls of cash. I dug a little deeper and found several hunks of gold nuggets. There was some kind of odd electronic device that I had no idea about, but I tossed it back in the bag satisfied that it would be one mystery I might never figure out.

"There must be thousands of dollars here," Sydney exclaimed.

I laughed when I found a treasure trove of gaudy touristy trinkets and several bars of lemongrass soap. "She must have found this stuff in one of the stores."

"You know, Mabs, with the diamonds she made for us, those gold nuggets, and the cash, we can have first class rings made and throw the biggest party this side of the Mississippi, after we get married of course. I hope you want a big wedding."

It was still a little too soon for me, because I still wasn't sure about our future. I needed to do a little work on myself to truly believe I was worthy of Sydney's promise of forever.

"Um, I would love to marry you, Sydney, but I want to make sure this is more than just a little shy librarian fantasy for you. I just told my parents, so I'd like to give them just a bit more time before I spring a wedding on them."

Sydney grinned. "Well you definitely have fulfilled my shy, sexy, librarian fantasy, but I hope you know my feelings go much deeper than that. I'll give you all the time you need, but you have to admit that's a boatload of cash and it would be a hell of a party. Just saying."

Even though I knew Sydney was joking around, I also knew this was her way of feeling me out. I was pretty sure that when she sensed I was ready, she would find a way to ask me properly.

Yazdi started to squirm in Sydney's lap, letting her know it was time to return to their former game of catch the red light before the phone call so rudely interrupted them. Eventually, Yazdi must have decided she'd had enough, because she ran to Sydney's leg and clawed her way up to her favorite perch on Sydney's shoulder.

I shook my head and plucked Yazdi off her shoulder. I thought of how she was so much like Gizmo, playful and friendly. It reminded me of Gizmo in outer space. I began to wonder how Celeste was faring with her new companion. I was startled when I heard Celeste's soothing voice in my head: *Gizmo and her four beautiful kittens are charming everyone on Sisterna. Everyone wants a kitten now.*

"Celeste," I whispered.

Sydney turned her head in my direction, "Did you say something, babe?"

I thought of all the times Celeste left me with a warm feeling and how sometimes even after she'd left, I'd still felt that connection. Now I knew she was still with me. Maybe it was the weird item she left in her pack that kept us bonded, or maybe it was something else that created the link. Now I had confirmation that energy was able to traverse across millions of miles. Anything was possible.

"I don't know how this is possible, but Celeste is talking to me," I answered.

Sydney smiled at me and kissed my cheek. "I think I'll just go into the bedroom and let you catch up, but I'll want to hear all about it later." She gathered my little ball of fur, Yazdi, and headed for our bedroom.

I wasn't sure if I could just think the words, so I spoke into the empty room like a total nerd, "Can you hear me, Celeste? Sydney wants an update too, but she just left the room to give us some privacy."

My sweet Bella, I did not wish to frighten you, but I will always have a connection to you.

"Oh, Celeste, it is so good to hear your voice. I miss you and Gizmo. Are you safe now?"

The invaders are limiting their aggression to the southern hemisphere and I have been teaching our people love and passion. We will be ready to defend when the time comes.

"Tell me about the return trip."

The return trip was uneventful and Gizmo is such a good little mama kitty. I accelerated the growth of her offspring because I wanted to maintain a safe, controlled environment for her to give birth. The caretakers approved another trip to planet Earth to obtain more cats so that we may breed them on Sisterna. They bring a certain amount of calming energy to those who are privileged enough to stroke them.

"Celeste, that is such wonderful news. When will you make the journey again?"

I still have more teaching to do on Sisterna. Perhaps we will be able to make the trip in another Earth year or two.

"We?"

I could almost hear the smile in her voice when she answered me.

You were right, Bella, I met someone and she is energy compatible. She would like to meet you. I hope you will not be disturbed by her appearance.

"Why on Earth would I be disturbed by her appearance?"

She is beautiful like you; she could easily pass for your twin.

"My twin?"

Yes, and when I described this concept of love, she understood immediately. I believe we are in love.

"Oh, Celeste, I am so happy for you," I gushed. "Hey, by the way, we found your little stash in the backpack, but couldn't quite figure out the electrical device you left behind. Is that the way you've been able to stay connected to me?"

I could hear her giggle in my head. I keep learning about Earth slang and your technology from the Kindle device you gave me. The device is what we call a communicator, but would more aptly be described as a videographer in Earth terms. I used this device to remain connected to my home planet and provide frequent updates on my learnings. I broke the rules when I left this technology, but it was worth the risk. I confessed this to the caretakers who have given me permission to utilize the device to remain connected. They believe you have more to teach us.

"So how does it work? Would I be able to use this device to send video messages?"

Yes, but there is a considerable delay in the transmission.

"Can you teach me how to use the device and then we can have another means of communication."

Of course, Bella, but I will always remain connected to you and anytime you wish to communicate with me, all you need to do is send a mind message. Emotion generates a greater amount of energy ensuring receipt of the message. When you wondered about how Gizmo and I were faring, your emotion must have been great because the message was the clearest one since my departure.

"Good to know. I miss you, Celeste."

I miss you too.

†

Sydney was tending to her garden and I walked out into the sunshine feeling the warmth of Mother Nature's rays caress my skin. It was late August and just sharing the same space with Sydney brought me incredible joy. I wasn't much of a gardener, but I would help Sydney harvest the fruits of her labor.

Sydney had an incredible green thumb, and it seemed like whatever she touched grew into luscious multicolored fruits and vegetables. August was prime time for picking blueberries, strawberries, and some of the early harvest tomatoes.

We'd evolved into a comfortable domesticity as we each gravitated to our natural talents. While Sydney pulled the weeds surrounding her prized tomato plants, I began harvesting the fruit. As I lifted my face to the sun, I thought of Celeste.

My Bella. It must be a glorious day there. I can almost feel the warmth of your Earth's sun.

"Oh, Celeste, it is so good to hear from you again. It has been too long."

Sydney turned to me and smiled. "Shall I give you some privacy?"

I shook my head.

"Celeste, Sydney is right here with me. Do you think you could talk us through how to use the videographer?"

Oh yes I can, but you must remember that the messages will be delayed. Between each communication, you can expect forty to sixty of your earth minutes to pass before receiving a response from Sisterna. Will this frustrate you?

I laughed. "It won't frustrate me, but I can't speak for Sydney. Hey babe, Celeste said she can teach us how to use the device but the messages are so delayed it will take an hour before we can expect to receive a response. I would love to see her and meet her new energy partner. We can just continue to work in the garden between messages. Okay?"

"Sounds good to me. As long as I can continue to dig in the dirt while we wait. Do you want me to get the device?"

"No, I'll go get it. Hang on Celeste. I'm going to get your fancy contraption and then we can give it a whirl."

Whirl? I have not come across that slang yet. I do not suppose you will be spinning the device around your head?

I chuckled. "Nope. It means test it out."

After I retrieved her videographer, Celeste talked me through how to work the strange device and when Celeste sent her first video message, it was eerie how much her energy partner looked like me. It was like looking in a mirror. They seemed so happy and I was looking forward to their future visit. Maybe I would allow Yazdi to have kittens and Celeste could bring one or two back to Sisterna so that they could breed with Gizmo's kittens.

†

Although it was awkward at first, Sydney and I learned how to keep in touch with Celeste and her energy partner, Pia. We made it a point to connect with them at least once a month. As the holiday season snuck up on all of us, we spent considerable time trying to help Celeste and Pia understand the concept of Thanksgiving and the tradition in my family to cite what we were all thankful for.

Christmas was just around the corner and I was looking forward to explaining that particular holiday to Celeste. I knew she would be interested in the origin of Christmas as well as what it meant to me. I sensed that Sydney had something special planned for Christmas Eve that would probably entail some grandiose romantic gesture. I was sure she was ready to pop the question because I think she sensed that I was finally ready to accept her love. My mom kept giving me sly looks, so I knew that Sydney probably let her in on the surprise.

I was racking my brain for what I could do to make her Christmas special. Maybe my alien best friend could give me an idea that would be unique and extraordinary. I'd have to ask her during one of our private talks. I wanted Sydney to feel as special as she made me feel every single day since we'd professed our love for one another.

I feel so blessed to have someone like Sydney as a partner because, not once, has she ever expressed any kind of discomfort about the connection Celeste and I have. When I reflect on my beautiful girlfriend, the love I feel for her at this minute is truly out of this world. The love we have transcends the universe and I have Celeste to thank for being the spark that ignited our love.

About the Author

Annette Mori

Annette is a health care executive living in the beautiful Pacific Northwest with her wife (got to love Washington state) and their five furry kids. Well actually, it might be more than five, but they do not count the ones they only feed. Annette is fifty-six years old and believes it is not too late to try something new. As an avid reader, she is pleased there are thousands of good books to choose from, and hopes that one day hers will be one of the many for readers to consider. She reads at least three to four books a week, so please keep them coming. She has a habit to feed after all.

No matter if you loved it or hated it, I would love your comments. Feel free to e-mail me at annettemori0859@gmail.com. I will always be a WIP (work in progress—just learned that) so feedback is a gift.

Other Books from Affinity eBook Press

Take Me As I Am by JM Dragon and Erin O'Reilly When Jo Lackerly and Thea Danvers meet, an unexpected friendship develops, proving a catalyst for both women to change their lives irrevocably. Follow them on a journey of discovery that will have your heart smiling, blood boiling, and senses entangled in a wonderful romance.

Carved in Stone by Jen Silver Join the characters from *Starting Over* and *Arc Over Time* in this final book from the Starling Hill trilogy. *Carved in Stone* has romance, adventure, a treasure hunt, and happy endings for all, living and dead.

Anywhere, Everywhere by Renee MacKenzie Gwen Martin's life in the Ten Thousand Islands area changes irrevocably when Piper Jackson comes into her life. Without trust, can the budding relationship between Gwen and Piper survive? Or will the answers to the questions continue to haunt them?

Venus Rising by Ali Spooner Levi Johnson arrives at Venus Rising, an exclusive lesbian only tropical resort in the Virgin Islands and finds more than she expected—a sizzling hot love triangle. Torn between her attraction to both women struggles to choose the right woman to share her life.

The Devil's Tree by Ali Spooner Torn between her love for the pack and her need to find what's missing in her life Devin Benoit travels to New Orleans. Will the previous happenings at the Devil's Tree help or hinder Devin in the fight of her life, and the life of Tia, the woman who now owns her heart?

The Case of the Beggars' Coppice by Erica Lawson Edda Case is a woman in crisis who discovers that things are not as they seem. Is it truly a message for her from beyond the grave or is something more sinister taking place? Can Edda solve the mystery of *The Beggars' Coppice*?

Locked Inside by Annette Mori How much does the power of love matter to someone who must overcome obstacles far greater than most people face in a lifetime.

Line of Sight by Ali Spooner Sasha and her lover Kara are back. Continue the thrilling adventures of this couple from the Sasha Thibodaux series.

Requiem for Vukovar by Angela Koenig Requiem for Vukovar continues the Refraction series and the exploits of Jeri O'Donnell and her partner, Kelly Corcoran. In an epic siege largely ignored by the wider world, Kelly, who was prepared to give up comforts and certainties when she became part of Jeri's nomadic life, encounters more than physical danger. Her ability to maintain her core integrity is assaulted by the inevitable ugliness of war. For Jeri, the true battle is confronting her attraction to violence as she struggles against losing herself in the exhilaration of combat.

The Settlement by Ali Spooner The outpouring of love and friendship toward Cadin helps her on her path to healing and learning to trust her heart to love once again. Join bestselling author Ali Spooner on this sensational journey that ends with a heartwarming romance.

Once Upon a Time by Alane Hotchkin Raven only wanted to escape the blows that life had dealt her. She longed to be on the open sea and free. When she came upon a beautiful young girl sitting alone in the middle of a meadow, little did she know that her destiny would be changed forever. Will they become the pawns of the ancient vision or will both paths lead to the same port of destiny? Find out it in this exciting high seas adventure that will capture your imagination.

Asset Management by Annette Mori Follow the twists and turns to the explosive conclusion. Not everything is black and white. There are many shades of gray and sometimes it's difficult to decipher who is good and who is evil. No one is all virtue or all malevolence, but sometimes love helps us rise above.

Do Dreams Come True? by JM Dragon How do two people who really shouldn't get on end up in a relationship? Find out in this deliciously ordinary romance.

Return to Me by Erin O'Reilly Will Salvation bring just that to Ellie, allowing her to find peace and happiness again, or will it have her questioning all that she believes in? A wonderful romance cloaked within an intriguing mystery.

Arc Over Time by Jen Silver This wonderful romantic continuation with the characters from *Starting Over* ties up loose ends. But the question is—does everyone have a happy ending? A must read.

The Presence by Charlene Neal Can Rebecca and Kayleigh overcome ghosts from the past and their own insecurities, or will a presence from the past tear them apart?

A Walk Away by Lacey Schmidt Sometimes chance brings you to the right person to help you resolve some of your baggage, and you learn to like yourself a little more. Kat and Rand are smart enough to recognize this chance in each other, but they also find that there is a catch to every opportunity—walking toward something is always walking away from something else.

Possessing Morgan by Erica Lawson The investigation has barely begun when Andrea becomes the target of a nearly fatal hit-

and-run. But was it really aimed at her? Can she and Morgan find the common ground they need to solve the case and stop the attacks, or are the gaps just too wide to bridge?

Twenty-three Miles by Renee MacKenzie This is a story about community, and how it comes together in dangerous and devastating times. Will Talia and Shay find the answers they need to the mystery of the murders on the parkway, or will justice be elusive? Will they survive their quest for the truth?

Reece's Star by TJ Vertigo Under Faith's guiding, loving hand, will Reece successfully traverse the rocky road of emotion and embrace the positive changes in her life? Or will she panic and be unable to control that Animal part of herself? Will she take that next step to declare herself fully capable of love and devotion? This third installment in the popular series that began with *Private Dancer* continues the passionate and often hilarious romance of Reece and Faith as they both grow in love and in trust.

Confined Spaces by Renee MacKenzie Corporate politics, complicated romance, and long distances conspire to keep Andie and Kara all boxed in. Can love triumph despite the Confined Spaces?

Cowgirl Up by Ali Spooner Ride along with the MC2, for boot scootin', butt kickin', dirt eatin', rodeo adventures, with a love story thrown into the mix.

If I Were a Boy by Erin O'Reilly Will Katie and Helen be able to make a life together work or succumb to doubts and the pressures of family? This story will fill you with the thrill of passion and the tenderness of love.

The Chronicles of Ratha: Book 2 A Lion Among the Lambs by Erica Lawson Can Jordana believe in herself like her Noorthi sisters do? Only then can she fulfill her destiny as The Chosen One. Follow the colorful cast of characters in this action-packed adventure sequel as they traverse the galaxy. Of course, nothing ever goes smoothly when Jordana is involved.

Terminal Event by Ali Spooner Will the killer be caught or continue to evade authorities? Can Tally and Blair's budding romance survive the possibility? Read this intense murder mystery romance and find out.

Love Forever, Live Forever by Annette Mori Fate intervenes and puts Nicky directly back into the path of her first love, Sara, and the corresponding events send her into a tailspin. Now she must decide—who will be the person she ends up living with and loving forever?

The One by JM Dragon *2015 GCLS Winner for Romance, Intrigue, and Adventure. The One* is a romance with everything, love, intrigue, misunderstandings with a happy conclusion—the only question—who gets the girl?

Reflected Passion by Erica Lawson Through a mirror, Françoise embraces life anew, while for Dale it is a powerful awakening, forcing her to discover not only her sensual nature, but the inner strength she possesses.

Flight by Renee Mackenzie Some lives will be lost and others changed forever when the sisters' lives intersect. Will they be consumed by the wreckage, or will they be able to pick themselves up and take flight?

Starting Over by Jen Silver Book 1 of the Starling Hill Trilogy. There's a mystery afoot—whose royal resting place is disturbed at Starling Hill? All is revealed in this classic romance of simmering passions, anguished loss, and the wonder of love.

Terminal Event by Ali Spooner Will the killer be caught or continue to evade authorities? Can Tally and Blair's budding romance survive the possibility? Read this intense murder mystery romance and find out.

Love Forever, Live Forever by Annette Mori Fate intervenes and puts Nicky directly back into the path of her first love, Sara, and the corresponding events send her into a tailspin. Now she must decide—who will be the person she ends up living with and loving forever?

The One by JM Dragon *2015 GCLS Winner for Romance, Intrigue, and Adventure. The One* is a romance with everything, love, intrigue, misunderstandings with a happy conclusion—the only question—who gets the girl?

Reflected Passion by Erica Lawson Through a mirror, Françoise embraces life anew, while for Dale it is a powerful awakening, forcing her to discover not only her sensual nature, but the inner strength she possesses.

Flight by Renee Mackenzie Some lives will be lost and others changed forever when the sisters' lives intersect. Will they be consumed by the wreckage, or will they be able to pick themselves up and take flight?

Starting Over by Jen Silver Book 1 of the Starling Hill Trilogy. There's a mystery afoot—whose royal resting place is disturbed at Starling Hill? All is revealed in this classic romance of simmering passions, anguished loss, and the wonder of love.

E-Books, Print, Free e-books

Visit our website for more publications available online.

www.affinityebooks.com

Published by Affinity E-Book Press NZ LTD
Canterbury, New Zealand

Registered Company 2517228

www.ingramcontent.com/pod-product-compliance
Lightning Source LLC
Chambersburg PA
CBHW051043050726
47592CB00002B/374